The Loyalist's Luck

Book Two of the Loyalist Trilogy

Elaine A. Cougler

Peache House Press

Peache House Press

Certain characters in this work are historical figures, and many events portrayed did actually take place. This is, however, a work of fiction. All of the other characters, names and events as well as all places, incidents, organizations, and dialogue in this novel are either the products of the author's imagination or are used fictitiously.

Cover by Spica Book Design.

Cover artwork provided through the Archives of Ontario.
RG 2-344-0-0-89
Department of Education. Provincial Museum art works.
Watercolour – Encampment of the Loyalists at Johnstown, on the St. Lawrence River, 1784, unknown artist after James Peachey, 1925.
10003081

Text layout and design by To The Letter Word Processing Inc.

Back cover photo of the author by Paula Tizzard.

ISBN 9781502898142

Acknowledgements

MY JOURNEY TO PUBLICATION for this novel has taken its own turns and I am indebted to several people for their help along the way. Author Barbara Kyle provided excellent feedback on my first thirty pages when I took one of her not-to-be-missed workshops. Millie Gremonprez, Alva Forsyth, Brian Garner, Allan Ramsay, and Betty Mathers, friends all, each read my early drafts and provided me with excellent feedback causing me to rethink and rewrite several times.

Museum and historical site curators, as well as a number of librarians, have pointed me toward books that I might not have found but for their interest in my project and their thorough understanding of the resources they have. Very old texts which I found online, placed there through various endeavors, allowed me to read from the comfort of my computer chair first-hand accounts of the times and places which are my subject matter. I am thankful these old sources have not been lost but have been made accessible to the world.

I thank all the wonderful readers of the first book whose encouragement kept me going to finish this sequel and whose unstinting support and praise has fed my fire. Especially I give thanks to the many who have gone out of their way to help me get the word out by inviting me to speak, by writing reviews, and by telling all and sundry about my books.

My family heads the list of those to whom I owe thanks for their unwavering support whenever I stumble. My husband joins me on my travels, gives me honest answers when I use him as a sounding board, and always listens intently as I think aloud about how some new research might fit into my novels. I am truly blessed.

Also by Elaine Cougler

The Loyalist's Wife

For Linda

The John Garner Family

John Garner (Butler's Ranger)
Lucinda Garner nee Harper (his wife)

Their Children:

1. Harper John Garner

2. William Garner m. Catherine Cain, daughter of John Cain (Butler's Ranger), three children

3. Robert Garner (twin) married Mary Anne, an American, one child

4. Thomas Garner (twin)

5. Helen Garner married Timothy Greenstone, an American soldier, two children

Contents

Part I: The New Land

Chapter One	Spring, 1780: Fort Niagara
Chapter Two	
Chapter Three	
Chapter Four	June, 1780
Chapter Five	Summer, 1780
Chapter Six	
Chapter Seven	April, 1783
Chapter Eight	May, 1783
Chapter Nine	Fall, 1783
Chapter Ten	June, 1784
Chapter Eleven	June, 1784
Chapter Twelve	July, 1784
Chapter Thirteen	August, 1784

Part II: The Capital Years

Chapter Fourteen	July, 1792
Chapter Fifteen	January, 1793
Chapter Sixteen	February, 1793
Chapter Seventeen	March, 1793 – February, 1794
Chapter Eighteen	March, 1794
Chapter Nineteen	March, 1794
Chapter Twenty	April, 1794
Chapter Twenty-One	July, 1794

Part Three: Border Wars

Chapter Twenty-Two   August, 1808
Chapter Twenty-Three
Chapter Twenty-Four   Fall, 1808
Chapter Twenty-Five   Spring, 1809
Chapter Twenty-Six   October 13, 1812: Home of William &
                              Catherine Cain in Stamford Township
Chapter Twenty-Seven   October, 1812
Chapter Twenty-Eight   December, 1813: Angel Inn, Newark
Chapter Twenty-Nine   January, 1814
Chapter Thirty   July, 1814
Chapter Thirty-One   July 25, 1814
Chapter Thirty-Two   August, 1814: Burlington Heights
Chapter Thirty-Three   March, 1815

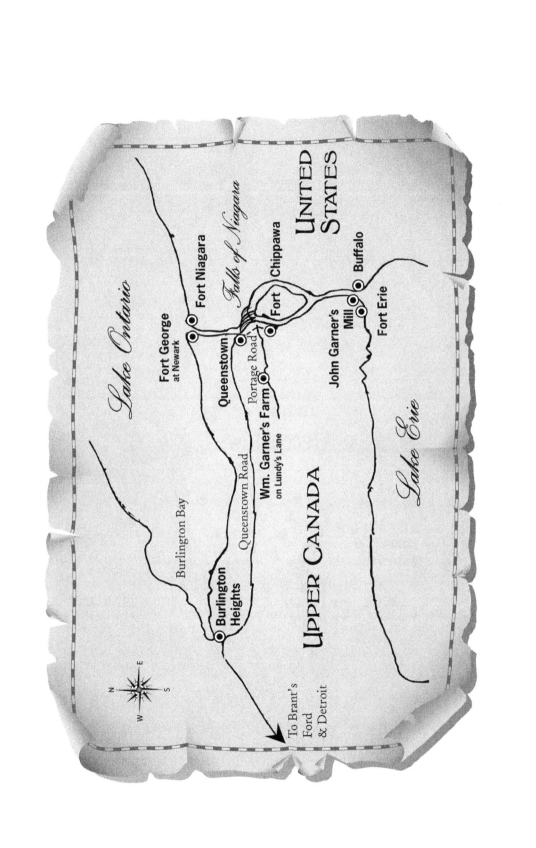

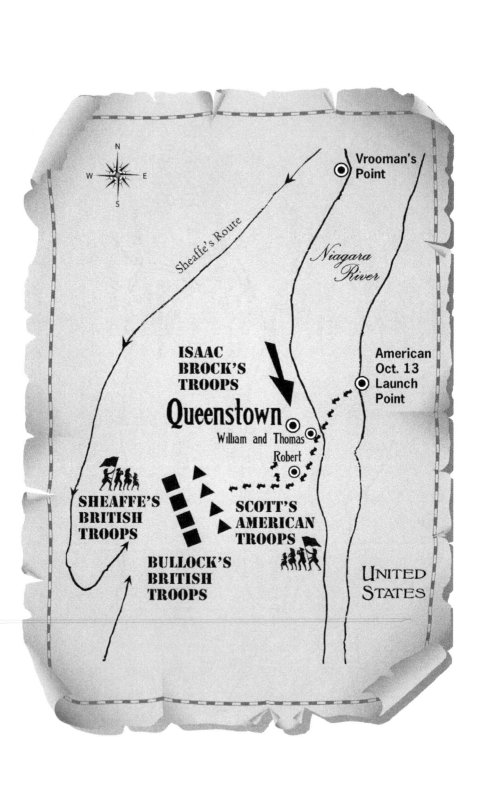

Part I
The New Land

Chapter One

Fort Niagara
Spring, 1780

CROSSING THE GRAY RIVER SEEMED SUCH A SHORT JOURNEY, only a few hundred feet. But Lucinda Garner was fleeing from all she knew. Crowded into the flat-bottomed bateau, clutching Harper John, and jammed against her husband amidst the others loyal to the King, she struggled to keep her footing as the boat pitched and tossed in the unruly waters. She glanced back one more time at the old French Castle high on the hill behind, almost lost in the morning mist.

"We'll never set foot on that side of the river again, mark my words." Her friend Nellie's voice was in her ear.

Why do you upset people like that, Nellie? "Of course we'll go back." Lucy turned to her husband. "Won't we, John?"

"No one knows for sure, but I'm one who's planning to return for what is mine. Ours," he added.

Lucy looked again. For six long months, she had waited and worried there with her child. Now John's arm held her again, but still her stomach clenched and the skin on her knees jerked up and down, a sign of her nervousness, as their boat neared the alien shore. She had one foot in the past and one in the future where, ahead, a wall of towering trees loomed black out of the fog.

"Ho! Man the lines!"

An elbow gouged her but John held tight and she choked back her scream. Harper John's arms tightened around her neck. She clutched him to her. "You're safe, little one," she murmured. "You're safe."

They landed on the narrow slip of stony beach, and the lines were tied. The push began to get the fugitives and their goods off the bateau, through the shallow frigid water, and up onto the rocky shore. Most people had boxes and barrels of cooking pots and quilts and blankets, all the possessions of a lifetime, but Lucinda and John had only a small satchel, two guns, and two saddled horses.

"Off now. Vite!" shouted the boatman. "We 'ave many load today."

John pushed ahead through the press of people, and lifted her and their child onto the shore. She turned to speak to him but he was already back on the boat for their horses. With no choice, she followed the other women, tripping and falling up the rocky shore to the path above. Finally, she set Harper John down to walk beside her, and he squealed and laughed, jerking to be free, but she held fast and pulled him along as she followed Nellie's dark skirts.

The wall of trees opened up and she recognized Butler's barracks, of which John had told her, standing firm and solid in the open field ahead. They would have shelter, at least. Until the King made good on his promise to take care of them and all the other Loyalists who had already lost their homes in the war.

The skies were dark with rain clouds and the damp permeated Lucinda's light skirts. She began to shiver but would not release the little hand struggling to be out of her own. Everything was gray—the sky, the hard-packed ground, the faces of the refugees arriving, even the soldiers barking out orders.

"Lucy! Over here!" John called to her as he struggled to pull the stubborn horses up the embankment.

She dropped Harper John's hand, told him to wait by the satchel, and ran to help.

"The baby! Catch him, Lucy!"

She whirled around. Harper John was hobbling across the field toward the barracks on pudgy little legs that threatened to pitch him to the ground at any moment. She raced through the wet grass. "Harper John!" she yelled, but he ran faster, his teasing laugh floating back to her, the only joy in the whole scene. He ran for the open door but, just as she reached him, stumbled and fell over the lintel into the dark building.

"Harper John, don't cry. You're not hurt." She brushed at his muddy trousers and his smudged hands.

"You need to slow down, young man."

Lucy heard boots behind her and looked up to see five Rangers, in their green jackets and khaki pants. They formed a smiling circle around her and her son. "He got away from me," she said. "Sorry to disturb you."

"You have no need to apologize, no need to apologize, Madam," said the short stocky man before her. "He is just a child."

"Lucy! Is he all right?" John pushed through the soldiers, their satchel in his hand, and grabbed her arm. Before she could answer, the man spoke again.

"Garner. Is that you?" he asked. "I thought you were dead. You never...never showed up after Newtown."

"Sir!" John's right hand flew into a salute.

Lucy stared from one to the other. The other soldiers had backed off and were silent. "Is this...are you...Colonel Butler?" She looked into his piercing eyes.

"Yes, madam, I am." He seemed to stare right through her but, in the rainy day gloom, she couldn't see his features clearly. "And you must be the lost wife...lost wife of Private Garner. If I'm not mistaken," he added.

"Yes, I am, sir. Pleased to make your acquaintance, sir." Lucy dipped her head as she spoke.

"Likewise, Mrs. Garner." He nodded and turned to John. "And you. You owe me a report, Garner. Right quickly, too." Butler stepped aside and headed out into the grey day.

John's shoulders slumped and he watched the soldiers drifting away. He held out his hands to her and Harper John, and led them out of the barracks.

"He wants me now, Lucy. I've got to go."

"Of course. But what will I do?"

"Hold on to Harper John, woman. That's the main thing."

His voice grated on her and she thought of all the months she had managed the farm without him, even birthed the baby, when he was nowhere to be found. She knew how to look after their child, for gracious sakes. She choked back the words she once would have given in reply. His return was too new. "Yes, John," she said. "Ask the Colonel where we are to live."

John nodded and turned from her. She picked up Harper John. "Look, there goes your father to get us a place to live."

"No father."

"Of course, he's your father. You just don't remember him, Johnny." She squeezed him tight and set him down. "Come on. Let's explore."

The barracks was a huge rough-hewn timber structure, newly built, but already starting to blacken from the weather, a small door in the middle of its hundred-foot length. Only a few small windows were propped open to allow air inside. How did the soldiers see anything? Facing the barracks a wide expanse of muddied parade ground held bedraggled Rangers drilling back and forth, their muskets and rifles clutched to their sides. Croaked orders hung weak in the air, from voices long tired of the monotony. Bordering this field was a collection of huts and cabins, some with thin snakes of smoke wisping into the grey skies, and others completely defenseless against the sleet, which now dripped into the mud.

The horses! Where did John tether them when he came running after Johnny? Along the barracks, hitched to the longest rail she had ever seen, the two stood still and silent, as though wishing away their inevitable drenching. She pulled her protesting son towards them, but the rain pounded harder and she retreated to the barracks and lifted Harper John back into the dark shelter.

The place was an abomination with bare earth underfoot, the sooty smell of smoldering fires assaulting her nostrils, and row upon row of berths, one above the other, covering the walls. Most sleeping places were empty, but some held dark forms huddled under thin grey blankets with only their bony faces showing above. She moved closer, drawn by the stark, staring orbs, but the smell of decay stopped her. Covering Harper John's eyes, she stumbled backwards, away from the stench, the smoke, and the despair.

In the straw around a small fire tended by a burly cook, she collapsed with Harper John and held him tight against her body. They could not stay here. She had thought there would be room in the barracks for families but, even if there were, she could not keep her wee child here in this black hole filled with death. The whole length of the barracks was lined with berths, one after another. There was no privacy, no clean air, and no hope. No wonder John had found his way home to her on the farm a year ago, rather than spend a punishing winter in this place.

The door burst open and daylight streaked through the smoky gloom as two men entered and tramped to the far end of the barracks, becoming shadows before the fire there. They dropped their coats and held their hands over the flames, not saying a word. Harper John's eyes sparkled in the firelight as he watched more soldiers come through the door, but Lucy held his pudgy hand tight in her own, and waited for the rain to stop, for John to come back, and for her stomach to settle.

"Daddy?" said Harper John, and Lucy followed his pointing finger to the door.

"Yes. That's your daddy, Johnny. Good for you!" She struggled to her feet with him and rushed to the doorway. "What did the Colonel say? Does he have a home for us? Was he very angry or…"

"Wait a minute, Lucy." He grabbed her arms. "I'll tell you all about it. But first, we must find a place to live."

"Not here, John," she cried.

He chuckled. "No, not here. This is for the single men. We'll have a cabin across the parade ground."

She took a step back and glared at him. "Those cabins?" As near as they stood to the feeble fire, her fingers were still like ice. She shivered.

"Come, I'll show you." Outside the rain had stopped and soldiers were again on the move all around the camp. The mud was so slick now her leather shoes slipped from one sinkhole to the next and, as the three of them slopped toward their cabin, her skirts became more and more waterlogged. She would have a job washing their clothes free of this filth. And not just today, but every time it rained. John carried Harper John now but he wouldn't be there all the time. The child would drown in the mud, she was sure.

WHILE JOHN HAD FETCHED THEIR SUPPER from the cookhouse, Lucy swept out the cabin with a borrowed broom and unpacked their meager possessions. The silver spoon, her last gift from her father, and her mother's buttons lay on the table. John's musket and her rifle leaned side by side against the wall under the tiny shuttered window and, beside the rope-slung bed covered with a dingy mattress, she had deposited their saddles. They sat together on the only seat in the cabin, a long bench against the wall, Harper John between them, picking away at the mess of colorless stew before them.

"What did Colonel Butler say, John?"

"He believed me."

"He just needs more soldiers, that's all. Who would ever have thought you'd make it back after that battle?"

John nodded but held his peace. "Whatever the reason, we're here now, and here we'll stay."

"But we have nothing, John." *We lost everything because we supported the King in this accursed war and what has it got us?* "Our farm is probably overrun with land grabbers by now and all our hard work has been for naught." She jumped to her feet and faced him. "Someone else is cooking on our beautiful stove while we take scraps from the camp cook. When will this war be over?"

A white light slivering through the shutters worried John's eyes as he wriggled and flailed on the coarse tick, trying to escape back into the blessed relief of forgetful slumber. Lucy lay scrunched beside him, and Harper John, next to her, all three under the two mangy blankets from the Ranger stores, trying to keep warm in the cold spring night. He settled against Lucy's warmth and draped his arm across her under the blanket, but she didn't stir. Her curls were damp and cold against his cheek and he held her closer.

He hadn't done much of a job of taking care of her. Left her alone on the farm while he went off with the Rangers, didn't force her to leave when he had the chance a year ago, and simply lost her and Harper John for most of the time since.

And now they had almost nothing left to start over. His eyes filled with tears and he inched his arm away from Lucy to wipe them away.

"We're all right, John," Lucy whispered.

She was awake.

She turned towards him and her arm crept around his waist. He held his breath as she pressed her face into his neck and kissed him. "We're safe now," she said. He wanted to answer, knew he should, hated the hurt he had caused her, but rolled over, and accepted the punishment of the cold, harsh tick.

✝

Chapter Two

"AT LEAST WE HAVE A ROOF OVER OUR HEADS," Lucy said. "That's something, I suppose."

"And we are safe here, safe from those Americans as they call themselves now." Nellie sat on the bench next to the table, her knees tight together and her feet tucked to one side. Her black hair was caught up in a tight bun, which protruded from her stiff bonnet, tightly tied under her chin.

Lucy remembered the perfect little doll her mother had dressed for her all those years ago in Boston. Nellie looked just like her. Lucy stifled a giggle. "And I have you, my friend, which counts for a lot. Are you sure you can spare this?" She stood up from her place on the bed and fingered the patchwork quilt lying on the table, a gift from Nellie this morning.

"I wish you would let me give you more, Lucy…another blanket or clothes for Harper John. We have plenty, you know."

"No. This generosity is ample, my friend." She turned and stood at the window, pressing her hands together but seeing nothing of the scene outside. "We have quite enough to get by." After a deep breath, she faced Nellie again, smiling. "Did you see, by chance, that the last gunboat is almost completed? Harper John has dragged me there every day since our arrival. What will he do when he sees there is no more building going on?"

"I am sure you'll find some other way to occupy him. Where is he, by the way?"

"His father took him for a walk over to where Colonel Butler is building his house.

"Really?" Nellie looked away from Lucy and fingered the grey homespun of her skirt. "And you let him go?"

"Of course. John is his father and it's high time they got to know each other."

"But he's, well, I just thought…"

"I know what you thought, Nellie. You and the whole camp here and you're all wrong. John is fully recovered and fit for duty. More fit than all those hulking shells gasping for breath in the barracks, I warrant!" She stopped. Her breath caught and her cheeks flushed. "I'm sorry, Nellie. I didn't mean to subject you to my tirade."

Nellie stood up and touched Lucy's arm. "Don't worry, my dear. And I apologize for offending you."

"It's just that everywhere I go, people whisper and look away. When I approach, they're polite enough, but the tongues start wagging as soon as I walk off. What is it they think John has done?"

"He deserted, Lucy. At least that's the word going around," Nellie said.

"But he didn't. He was wounded and almost died, for heaven's sake! And all for the King."

Nellie stepped across the bare floor and squeaked the door open. She turned to Lucy. "I will be on my way, my dear. Remember, we are only just across the marching field."

"Goodbye, Nellie. Thank you once more for the quilt." Lucy watched the door close and heard the latch click. She stood staring at the rough, hand-hewn wood but her mind was on the lovely, two-room cabin John had built in the wilds of New York State when their love was new, Harper John not even thought of, and the war a distant haze on the horizon.

"Momma, momma," Harper John called and the door crashed back against the wall as he ran inside, John behind him.

She clasped his wee body to her and breathed in his damp sweat. She looked at John with a silent question.

"Yes, Momma, we got along well. Didn't we, Johnny?"

As he took the boy from her, she smiled into his green eyes and relaxed. "Shall we go to get our dinner, Harper John?"

Without warning the door banged open and a soldier stood on the threshold, his shoulders heaving up and down as he gasped out his message. "Garner! The Colonel wants you. Now!"

"Why? What has happened?" John asked.

"The river. Come! We need you, now." He grabbed John's arm and pulled him out of the cabin. Harper John whimpered and Lucy held him to her. "Don't cry, little one. Daddy's a soldier and they need him for a while." But her stomach tightened as she held her boy and tried to breathe evenly. John disappeared with the soldier. The mess bell sounded. Lucy took the child and went to eat.

As the days went by and spring gave way to the promise of summer, Lucy settled into her life as part of the entourage of Butler's Rangers. No homes existed for those who were not soldiers, no streets, and certainly no towns. This new land had to be hacked and hewn, ploughed and sown with the daily sweat of the few Loyalists who had crossed the Niagara River to escape the Americans and start again. With John occupied every day by Ranger business, at the beck and call of his superiors as he was, Lucy's shoulders bore the brunt of finding a way for them to start again. She soon knew the limitations of the facilities available and began to see the many problems they all had to face.

There were no land divisions drawn up yet, but the new settlers had only a couple of years to start their farms before their rations would be cut off. Brave couples made forays into the woods, surveyed their situations, and began clearing and building on the land even though they had no title. Colonel Butler had even marked off his own acreage and begun his farm on it.

Over and over Lucy walked across the parade ground toward the woods, always ending in a different part of the cleared areas. The question of where she and John might settle became a burning quest for her. Farther and farther she ranged past the military buildings, the ship building down by the river, and out into the woods. As she had always done on her spring jaunts, she walked with her eyes to the ground looking for food and medicinal plants to replenish her stores.

On one such foray she held Harper John's hand as they followed a faint trail under the giant oak trees and reveled in the somber quiet, broken only by the trilling of birds high above and the swishing of branches in the wind. She heard water and followed the sound to a running stream that tumbled with airy specks of wet light over an outcropping of rocks, black and grey, to splash into a small pool a few feet below. It was hardly a match for the might of the huge falls a few miles away, but still thrilling in its own right.

Lucy ran, tugging her child, all the way back to the barracks and their cabin. Even though the day was only half spent, John was there, sitting at the table, his empty plate before him on the bare table.

"John, we found it. Harper John and I, we found it!"

"What are you talking about?"

"The place for our new home. We found it!"

He jumped up from the bench and grabbed her shoulders. "Lucy. Slow down. We already have a home."

"We found the place for our new farm, John. With a beautiful stream, and falls. Falls, John. Just like we had in New York. You must come."

"Lucy, I don't know what you're saying. We'll be going back to our home when we win this war." His green eyes flashed with gold specks and his thumbs dug into her arms. "You have to hear my news." He released her and sat, patting the bench beside him. "Join me, Lucy."

She sat. Still panting from her run, she stared at John. Why was he not excited? Something was wrong. Harper John pulled at her arm and she realized she was still clutching his little hand in hers. She let go. The child crawled up on the bed, drew the blanket into his hand, and thrust his thumb into his mouth as he lay watching them.

"What is it, John?"

He took her hands in his and pulled her to face him on the bench. The small cleft in his cheek twitched as he opened his mouth and then closed it again. His eyes closed, too, just for a second, and she held his hand tight as though she might stop him from saying whatever bad news he had. But it was no good.

"The Colonel has given me new orders."

She stared at him, unable to believe that, so soon, the Colonel was sending him away from her when they had only been reunited for a matter of weeks. She thought of the trail of disasters along which she, without John, had managed to bring Harper John after fleeing from their farm: her father's murder, the rebel attacks when she was with the Seneca, and that despicable beast of a man who had tied her up and abused her and her child at will.

A shiver shook her and her body twisted but John held tight to her hands. She forced her thoughts back to John's sad eyes. "When?" she asked.

"Immediately, he told me."

"What are you doing this time?" She moved to the bed and stroked Harper John's back. "Another reconnaissance mission to go bad?"

"Yes." His voice caught but he went on. "I will be going by myself to mix with the rebels and send back information. This could help us win the war, Lucy."

"I suppose you have no choice. And neither do I." She looked for him to refute this but his hooded eyes and slumped shoulders told her he could not.

"I'll be back as soon as I can," he said, head nodding. "You'll see. This will help our cause, I know it will." His eyes shone as he spoke and she saw his pain.

"When will we ever get our lives back? When?" she whispered, and, for the first time in weeks, they clung to each other with a desperate urgency.

John had little to pack up; next morning he rode off again to ferry across the river to Fort Niagara and beyond. Lucy and Harper John had gone with him to the river, hugged him one last time, and watched and waved until they saw the boat land on the other side and John lead his horse up onto the shore. He turned toward them, held his hat high in the air in a final wave, and rode away up the cliff trail.

"Daddy all gone," whispered Harper John and Lucy picked him up and held his tiny warm body tight.

"He's coming back, you'll see," she said, as much to herself as to him, and started back up the trail to their tiny ramshackle pile of logs, the only home they had. And now, John was gone again.

Chapter Three

THE LAST TIME JOHN HAD RIDDEN OFF on a secret mission, he had been part of a small group of six Rangers and three Indians. Staying off the main trails, they had hoped to reconnoiter the placement of the Americans without being discovered, but within a couple of days of setting out they were attacked, and his best friend, Frank, had been murdered along with everyone else in their party. What would happen on this trip?

He rode past Fort Niagara with its old French castle a hive of colorful soldiers and Indians bustling about. Children ran in front of one-room cabins, their mothers hanging homespun garments to dry on the bushes outside. In the background officers barked commands at soldiers drilling in front of the fort.

John turned his eyes to the forest ahead and swallowed the bitter bile of leaving once more. Soon the sounds of the fort softened and disappeared and he began to ponder the journey ahead. Butler expected him to infiltrate the rebels in Boston, the flaming heart of revolutionary zeal in the colonies, from which all loyalists had been driven. He wished Frank were with him but his good friend was gone forever.

As the trail narrowed into the trees, he began to think of the last time he had ridden in the other direction, a few short weeks ago. He had totally lost track of Lucy and Harper John and hoped against all hope to find them at the fort after his long wounded winter with the Senecas who nursed him back to health. Now he was leaving his family again, and though he had told Lucy there was no danger to this trip, he knew better. The Americans were combing the forests and farms looking for enemies among the settlers and the Indians and giving no quarter when they found them.

He scanned the forest trail ahead but saw nothing beyond the pain on Lucy's face. The trees, however, were so thick that he had no choice but to stay on the trail as long as he could and watch closely. There would be no losing himself in thoughts of Lucy. He must stay alert.

The horse neighed and pulled up short. She chewed at the bit, her hoofs trampling the grass underfoot, and he struggled to hold her while all his senses strained to discover what had frightened her. He could see nothing ahead or behind. A lone call echoed in the strangely silent woods, an owl's hoot, yet the sun had risen well above the trees. He slid down and pulled his horse into the thick branches and prickly underbrush, not knowing if he was escaping the danger or running directly into it.

A few feet in was all John could manage and the wild-eyed horse fought to escape the tight space. He stood inches from the mare, desperate to calm her. He stroked the damp head over and over, murmuring soft sounds, and leaning against her heat. Gradually her eyes closed a little and they both breathed easier.

Able to refocus on the trail sounds now, he heard only a lone robin's call, and then nothing. The faint snap of a twig made him jerk to the left. The sound came again, closer. He held his breath and didn't dare move. Even when his horse shifted from one foot to the other, John only leaned his head ever so slightly to rest against the animal's head. He picked up a slight rustling sound. Something or someone was definitely close.

And then he saw just a small spot of red through the fresh green of the maple leaves. It moved. He should have grabbed his musket off the horse, glanced back to see if he could reach it. Damn! The red came closer. Someone's shirt? His hands were wet now and rivulets of sweat snaked down his forehead. A quick rub against the horse's face kept the sweat from his eyes.

"I will court her for her beauty. She must answer yes or no." A woman's soft singing broke the stillness. The red patch moved as she stepped along the trail toward him. His nose itched; he was desperate to scratch it. Between the horse hair and leaves against his face, he just couldn't breathe. She was close by. A few seconds more and she'd be gone.

His sneeze broke the silence and the horse bolted out of the hiding place. He had no choice but to follow her into the open. The woman a few feet away had turned.

"Who are you?" she shouted. "Why are you spying on me?" She held a small knife in her hand and her eyes showed she was prepared to use it if she could.

"I'm not spying on you, madam." She was probably on her way to the fort. He thought of Lucy and Harper John alone on the trail last summer and fall. Perhaps this woman was escaping, too; he heard fear in her voice.

"Are you a soldier?" she asked as she took a step closer to him.

John's whole body stiffened. He had to begin his story right then and there. "No. Definitely not, madam." She didn't comment and he continued. "I've been trying to get back to Boston or at least somewhere away from these British forts." He smiled as best he could and waited.

"It's a strange time to be travelling, sir."

"Yes, it is. For me and for you." He noticed her drop her glance and the knife, just a little.

She remained silent as she stepped so close he could see the sun shining in her beautiful brown eyes. "I'm on the run," she said, "all alone."

John heard another sound in the distance. "Horses!" He pulled his own mount back into the brush and she followed him into the tight space. He had to put his arm around her and pull her to him. Together they stood and listened to pounding hoofs of a few soldiers mere feet away. John's breath was full of her dark hair this time; her bonnet had snagged on the overhead branches and uncovered her tresses.

When the sounds on the trail ceased and silence reigned again, they squeezed out of their hiding place. "Could I go with you?" the petite woman asked. Seeing his shocked look, she continued, "I've no one and need protection. And two would be better than one travelling, don't you think?" She looked down to pull her bonnet strings together and tie them.

What could he say? She certainly needed help and she would help his disguise. In short order he mounted, pulled her up in front of him and struck out east. This time he made sure his musket was close at hand. He rode with the woman, whose name he didn't know, even further away from his Lucy and Harper John, towards he knew not what.

Chapter Four

June, 1780

LUCY LAY NEXT TO HARPER JOHN IN THE BED, her fingers running over his steaming forehead. His whimpering barely penetrated her fever-ridden brain. The whole camp was afflicted with the ague. First to succumb were the youngest and oldest and she had not been far behind. Her child's body lay limp and listless. She forced herself half way up to check him once again, wiped the drops from his face with her hot hand, and fell back again. Her stomach roiled and she barely managed to flop over to retch in the pail beside the bed, still soiled from the times in the night when she had thrown up.

"Help…" The word barely escaped her dry lips. She slid her feet off the bed to the cool floor and pushed up from the bed. She staggered the few feet to the door. Her head was heavy on her shoulders and she leaned against the hard surface, trying to get her eyes to focus. The latch was loose in her slippery hand but it lifted and she pulled with all her strength to open the door. She tried to take a step but fell through the doorway to lie full out, on her back, in the mud. The cooling rain splashed over her. She could not move. *Must rise. Harper John…*Some force prodded her. *Get up. Get help for Harper….*

No sound came to her ears but the soft silence of the rain. Its coolness calmed and comforted her and sleep came easily for the first time in days. Years? She didn't know. A great weight lifted from her tired body. But deep within, a niggling something pricked at her. *Go away, go away, let me go.* It would not. And she remembered her child, lying helpless mere feet away. Again, she lifted her head and opened her mouth to call out. No sound came.

In this driving rain, the parade ground was empty, as all sensible people were cocooned in their cabins or in the barracks. No one was hurrying for their supper or caring for their horses. Nellie's cabin, across the way, was closed up tight and Lucy couldn't possibly make it there anyway. She watched the rain-black door and willed Nellie to come out, but nothing and no one moved this desperate, dank day. She shuddered at the thought of not getting help. The mud, which had felt so good scant minutes before, now wrapped her in icy cold and she shivered and shook as she lay sunk in the slop. And lost all feeling.

Hard hands held her and voices, a voice, shouted. What were the words? *No, let me be.* The fingers dug into her, lifted, she drifted, and the wet stopped hitting her face.

"Where shall I put her?"

A man. John?

"On the floor. I'll never get all that mud off the bed."

Mother?

LUCY LAY IN THE BED AND STARED AT THE SWAYING COBWEB above her. Suspended in mid-air with seemingly nothing to support it, still it persevered and kept its place in the sunlight streaming through the window. For the first time in weeks, she felt she might get out of bed and sweep that cobweb away, but for the moment she was content to observe it. A light knock came on the door before it swung open with all the force a boisterous two-and-a-half-year-old could muster. He flung himself on the bed beside her.

"Harper John!" She wrapped her arms around his tiny warm body.

"He was just that anxious to come see you this morning, Lucy. How are you feeling?" Nellie asked, her brown eyes taking in the whole room before they settled on Lucy with a look of deep concern. "Did you sleep?"

"Oh, I did, Nellie, and I feel so good this morning. For the first time, I'm thinking about John's homecoming and building a new farm and a new life again. Thank you so much for caring for us both." She sat up in bed and slipped her feet to the floor. "Move over, Harper John. Mother is getting up!"

"Don't rush, Lucinda."

"How nice, Nellie. No one has called me Lucinda since my father died. Thank you." She inched to her feet and smiled. "The dizziness is gone."

"Good. I have something to tell you," Nellie said.

"Yes?"

Nellie stepped toward the window, was silent for a moment, and turned back, blocking out the sunlight.

"What is it, Nellie? You look like someone has died." Suddenly Lucy felt weak again. "Is it John?"

"Well, that's just it, Lucy. No one knows where he is."

"He's on a mission, for the Colonel, you know that."

"The Colonel says not. He has put out the word that John is absent without leave." She put her hand on Lucy's arm. "I'm sorry, my dear."

Lucy squeezed her hands together, fighting the urge to slap Nellie. "You're wrong. And everyone who says that is wrong." She reached for her gown on the hook above the bed. "No one is going to spread lies about my husband while I'm lying here in bed, sick in body and mind."

Nellie moved in front of the door. "Don't go, Lucy. You're still so weak and the Colonel isn't here anyway."

"Where is he?" She stood inches away from Nellie, prepared to walk right through her friend to get out the door.

"He's off fighting somewhere. And so are most of the soldiers, except for those who are too sick. Don't go, Lucy. Think of Harper John."

"What about Harper John?" Her eyes widened with fear as she wondered what else Nellie hadn't told her.

"I didn't want to say this, but," she paused. "With John branded a traitor, your safety here is in jeopardy. Do you not see? The British might just refuse to feed and house you. And your child."

"Children," Lucy whispered as she reached behind her for the edge of the table. "I think I'm going to have another one." She sank to the bench and lifted her eyes to Nellie. "What shall I do?"

That night, for the first time in weeks, Lucy crossed the parade ground, Harper John's hand in hers, to get their evening meal from the cook's hut. A small number of other women, children, and scrawny men so shrunk up they looked like wraiths from another world shuffled in line beside her. Only those unable to fight and a very few Loyalist men who daily went into the woods to clear land for farming were left in the encampment around Butler's Barracks. The late afternoon sun struggling through the trees fell on a sorry summer camp with no joy, no peace, and certainly no contentment.

With some of the women she had struck up at least a nodding acquaintance before her illness, but none would meet her eyes. One turned around and headed the other way as soon as she saw Lucy, even though her two children whined for their supper and looked back with sad eyes in long faces. Nellie had been right. The camp had turned against her and her child, for no good reason. John was not a traitor. He was not. He would never abandon them or his beliefs. Would he?

Alone in her bare cabin, Lucy watched her child sleep as, once more, the camp became quiet as death. She must confront whoever was in charge tomorrow and set things right. The whispers about John had to be stopped, once and for all. In the last daylight streaking across the bed, Harper John's curls shone bright and blonde. She must be strong, for him. And for the new baby.

"YOU MUSTN'T WORRY, MRS. GARNER," the dark-haired Sergeant Crawford across the table said. "There is no plan to cut off you or your child. These are just idle rumors."

"But, sir, because of these rumors no one will speak to me. Only my friend, Mrs. Watters. And they won't let their children near my son. Surely you can put out the truth about John!"

"I can only follow my orders, ma'am," he whispered, "but, ah, perhaps there is some other service I can offer you, a woman… alone…unprotected here…in a virtual wilderness." He raised his black eyebrows and his hand came across the table toward her.

As though struck in the face, Lucy jerked her hand from the table and stood, the hot blood rushing to her face. She groped for the door behind her. "Thank you, Sergeant Crawford," she said. "I've got to see to my son." Like a deer escaping a trap, she stumbled from the small room, fighting tears, her head pounding. But she held those tears at bay, straightened her back, and marched across the parade ground, the sun hot on her face, towards Nellie and Harper John playing with James and Robert, Nellie's twins, in a game of toss-the-stick.

That afternoon a sharp rap on the door startled Lucy as she sat at the table sewing a pair of britches. She pricked her finger. Immediately blood oozed but she stood up and pulled the door towards her. As soon as she saw who it was, however, she stepped forward into the opening and blocked his advance. Sergeant Crawford's broad smile narrowed a little; however, he put on a brave face.

"I've come to offer my assistance, madam." In a soft voice he spoke again, but his eyes were black and hard. "We parted on less than desirable terms this morning. I hope to remedy that. Can I do anything to assist you?"

Lucy wondered what to say. If she made an enemy of this man, her situation would be worse in the camp, but she could not encourage him for fear of how he might take it. "No…I…no, not just now, thank you," she said. "But I thank you for your offer." She offered a slight smile and turned to go in.

He grabbed her elbow. "Please, Mrs. Garner. I would like to make amends. If there is anything I can do, please tell me." He stepped back a pace, tipped his hat to her, and walked away.

She watched him stride across the parade ground and wondered if she had been mistaken about his attentions. Perhaps he was sincere.

Inside the cabin again, her hands found their way to the small pocket in her worn satchel. She pulled out the letter John had sent to her back when he first joined the Rangers and left her alone on their farm. She had kept it all these frightening two years and knew it by heart, but opened it anyhow to read the worn words again. Her bloody finger smudged the wrinkled paper and she tried to wipe it clean but could not. Where was he?

Chapter Five

Summer, 1780

IN THE DAYS THAT FOLLOWED Sergeant Crawford seemed to be everywhere that Lucy and Harper John went. Twice a day he would magically appear in the food line at her elbow, offering to carry Harper John's plate and reaching across the broad serving table to spear some larger piece of meat for her. His smile was constant, broken only when he showed concern for her and her son, and her own wariness faded to the far reaches of her mind. Amidst all the averted faces and exaggerated sniffs she endured from almost everyone in the camp, the sergeant's company was balm to her bruised soul.

She found herself smiling again. Walks with Harper John into the woods almost every day brought her back to searching for medicinal plants as she had done in the woods surrounding their farm, and her cabin began to look like home with herbal bits bound and hung from the rafters to dry. Even the very hot days of summer were pleasant under the canopy of maples, oaks, and hemlocks which all protected her just as surely as the sergeant's friendship and presence in the camp itself.

He was the soul of propriety whenever he saw her and she never thought of her earlier fears about his intentions. He was an even better friend to her than Nellie as no tension existed between them as it did whenever Nellie's twins poked at Harper John in the food line or pulled his hair until he cried on one of Lucy's visits to their cabin.

Today Sergeant Crawford appeared at the edge of the forest path just as Lucy was about to take her customary afternoon walk after Harper John's nap.

"Hello! Mrs. Garner!" he called.

Lucy grabbed her son's hand to stop him from chasing into the woods, his favorite part of the ritual. "Good day, Sergeant Crawford." She waited for him to catch up.

"Would you permit me to accompany you on your walk today, Mrs. Garner?" He removed his hat and gave a slight bow.

"I, well, Harper John and I are looking for toadstools, aren't we, son?" She looked down at Harper John, and away from the sergeant.

"A wondrously interesting pastime, I'm sure. Would you allow me to accompany you both?" He reached for the little boy's other hand and his full lips parted in a smile when Harper John put a tiny hand into his own.

Lucy glanced around to see if anyone was watching but the parade ground was empty and the cabin doors were all closed against the heat. "Yes, all right, Sergeant Crawford, if Harper John wishes it." And they set off down the leafy trail, the little boy running merrily between them.

An hour later the parade ground was no longer empty. Groups of children ran in and out of the sun while their mothers clustered in shady porches, the din of their shouts to their children filling the sultry air. All eyes turned to watch her and the sergeant as they approached the camp, he at her side, carrying the tired child, and the three of them chuckling over Harper John's attempt to croak like a frog.

Lucy glanced at the sergeant but he stared straight ahead and held tight to Harper John. She choked back her laughter but her child still gurgled and giggled, oblivious of the tension that mounted with every step they took towards the parade ground. She ignored the errant curls sticking to her wet skin and stared straight ahead, willing her feet to walk on no matter how her stomach churned. What would these women say this time? What would they think?

The boys stopped their running and their laughing and stared. Lucy's feet were like heavy wooden lumps but she forged ahead, her own cabin door her only goal. Almost abreast of the porch women, her chest tightened. She took a deep breath, full of dust and heat, and focused on her cabin.

From the corner of her eye, she could see her son, now silent and staring ahead, and she felt the heat of the man walking beside her. Was he angry with her? With the women? She walked on.

One by one, three of the women on the porch stared right through her and then slowly turned their backs in a silent pantomime whose meaning was only too clear. Nellie was the only one left. Her friend. Would she snub them, too? Lucy looked into Nellie's eyes, beseeching her. Nellie stood still. She glanced at the children, at the other women, and back at Lucy, who tore her gaze away. She passed the group and crossed the parade ground, willing her hands away from her brimming eyes. She would not let them see her pain. She would not.

As she stepped on to her own porch, a hand touched her elbow—the one opposite the sergeant—and she whirled around.

It was Nellie.

THE SUMMER SETTLED UPON THE STEAMING CAMP as wagons guarded by small groups of Rangers came in empty and left loaded up over the top with food, muskets, cartridge papers, gun powder, and mail pouches, all for the struggling soldiers pushing back against the Americans. Tagalong children ran beside the wagons until they could no longer keep up on the narrow trail to the river where, one by one, the wagons were loaded onto flat-bottomed boats and ferried the short distance to the other side.

The parade ground was empty except for the children still running in the sun and the sickly soldiers sliding along beaten paths toward the food lineup whenever the leaden gong sounded the call.

Even the gossiping women held their tongues as though walking to the food line was all they could do in the blistering heat.

Outside their cabin door, Lucy held fast to Harper John's hand as they walked alone to get their supper. She carried the two tin plates but coming back she would have Harper John carry his own. If she carried them herself, he would run off and there was no telling what kind of trouble he might get into. Nellie waved from her porch and Lucy smiled and nodded. She knew better than to wait as Nellie always walked with her other friends in a laughing, boisterous group, with no room for Lucy. Still, she was grateful for Nellie's furtive visits to her cabin in the darkening evenings and for the sage advice her friend brought with her. Even news about the war and the endless rumors about John were welcome tidbits to Lucy.

This night, though, Nellie was held up with her children in a tantrum on the porch and the other ladies walked on. Instead of averting their glances as they usually did, the three of them, Mrs. Smith, Mrs. Butcher, and Mrs. Zebulon, all stared straight at Lucy, almost as though they had planned it. She smoothed her hair back under her bonnet and clasped her hands over her bulging stomach. Her nose suddenly ran and she sniffed to clear it. Harper John tugged her arm, wanting to run ahead. She yanked him back.

As their separate paths converged, Lucy had no choice but to stop and let the three go ahead of her.

"She has no pride," Mrs. Smith whispered loud enough for Lucy to hear.

"And no virtue, either," Mrs. Butcher added.

"What do you mean?" This was Mrs. Zebulon.

"No husband here for months and look at her. There's a baby coming, for sure."

All three of the women suddenly turned on Lucy and studied her stomach. She stepped back and Harper John whined. "Mama! Eat!"

Others filed by as Lucy knelt by her son. "I know, darling." She let the line move ahead and then stood again. "Come along. We can eat now," she whispered, but food was the farthest thing from her thoughts as she held her first child's hand and felt the flutter of her second.

"Mrs. Garner!"

Lucy's stomach relaxed. Finally, a friendly soul.

"How is Harper John this evening? Is he hungry?" asked Sergeant Crawford as he bent to smooth the boy's hair.

"Oh, Sergeant Crawford, he is just that anxious to get his food, I've had a time holding him back until the gong sounded." She swallowed and forced a smile.

The sergeant stood up and looked into her eyes. "Are you all right, Mrs. Garner?"

"Yes, yes, thank you. Just a little tired." She turned and began dishing stew onto the two plates, glad of the distraction.

"Come and eat with me, Mrs. Garner. There is a table near the barracks door. Would you?"

She shook her head. "No, no. We'll eat in our cabin. It's easier with the boy, you understand." And, much as she would have enjoyed his company, she turned toward the solitary cabin across the parade ground. "Come along, my son. Hold your plate steady."

THE NEXT DAY NELLIE CAME TO CALL first thing in the morning, right after Lucy had dressed Harper John and tidied up the cabin. It was more comfortable now with the muslin curtains Nellie had given her and a strip of a blue cloth over the bare table. In the corner beside her bed, a small mattress was made up for Harper John right on the plank floor so that he wouldn't fall out. The broom in the corner she had inveigled out of the camp stores by offering to mend some homespun shirts for the soldier in charge. It was a prized possession.

Into this clean but spare space Nellie swept with her swishing skirts and her full-sleeved blouse, both a drab brown but brightened at the neck with a sprig of dandelion. She was scowling.

"Lucy, there is a story about you, did you know?"

Lucy shook her head and frowned as she motioned toward the bench and Nellie sat. "What story?" she asked.

"Well, I, it..." Nellie stood and went to the window, drawing back the curtain. "They say this baby, it...is not your husband's." She faced Lucy who sat on the edge of the bed. "They say he's been gone too long and you've taken up with Sergeant Crawford. People have even seen you sneaking off with him." Her brown eyes flashed on Lucy and then looked away. "They say."

"So now it's out, is it?"

Nellie jerked her head up. "You mean it's true?" The cords in her neck tightened and her eyes took on a look of horror mixed with pleasure.

"That I'm pregnant? Of course. You knew that. But I didn't realize others knew. What have you said?"

"Nothing, I swear. People can see, that's all. And you're so friendly with Sergeant Crawford..." she went back to the window.

"How dare you? I thought you were my friend even though you're so thick with those three witches. How could you think that of me?"

Nellie's face was shadowed. Her head dipped down as she studied something on the floor. She nodded, imperceptibly at first, and then more vigorously, a sure sign that she believed Lucy.

They sat again, Nellie on the bench, Lucy on the bed, and talked a little. Harper John played with a stick and a stone on the floor next to his mother but he uttered not a word. Soon Nellie rose and took her leave, a fixed smile on her face but over it her brow was furrowed like a fresh-plowed field.

Chapter Six

THE SETTLEMENT BEGAN TO LOOK more and more permanent that summer as the number of small cabins surrounding the parade ground increased whenever the few soldiers left behind had a spare moment. Settlers fleeing from Fort Niagara across the river to safety came whenever boats docked at the landing below and they trudged up the incline with their possessions and their sad eyes, wearing their desperate fear of the unknown. Finding space for them was almost impossible and many a fine night in summer, newcomers slept on the parade ground in the open air, finally safe from attack.

Butler's orders were to find shelter for all who came but the wherewithal to do that was glossed over. And with the Colonel himself off fighting in the colonies, those left behind soon learned to do whatever they could to provide shelter. One particularly rainy night, Lucy even had a man and his wife squeeze their belongings and themselves into her tiny cabin rather than lie in the puddled parade ground. With the damp and the heat and four people cooped up in the small space, Lucy lay awake most of the night just trying to breathe.

The weather cooled as fall came on, making the nights more bearable but also tending to make the landings fewer as the Loyalists prepared for winter where they were rather than try to make the arduous journey to British territory. Still the shipbuilding down by the docks went on and Harper John loved to go walking there with his mother and, often, Sergeant Crawford.

One day, however, Crawford arrived at Lucy's cabin door to accompany the two and Lucy went back for a shawl. As she threw it over her shoulders, the sergeant's eyes were on her. He stepped back off the porch.

"It's true, then," he muttered.

"What do you mean?" Lucy asked, as she stepped down beside him.

"You're...you are...you're with child!"

At the somber tone of his voice, she glanced at him. "Yes. I thought you knew."

"No. I didn't know. And I supposed the talk I heard was just gossip." He turned away. "Who is the father?"

She grabbed his arm and forced him to look at her. "Who do you think is the father? My husband!"

He blanched. "I'm sorry, Lu...Mrs. Garner. I just didn't think. Please forgive me."

With one hand Lucy held tight to Harper John and with the other she lightly touched her stomach, so quickly no one would even notice. But the sergeant did.

"I am so sorry, Mrs. Garner. I, I cannot do this." He started to walk away from her.

"You cannot do what?" she called.

He stopped, and slowly turned. "Another man's wife. Another soldier's wife. I must not." He did not touch her but his eyes found hers with such a look of pain in them as she had never seen before.

"I, I..." she could think of no reply in the face of his hurt. She dropped her hand and looked down at her son. The sergeant's scuffed boots moved away, Harper John moved in front of her, and for once was silent as he looked up at her in confusion.

"Mama cry?" he said.

"YOU'RE BETTER OFF WITHOUT HIM hanging around all the time, aren't you?" Nellie sat on the chair in Lucy's cabin, a cup of tea cooling before her. "Well, aren't you?"

"He was just so pleasant with Harper John," she said. "I feel the loss." *And I miss his kind words to me.* She leaned over to pick up one of Harper John's blocks from the floor.

Nellie sniffed and sat silent a moment before speaking. "Perhaps this will be better for you, Lucy."

"What do you mean 'better'?" She stood and faced her friend, hands on her hips and tried to meet Nellie's averted eyes. But Nellie wouldn't look at her. Instead she stirred her tea over and over rather than letting the tea leaves settle to the bottom of the cup.

"People are talking about you, the two of you. Together all the time. It's just not decent, Lucy!" The spoon clattered against the clay cup.

Lucy took a step back, dropped her arms, and choked out her reply. "Yes. I'm sure you're right." She moved to the window and yanked aside the curtain.

Soldiers drilled on the parade ground and she had allowed Harper John to sit on their one step to watch, cold as it was. He wore a long coat buttoned to his knees and a stiff blue scarf over his head which crossed back around to tie behind. As she watched his little head bobbing up and down, his shoulders rocked from side to side in the same rhythm as the marchers. Suddenly he jumped up and began clapping and shouting.

"Lef'… lef'… lef', ri', lef'!" He marched off across the frozen grass toward the red-coated soldiers.

Out the door she ran and caught her son's arm. "Come back inside," she said to her wailing child as she tugged him away from the approaching soldiers. Nellie held the cabin door open.

"I'll be leaving then, Lucy." She flounced down off the porch and across one end of the parade ground, careful to avoid the drill sergeant. Her bonnet strings flew out behind, drab as the day. Her skirts whipped against her legs as she leaned into the wintry wind.

Heading for the food line that night, Lucy spied Nellie. "Walk a little faster," she said to her son and pulled him across the parade ground to catch up to her friend. They had parted on poor terms earlier and she needed to soothe Nellie's ruffled feathers. If Nellie turned against her, she and Harper John would be totally alone in this godforsaken outpost on the edge of the world.

"Nellie, wait," she called, but Nellie didn't turn and even seemed to walk faster. "Nellie, I need to speak with you." Coming up behind she reached out to touch the heavy shawl Nellie wore.

"Keep away from me!" She jerked toward Lucy but the look on her face was not friendly. It was as if they had never met.

Lucy dropped her hand. "Nellie, please," Lucy began but Nellie walked on. "We need to talk!"

The woman stopped and faced Lucy. "That's Mrs. Watters to you, madam, and we don't need to talk. Keep away from me!"

As though prodded by a hot poker Lucy jumped away, her face hot and her free hand covering her mouth. Her stomach tensed into a hard ball and all her muscles seized. She couldn't move. She saw the other ladies fall into line with their children, the soldiers, too, the red-coated, the green-coated, and those whose homespun clothes were tattered and torn, and she stood, unable to join them, her feet stuck fast to the spot. She would not cry. Though her hope was gone and her will worn to the bone, she would not cry.

"Mama, Mama!"

A sob started deep down in the place where she had buried all her hurts and disappointments. She felt it rise with her breath, a slow, jagged knot of pain which she willed to stay hidden, exposed as she was on the broad parade ground with all the hungry bodies filing past, silently stabbing her with their accusing eyes. Her stomach muscles jerked and the sob, breaking free, pained as it escaped its prison for all the world to see. And hear. But she sucked in a breath, and another, and held her tears at bay.

"Mama!" The little boy's words crashed into her brain. He was pulling and jerking her hand and leaning toward the path to his supper, aware only of his need.

I must be strong. I...must...be...strong. She licked her lips and swallowed. "Yes," she whispered to her boy and put one foot in front of the other.

In the lineup Lucy looked only at her two plates as the cook ladled steaming stew onto them and plopped a blob of white in the middle. Potatoes, she thought. So thinned out, though, she wasn't sure. But she put the plate in her son's hands and pointed him toward their cabin. Grabbing her own and still looking at the ground, she bumped into someone and muttered an apology.

"Mrs. Garner, is it?" the woman asked.

She heard the pleasant tone and a bit of a Scottish brogue and raised her head. Who was this person?

"Ya dinna remember me?"

Lucy studied her swarthy complexion, the way her chin seemed not to be finished, and the woman's raised eyebrows. "Ah, of course. You stayed in my cabin when you arrived. With your husband." She nodded and a tiny smile broke forth as she remembered the woman's kind words to Harper John at the time. "You fixed my boy's scratched finger."

"Aye, that I did." She walked beside Lucy and Harper John. "My man is off with the soldiers gathering firewood. Might I eat with you?"

"Of course. You are most welcome."

Lucy felt the tears coming again but this time for a different reason as she led the woman and Harper John across the field. A thought crossed her mind. "I am sorry," she said, "but what is your name? I am afraid I have forgotten it."

"McKie, Mrs. Dorothea McKie." Her voice carried a song with it and Lucy relaxed for the first time in months.

HARPER JOHN HAD HIS SECOND BIRTHDAY IN DECEMBER, another occasion when Lucy longed for her missing husband, but Mrs. McKie invited them to her cabin for a wee celebration and the gloom lifted. Lucy held her son's hand to keep him from slipping in the fresh fallen snow as they trudged across the parade ground, around the barracks to the new cabin where her friend lived. A sprig of holly had been nailed above the door, its pointy green leaves and perfect red berries a welcome sight amidst all the white surrounding them. On the porch mother and son stamped the snow from their boots as the door opened.

"Look at the wee snow monsters who've come to visit me," Mrs. Mckie exclaimed as she opened the door wide to let them in. "Happy birthday, wee boy."

Their coats hung to dry, Lucy, Harper John, and the McKie's sat round the table.

"Mrs. McKie, this is good of you to have us," Lucy said. "Your home is very welcoming with all its spruce boughs and holly berries." She looked at Harper John's bright eyes. "Isn't it, my son?"

"We must celebrate the wee bairn's day, Mrs. Garner."

"Of course we must," Mr. McKie added, "and we have a bit of a surprise."

Mrs. McKie went to a wooden cupboard near the table and grasped the door handle. She looked at Harper John. "What might be in here, my young man?" Her wide mouth opened in a broad smile as she paused. "Can you guess, wee one?"

Harper John's eyes shone wide and wondrous as he looked at his mother and then back to the cupboard door.

"What do you think it is?" Lucy prodded him to answer.

As they all watched Mrs. McKie slowly tugged the squeaky door open and drew out a platter with a large frosted cake on it.

"Ah!" "Oh my!" The gasps tumbled together and the little boy jumped off his chair to get closer to his first birthday cake ever. Around the bottom of the plate green sprigs circled the creamy covered cake and a lone figure stood on the top, dressed in the green jacket and tan leggings.

"Marzipan!" Lucy said. "Where on earth…?"

"That army cook made it for me. Imagine. He knew how to do this beautiful marzipan soldier." She looked at Harper John. "Looks like your daddy, doesn't it, wee one?"

Harper John jumped up on his chair again and plunged his hand into the middle of the cake. Of course Lucy immediately stopped him but all the adults laughed uproariously at the first really funny thing they had experienced in a long, long time.

Chapter Seven

April, 1783

SPRING CAME EARLY THAT YEAR and with it a new name for the settlement which seemed to expand every day. Lucy watched as land was snatched without real title and ramshackle barns and cabins quickly filled the landscape. Every day the sounds of saws and hammers, shouts and falling trees drifted on the wind as it swept across the parade ground. Colonel Butler called the place Butlersburg and, wearing its very own name, the settlement took on more importance, like an attorney who donned his wig and robes and became someone to be respected and feared.

The soldiers had not left this spring. Colonel Butler was ensconced in the new home he had not even finished yet, looking for all the world as though he knew the Loyalists would never be returning to their homes in the colonies. With the addition of the French ships and soldiers, the Americans were winning the war. Those loyal to the British king had gambled. And for their troubles they had lost their homes, their wealth, and those dear to them. There was hardly a family whose tale of survival did not include a theft, a murder, a hanging, a scalping, and at least one narrow escape.

Lucy had still heard nothing from John, nor any word as to whether he was alive or dead. Her two boys, Harper John, now almost four and a half and William, in his second year, kept her entertained and on her toes from the first streaks of daylight to evening prayers before she tucked them into bed. Only then could she think of the future and what might be if John never returned. The sergeant had never come back to befriend her after William's birth and as the days turned into months and still no sign of John, she was lonely. She saw the sergeant walking with a widow from time to time but he kept his eyes on his companion, as though Lucy didn't even exist.

The lines for food were shorter now that many people grew their own and traded the excess for staples at the company store that did a brisk business every day except Sunday. Lucy had her eye on a plot of land for her family. She couldn't wait for John any longer as her two years were running out, with still no word of him. The acreage was small and covered with trees but with the help of her boys, she hoped she could make a start.

Today she planned to visit Colonel Butler at his home where he kept office hours during the afternoon. With her two sons in tow, she crossed the parade ground as the spring sun beat down on her bonneted head and little beads of moisture formed on her brow.

"Slow down, Mama," whined William.

"Yes, dear. I'm sorry." She smiled at him and forced herself to take slower steps.

They walked the path all the way to the Colonel's new house. Hammers tapped the fresh tongue and groove boards together on a broad porch that was set up to go along the east wall and halfway down the south one as well. The smell of fresh cut lumber filled Lucy's nostrils and she breathed in the welcome scent. She helped her boys up the steps, across the porch, to the open front door.

"Colonel Butler," she called. "Could you spare a moment?"

From the back of the house footsteps approached. Lucy licked her finger and smoothed Harper John's hair off his face.

"Yes?" The Colonel called out to her as he came through an interior doorway. "Can I help you, madam?" His voice fairly sang out the question.

"Ah, yes, sir," she began, and stopped. "You don't remember me?"

He looked into her eyes and down towards the two boys whose hands she held. "No, I'm sorry, ma'am, I do not." He stepped back. "But do come inside where we can talk more comfortably."

He led the three of them into a sparsely furnished parlor where a fine leather settee and two matching side chairs were placed at the edges of a large braided rug. "This is lovely. Thank you, sir," Lucy said in what she hoped was a pleasant and polite tone.

"I am sorry to have no refreshments…no refreshments to offer you, madam, but I haven't really moved in yet." As he indicated the settee to Lucy, the Colonel squeezed his bulky form into one of the chairs.

She flicked her tongue over her dry lips and lifted her chin. "I am Mrs. John Garner, sir. We have talked before."

"Garner!" The Colonel spat out the word. "I…I do not wish to hear that name, madam."

"But, sir," she began again. "We must talk about this, come to some arrangement." She struggled to control her shaking voice. His eyes blinked over and over. "I must know what provision is being made for us, the family of a Ranger who has been and still is very loyal to the British King." She forced herself to breathe.

"Your husband, madam, is a traitor to the King and you have no right to any bounty from His Majesty's largesse." He stood up quickly and turned his back on her. William began to whimper but Lucy ignored him. The Colonel, however, turned toward her again. "I did send your husband to the other side, madam." He took a step toward her and took a deep breath as he stared into her face. His left cheek seemed to twitch of its own accord. "I sent him to spy but I have received nothing from him. Not a word. About him, though, I have heard plenty."

He turned away, "You would be very wise to marry…to marry… to solve your own problems, madam. John Garner has NOT served his king well and he is dead to us—a traitor! Do you understand?"

"But you sent him to spy!" Lucy shouted. "How can you turn your back on us and him?" Both boys cried softly at her side and she drew them to her. "These are his children, sir. See how your words have offended!" She pulled the boys up and staggered from the fresh-smelling room, but not before Butler spoke again.

"If your husband comes back here, we'll hang him as a traitor. Look to your own future, madam!"

Chapter Eight

May, 1783

"MAMA! MAMA!" HARPER JOHN'S VOICE brought Lucy to the window where she watched him run from Nellie's house across the parade ground. She pulled the door open just in time for the four-year-old to run into her arms.

"What is it, my son?" she pulled him to her as she sat down. "Is a wild boar chasing you?"

"Peter and James, mama. They say I can go with them!"

She could hardly hold him, he was so excited, and the smile came to her face unbidden, especially as she had waited so long to hear the other children accepted him. With the war almost over and tensions lessening, the rest of the camp was beginning to forget their hatred for John, supposedly a traitor, and Nellie had begun speaking to Lucy once more. *Finally*, she thought. *My boy can play with the other children.*

"May I, mama? May I go?"

"Of course you may, my dear. Stay with the bigger boys, though. You will, won't you?" She held his arm to keep him from immediately running out the door.

"Yes, mama. I will."

She kissed the top of his golden head and released his hand. Out the door and back to the three boys waiting by Nellie's cabin he ran, as fast as his short legs could take him. She watched as the children ruffled Harper John's hair and pulled him along with them towards the woods. And she took a smile back to her chair and her mending of William's trousers.

THE AFTERNOON SUN SLANTED across the parade ground as Lucy looked out the window once more. William whined beside her. He wanted to go walking but she was reluctant to take him until Harper John returned. A shiver shook her as her fingernail scraped the dull glass.

"Come along, little one," she said. "We're going walking. Perhaps we'll meet Harper John and his friends on the way." Friends. How long she had waited to see her son playing with the other children.

William had tugged the door open already and she laughed at his bright cheeks, all scrunched up by his wide grin. Like rosy apples, she thought, and took his little outstretched hand in hers. Across the parade ground toward the forest trail they went, William running so fast to reach the trees she almost had to run herself.

"Mrs. Garner! Mrs. Garner!"

The voices came from ahead. Three small figures were running toward her, so far away she could hardly make them out. The boys. A broad smile sprang to her face as she waved and shouted. "Hello, hello."

She began to run, tugging William along with her, so happy was she to see the children, who were now running, too. Peter and James were in front. In behind was…No! This tall gangly boy who ran with legs that turned out at the knees, this was not Harper John. She stopped. But William loosened his hand and kept going, oblivious to the dread that held her back. And then she was running again, a loping, slipping, sliding run that turned to full out racing toward the boys.

"Harper John, where is he?" Her words poured out of her at the stricken faces of the boys. "What have you done with my son?" She grabbed Peter's arms and shook him.

....

"We didn't do it, Mrs. Garner. We didn't," he shrieked, as tears streamed down his muddy cheeks. The other boys nodded their heads, fear glowing in their wide eyes.

"Do what? What didn't you do?" Lucy shook Peter again. "Where is Harper John?" she cried.

"He fell."

"In a hole," added James. Nathan nodded.

Like a thunderbolt in the black of night that crashes just before the lightning, Lucy's stomach wrenched. The fear started deep inside, further down than her stomach, in the very base of her soul, and held her in thrall. She struggled for control.

"Where?" she gasped.

Peter's finger pointed back down the trail. She yelled at him. "Go! Get help." The boy tore off. "You two, show me where." The four of them ran down the trail.

LANTERNS LIT THE DESPERATE SCENE as Sergeant Crawford directed efforts to free Harper John from his earthy prison. He had fallen through an opening no wider than a milk bucket and lay trapped about twelve feet below the surface. His crying had stopped as Lucy spoke gently to him. The only sound was the subdued voices of men trying to figure how to get the wee boy out and the soft sobbing of women, stricken with the thought of losing one of their own in this way.

The sergeant dropped a rope weighted with a heavy stone and Harper John grabbed on to it. The men pulled gently on the rope but fell backward as it went slack in their hands. Harper John had let go. His voice seeped out of the hole. "Can't get out. Too tight."

"What do you mean, my son?" Lucy leaned over the opening.

"I'm stuck, mama."

A collective gasp escaped into the branches above.

"It's dark, mama. Pull me out," the child wailed, and Lucy turned to the men, hoping for a miracle.

"We'll try again." Sergeant Crawford's voice was strong but desperate. "We'll get him out, we will." And try again they did, over and over, and each time Harper John let go. Soon the slipping rope burned his hands so that he could not hold on any more and despair settled into the silence of the night.

"We'll wait until morning." The sergeant took Lucy's hands in his own and tried to get her to look at him. "There is just no way to do this in the dark. In the daylight, we'll get him out, Lucy. We will." He called her Lucy but she didn't even notice.

She slipped away from him and lay down on the ground beside the hole. "Harper John," she called. "I'm here. I won't go anywhere. I'll stay with you, my sweet boy. Don't be afraid." She listened a moment for a reply but there was none. "See the light? We're here, Harper John. We're here."

Sometime in the night the rain came and Lucy wakened stiff, sore, and wet with cold. "Harper John," she called into the dark hole. "Perhaps he's sleeping," she said to no one in particular.

"I'm sure that's it," a voice quite near replied.

She turned and saw Sergeant Crawford, his forehead creased with worry as he, too, stared at the black opening in the wet ground.

"We must cover the hole. And stand back." He took Lucy's arm and gently pulled her away.

"Whatever for?" she cried, but knew they needed to keep out the rain. Harper John would be in total darkness. The sergeant directed the faceless figures as they placed planks and pieces of oil cloth across the hole, the hole where her firstborn child, the child she had birthed all alone in the cabin those desperate years ago, where that very child lay wedged.

A heavy coat settled over her shoulders. Hands pulled her away from the working men. Cold drops of moisture streaked her face, slicking her hair to her cheeks and mixing with the hot tears she could not stop.

"Come, Lucy. We need to get out of the rain."

The voice sounded miles away, too far away to help or to heed and she shook her head, pulling away from the hands holding her back from her boy. If she could just dig, she could reach him. She knew she could. And she ran forward, collapsed to her knees, her hands hauling at the boards and then flinging bits of muck and grass in every direction. "Harper John, Harper John!" she wailed.

But no sweet voice answered.

Again hands held her and pulled her away from the soggy earth circling the hole. "Lucy, come back," he said. "Try to bear it. We'll get him in the morning." She gave up her fight and sank into those arms that dragged her through the black rain.

"John?" she whispered.

"No," he said but still held her tight.

He led her a few feet away to a tent erected as shelter from the rain. Nellie was there and pulled Lucy to a seat beside her on a plank bench. Sergeant Crawford was right beside her, squeezed onto the short bench with the two women, while across from them two men in uniform sat. All were dripping with rain, their faces ghoulish scars in the dim lantern light. She saw not a glimmer of hope on any of them.

Until the dim light of daybreak seeped through the rain-soaked canvas they sat in silence. Lucy heard no word of encouragement or of plans to save her child. They were all here just to support her. Nothing could be done for Harper John. The cold light of day brought with it that harshest of realities and she died inside.

"We must try again," the sergeant said as he half stood and pushed through the flap to the outside. One by one the other men crept out, followed by Nellie and Lucy. She slipped in the muddy grass and only missed falling flat when Nellie grabbed her arm. Mr. McKie and Mr. Johnson lifted the planks away from the hole now ringed with slimy mud. The rain had caused a small rivulet of water to run right into the hole and there was no telling how long it had been running.

Lucy gasped. She pulled away from Nellie. "Let me call to him." Her voice barely crept out of her and the sergeant turned to look into her face.

"Yes," he said.

"Harper John, are you awake, my son?"

They surrounded the narrow opening and leaned over it.

She called again. "Harper John, answer your mama."

"Uhhhh." A tiny whimper floated up toward the listeners. In unison the five let out a gasp that was choked off as they listened again.

"Yes, Harper John!" Lucy called. "We're going to get you out now." She began to talk in a low crooning voice, encouraging Harper John as the men began to shovel in a ring a couple of feet away from the hole. Lucy talked to her boy as the sergeant directed the digging. Nellie left to go get food for all of them and more dry blankets. The child would need those.

She sat by the hole, oblivious to the mud and muck covering every inch of her clothing. The men dug deeper and deeper until they needed her to move so they could continue. Reaching for the sergeant's outstretched hand, she stepped across the yawning trench away from her son, but she didn't stop talking to him. She just spoke louder until her voice almost drowned out the shovels striking the stones as the men hurried to save her boy.

"Stop!" The sergeant's voice shattered the din. All were silent as Lucy and the diggers looked first at the sergeant and then to where he was pointing. Beside the opening to the yawning hole, bits of wet soil were slipping from the edge into the hole.

As Lucy watched, the earth slipped slowly away but soon began to go faster and faster. "Nooo!" she cried and sprang for the hole but the sergeant held her back. "Let me go," she cried just as the whole side collapsed and all of them had to jump away. Sergeant Crawford held her against his chest so tightly that she couldn't see, couldn't move, but couldn't help her child either. She struggled and struggled against him until his arms released her and she turned to look.

Earth flew in all directions as shovels dug and tossed, dug and tossed, and the women—Lucy and Nellie both—knelt side by side on the ground raking their bare hands back and forth over the ground and flinging the muck behind them in a desperate drive to open the hole again. But it was no use. Each time they had the hole dug down a short distance, the sides gave way and more earth tumbled in. There was no sound but the shovels scratching on stones, the ragged breathing of the men, and the low moaning sobs of Lucy, and now Nellie, beside her.

They worked and they sweated, not stopping a moment, until the sergeant stepped away from the others. Lucy glanced up but her bloodied hands went right on flinging gobs of earth and stones behind her. The other shovels stopped. And Nellie sat back. The silence was broken only by the soft plops of dirt hitting the ground behind Lucy. She blocked out the others from her thoughts. *I must save him. I must, I must, I must.* In her desolate world she heard only her own words as she dug and threw, over and over. Her boy's life depended on her.

"Lucy."

From somewhere far off the soft voice broke into her painful prison. Hands stilled her arms and she struggled against them. "Lucy." A different voice, deeper, the tones ringed with sorrow. "Come away, Lucy." He pulled her to her feet but she began to fall. Quickly Sergeant Crawford's arm circled her and he held her to his chest. She dropped her head against him and gave up.

HARPER JOHN LAY CLEAN and white-faced on top of the patchwork quilt that covered his tiny cot. His clothes were clean and sweet smelling again and, but for the sheen of the pearled pallor on his face, he could almost be sleeping. He wasn't. Her lovely son was dead. And would have stayed buried in that punishing hole out in the woods if the sergeant had not taken pity on her and, with the other men, moved mountains of earth to free him for her.

The barest of knocks sounded on the door and Nellie slipped in. She, too, was in clean clothes, black, with her hair slicked back under her bonnet. "It's time, my dear." She held out her hand and Lucy stood to take it. Mr. McKie and Mr. Johnson carried in a short wooden box and set it on the floor beside the cot. Ever so gently Mr. McKie slipped his arms around her son and eased him into the box. He moved back and looked at her.

"Time, Mrs. Garner," Mr. McKie whispered.

Time? She didn't understand. Time for what? Nellie's arm tightened around her and she took a step. Then another. Toward the box. She began to kneel but fell right over her son, his cold little face right under hers, but she felt nothing. No pain, no tears, nothing. Nellie helped her to her feet where she stood to one side as Mr. McKie positioned the lid over the box shutting out the light on her dear boy.

"No!" she screamed.

"Lucy, we must," whispered Nellie.

But Lucy threw off the lid and reached for the patchwork quilt. She spread it over Harper John and tucked the edges around him, one last time. Her lips grazed his forehead; her hand lingered on his hair. Finally she stood, turned to Mr. McKie, and nodded.

Quickly, the men nailed the cover over her dear boy, shouldered the box between them, and carried her son from her life.

Chapter Nine

Fall, 1783

LUCY HAD DRAGGED A SLATTED WOODEN CHAIR outside to sit in the late September sun as she kept a close eye on William who was tossing a stick for the mangy mutt that plagued the camp at mealtimes. Her boy could barely throw twenty feet; each time the dog was back almost immediately, but William's laugh filled the air and they played the game over and over as the sun dipped in the west. She thought of another boy tossing a stick but tears threatened and she bit down on the thread she was moistening to put through her needle.

Across the parade ground Sergeant Crawford waved. She forced a smile. He had been very courteous and kind since…Well, she wouldn't think of that. The sergeant was heading her way. She was glad. Even though people had been kind to her since the accident, she was still lonely for someone, someone male, to talk to and the sergeant had helped her through the worst of her grief.

"Hello, Mrs. Garner. How are you this fine day?" He waited a moment but Lucy just cracked a slow smile. "I've news," he said.

"Of John?" She put aside her mending and stood before him, excited for the first time in months. Maybe John was finally coming home.

"No. Not of your husband." He stepped back a pace, his eyes leaving her face to study something on the ground between them.

Lucy looked but saw nothing. "Well?"

"The war is over!"

"But that means John will come home, doesn't it?"

"That I do not know, Mrs. Garner."

"What reason would he have not to come home now?" she asked. "And clear his name once and for all?"

"Perhaps you are right. He will come home. For your sake I surely hope so."

THE DAYS GREW SHORTER and the leaves fell but nothing seemed to change for Lucy except the new nip in the air and William's need for an extra blanket at night. For her own bed she had made a snug comforter from scraps of fabric Nellie had collected from many of the other women in the surrounding cabins. It was warm. That was the main thing. And tied with bright bits of red wool. But the colorless squares of pieced together remnants of worn shirts and skirts made her think of the treasured quilt she had wrapped around Harper John.

It was blues and off whites, with the odd bit of brown, and made from her childhood dresses and the fine stitches binding it all together had actually been sewn by her mother's hand. Until forced to do without it, she had not realized what an anchor it had been. Still, knowing it lay wrapped around her little son was some comfort.

Lately Sergeant Crawford had taken to searching her out in the food lines and talking to her again; in fact, she almost thought he was making excuses to come by her cabin. He had come with the news about the treaty being formally signed by Great Britain and the United States. She had to get used to saying that and not the Thirteen Colonies, as they were colonies no more and all that she and John had left behind was gone forever. There was some promise of compensation to the Loyalists but no one knew when that might be. Meanwhile the weather worsened and the winds whistled through the floorboards at night as she lay in her bed and prayed for John's footsteps at the door.

He did not come.

The snow fell one December morning, making William toddle to the window squealing his joy at his first sight of the fluffy white all over the ground. As soon as she could, Lucy dressed him and they set off for the breakfast line. To keep his feet dry, she tried carrying the child but he would have none of it and she soon set him down to touch and taste the marvelous white covering the ground.

In the line she happened to be just ahead of Peter and James, Nellie's boys who had been with Harper John when he fell. "I've been wondering, boys. Just what were you doing when my son slipped that day?" She tried to keep her voice light but her insides seized tight and she could barely look at the porridge she was spooning onto plates for her and William.

The boys stole a quick glance at each other. She hesitated, the spoon in midair, and turned to face them. "What were you doing?"

"Move along, woman," a male voice called from down the line. Angry faces looked her way but she held her ground, waiting for an answer.

"What? You can tell me." She nodded at them but the boys said nothing and busied themselves with their food.

Finally Lucy gave in to William's urging. She grabbed johnny-cakes and worked her way to the end of the line.

Back in the cabin she sat at the table long after William had finished his food and scrambled down to play with his makeshift ball on the floor. Those boys were hiding something and she needed to find out just what. Why couldn't they look at her?

That afternoon at Nellie's, she sat brooding while the ladies spoke of the end of the war, their hope for settlement of the land claims, and their plans for celebrating Christmas. Finally the war was over and the exhausted Loyalists could concentrate on planning some fun. The soldiers were all back in camp, anxious to settle their land grants and rebuild their homes here in this new British land.

Lucy's mind kept going back to the shameful looks she had seen on Peter and James that morning. She must get them alone and find out just what happened that horrible day last May. As she was leaving, she turned to Nellie. "Could Peter and James come over to my cabin tomorrow? And Nathan, too," she added when she saw his mother. "I have a surprise for them."

"That will be wonderful, Mrs. Garner," Nathan's mother said, her double chin wobbling as she spoke. "Of course." Nellie chimed in and the date was made.

The next morning was blustery and cold but Peter, Nathan, and James arrived in a flurry of stamping feet, steaming mufflers and snowy coats, too many to hang on the door hooks so Lucy draped them over the chair backs. The boys sat squeezed onto the bench before the table and she and William took the chairs. Plates of buttered bread tantalized the children and she was glad she had begged five slices from the camp cook that morning.

"Go ahead, children." She sat back and watched as their guarded eyes gave way to smacking lips and smiles at her between bites. Crumbs fell to the table but the children, even William, made a game out of snagging each and every one and licking them off their fingers. All too soon the treat was gone. The children turned their pleading eyes to her.

"I'm sorry, but that is all I have. Come, let's play a game." With the boys' help she pushed the table and chairs aside and led them through several rounds of "ring around the rosie" until wee William began to cry when Peter fell on top of him. Lucy took him on her knee while the bigger boys settled with the box of toy soldiers in the corner.

William was too young to play with his brother's soldiers but, as she comforted him, she thought of Harper John sitting just so, placing each musket-toting man in a line before the imagined enemy. Some of the soldiers were kneeling to shoot and others stood behind. Small fingers moved them steadily forward as though in a real battle. She thought only of the battle she had fought to free Harper John—fought and lost—and gripped William tighter.

....

"Mama!" he cried, and she let him go. He scrambled off her lap and plopped down in the midst of the line of soldiers. "Bang bang! Killt," he yelled.

"What other games do you know, boys?"

Peter tore his eyes away from the fractured line of soldiers to answer her. "Lots."

"Can you tell me?...Any of you?" she looked at each in turn but they paid her no heed. "Boys! Answer me."

And they did. One by one they described a host of games they enjoyed, even one with makeshift javelins that they had learned from some of the Indian children.

"What's this jump-the-hole you mentioned?"

Suddenly the banter stopped and the smiles ceased. Hanging their heads as though some inner signal had been given, they sidled toward the door and tugged on their outdoor clothing.

"Where are you going? We've barely had any time together," Lucy said but the boys hurried to grab their things and open the door. "Thank you, Mrs. Garner," said Peter. James and Nathan nodded at her. As they pulled the door shut a gust of frigid air swept into the room.

THE WAR WEARY INHABITANTS OF BUTLERSBURG celebrated Christmas with gusto. The peace had been signed and all the soldiers had returned. All except John, that is. Still no one knew his whereabouts and precious few were interested in even considering the subject. Lucy, however, was lonely and bereft even though she tried to put up a brave face in the camp and for wee William. Almost two years old now, he was the spitting image of his father, right down to the dimple in his chin, a fact that both pleased and troubled her. She didn't need any more reminders of the husband who had abandoned her.

Of late Sergeant Crawford had taken to dropping by her cabin or accosting her in the food line but so far she had ignored his obvious interest. The day was coming, she knew, when Colonel Butler would give the command to refuse her food and bar her from the cabin. She could not live on the largesse of the king any longer. She would visit the Colonel one more time.

"WHEN LAST WE TALKED, Colonel, your words were most unkind." She had refused a seat in the finished parlor but, instead, stood eye to eye with the portly leader of their small settlement here in Butlersburg.

"Madam…"

Lucy pushed on. "And at that time I had my two sons, OUR two sons, with me, who cried at the shameful way you spoke of their father. And you told me to marry!"

"Madam, I did not mean…"

"I am already married, sir. And to a very good man." She paused before stepping toward him and speaking in a low voice. "As. You. Know."

"Mrs. Garner, I…uh, I don't know how to answer you."

"But answer me you must, sir."

"Please. Take a seat, Mrs. Garner, I beg you."

He reached past her to indicate the settee where she had sat last time she had been here. Across the room was the chair he had held. She glanced back at him and stepped smartly to that chair where she positioned herself comfortably and watched him settle on the couch, a look of resignation on his sober brow.

"Well, Colonel. What do you intend to do for me and my son, William?"

"I am sorry about your other son, other son, madam." He shifted his thick legs to one side as he leaned forward. "I truly am, Mrs. Garner."

The pain, so long buried in her fight to survive, now threatened to overwhelm her. Deep breaths and a stoic tightening of her jaw were Lucy's only weapons against this worst of all foes. She stared into the man's watery eyes. And spoke. "Thank you."

"I am sorry to tell you, madam, your traitorous husband has not been heard of. We think he is dead." When Lucy tried to interrupt, he hastened to add, "I will do what I can for you and your remaining son."

"What do you mean, sir?"

"As you know, I am giving out land grants, even though as yet a proper survey has not been done. Our people need to get on...get on with their lives!" He rose and crossed to the window. "Out there is a bustling village, madam. A village full of industrious people, industrious people, who have lost almost everything. Why? Because they followed their king."

"Yes," she said and tried to ignore his constant repeating of words. She joined him at the window.

"We must see them rewarded for their loyalty." He turned. "And I will see you rewarded, too, Mrs. Garner. With land."

Footsteps sounded along the passageway and Sergeant Crawford came into the room. "I hope I am not disturbing you, sir," he said, glancing from Lucy to the Colonel.

"I was just leaving, Sergeant. My son will be waiting for me to gather him from Mrs. McKie's new cabin and get his supper." She took the Colonel's outstretched hand. "Thank you, sir."

IN THE DAYS THAT FOLLOWED Sergeant Crawford accompanied Lucy and William as they tramped through the snow looking for a suitable tract that Lucy might request. She still had hope that John would return and looked for a few acres where they might build a life together. This thought she kept from the sergeant.

When the surveyor finally took up residence that spring in an office in the new town, Lucy was quick to get in line with Colonel Butler's backing and the location for her new farm. A shortage of paper on which to print deeds and the like meant that she was handed a playing card as proof of John's and her ownership of one hundred acres to the east of Butlersburg along the bluffs which overlooked the mighty Niagara River. On the plain side of the card, the surveyor had written the location of her land.

As a Loyalist settler Lucy was granted a plough, a horse, a ticket for various stores from the barracks storehouse, and the use of a team of oxen to pull stumps from the land as it was cleared. A cabin, barn, and even an outhouse the settlers had to build themselves; for Lucy this presented a great burden. She had no husband.

With the sergeant's help, one fine morning in early April she loaded her possessions on to a wagon he had brought, tied the borrowed oxen on behind and climbed up beside William and Sergeant Crawford. Nellie had given Lucy a quick hug and stood to one side as they slowly made their way out of Butlersburg. By mid morning the two friends had marked off the acreage, chosen a spot overlooking the river for the cabin and started sawing through huge trees.

Lucy had never done such heavy work and was ill equipped to match the sergeant's strength on the other side of the saw. Even though she had tied William with a long line to a tree nearby, she worried that, left to his own devices for such a long time, he might get into trouble and need her help. Her curly hair blew across her sweaty face and stuck there. Flies and pesky mosquitoes landed on her exposed arms as she pushed and pulled the saw, trying with all her might to match the Sergeant's strength.

"Stop! I can't," she called and fell against the tree trunk. Sergeant Crawford took one look at her and dropped the saw that had barely cut through an inch into the tree trunk.

"We need some water." Off he went slipping and sliding down the steep slope to the river, a large pail in hand.

Just as he disappeared over the edge, a shout came from the other direction. Lucy ran for William but he was perfectly happy pulling leaves off a newly sprouted dandelion.

"Hello! Mrs. Garner, where are you?" The voice was closer. Horses came through the trees and on them, soldiers.

"Over here," she called, and waved at the crowd of men coming her way.

"We've come to help."

By sundown huge white pines lay on the ground and a small canvas tent was pitched where later would be a cabin. William was already asleep and Lucy knew she would not be long crawling in beside him. For the moment she sat with the men around the fire finishing the last of the stew the camp cook had sent out with their helpers.

"Thank you for coming, all of you." She stood up and looked at each of them in turn. Sergeant Crawford, Mr. McKie, and the rest all smiled back at her. "Where will you sleep?"

"Under that fine set of stars, Mrs. Garner," said Mr. McKie.

She knew they would be cold and missing their warm beds but was too tired to argue.

Chapter Ten

June, 1784

ONCE AGAIN HE HELD HIS HORSE STEADY in the flat-bottomed boat as they neared the shore. The ferryman grunted with every stroke of the oars and John struggled to keep upright and to calm the horse while he scanned the faces on the shore. He longed for a glimpse of flyaway curls and a wee boy, but all he saw were men in ragged remnants of uniforms, some red and others forest green. All were worn and in need of a good washing.

The boatman tossed the line to waiting hands on the sun-streaked shore and he and John made quick work of unloading the horse and the few crates. For the huge stove more hands were needed to lift it safely to shore where its silvery bits glinted in the spring sunshine. *Lucy will be delighted.* He glanced around again but saw no one he knew. Leaving the stove, and his crates on top of it, he pulled the horse up the path.

A lot had changed in three years. Where once uniformed soldiers had drilled in the parade ground, now two small boys tossed sticks and yelled at an angry dog. His was the only horse tied to the rail outside the barracks building. He would have to check in with the Colonel but first he headed for the cabin and Lucy.

Three years it had been. Three years since he had waved to her and Harper John from the other side of the river and rode off on his spying mission. He shook off his thoughts and walked faster. "Lucy," he called. "Lucy, where are you?" The door flew open and he began to smile in anticipation. His breath was quick and his arms stretched before him. How he had longed for this moment. But he stopped. And stammered, "I'm sorry, ma'am." His arms dropped.

"What do you want?" The woman's loud voice forced him back a step.

"My wife, where is she?"

"For certain she's not here. Who are you?"

"Garner. John Garner." He paused, looked around at the other cabins, and spoke again. "When I left to fight, she lived here. Where has she gone?"

"There was a woman here but she left. Took her child and went to claim her land."

"By…by herself?" She was headstrong and capable but surely she couldn't start a farm alone.

"No. That sergeant who was always sniffing around her, he went, too."

He staggered back, away from the door, now closed to him, a hitherto unimaginable thought rooting in his mind. She did not wait for him. Did she think he wasn't coming back? That he would abandon her? And their son? He untied his horse, mounted, and trotted away, he knew not where, oblivious to the growing brightness of the day, the boys still running, and the women's voices calling to them. He was completely alone.

LUCY HAD INSISTED THAT THE CABIN in the woods have two rooms, just like the one John had built. What with the generosity of the Colonel who directed her to take what she needed to start again, her new home was comfortable but lonely. The sergeant had taken up residence in the tent outside and spent his days helping her plant a garden and fence in the chickens, but mostly he worked at clearing the land. From dawn till dusk he chopped trees, cleared and burned brush, dug a pit for the outhouse, and attacked whatever other of the mountain of chores she gave him.

Immediately. Everything needed doing immediately. And she had no time to worry about her long lost husband who, if he even thought about her at all, would have sent her some message sometime over this last three years. He was either dead or he didn't care. Best get on with life, she thought.

Each day the sergeant became more and more insistent that she abandon all hopes of ever seeing John again, and marry him. At first he had played the role of a good friend helping her out in her time of need. And she had been in need. Now, however, every day, with some word or glance or smile, she felt the pressure to give him an answer. She sat at the table and stared into space. *He is a good man. And I do enjoy his company.* Her eyes focused on William's wee cot, the sling shot that the sergeant had made lying on the coverlet. *William needs a father.*

The door burst open. "Mama, mama! I can go to the river!" The boy ran into her arms and she scooped him up. Sergeant Crawford—Tom—stood smiling at her. She nodded her head and smiled back. "Thank you," she mouthed to him.

"You can go to the river and I'll go walking in the woods. I need to collect some sprigs and shoots for my medicine bag. Off you go!"

SHE REMEMBERED WALKING IN THE WOODS with John before the war and before their lives had taken such a desperate turn. Animals had worn a pleasant pathway under the canopy of green that protected her from the heat of the sun and she ambled along the path, her eyes peeled for medicinal plants, particularly slippery elm and witch hazel.

Deep in her own green and sunny world Lucy allowed herself, for the first time since Harper John's death, to smile. If she married Tom, William would have a father and she would have a partner once more. Perhaps there would even be more children. She stopped a moment. Could she go through all of that again?

In the silent forest she stood, watching. What had she heard? But nothing stirred and presently she relaxed and resumed her search until a lone bird call sounded. Down the path she thought something moved. "Hello," she called. "Is someone there?" She forced her voice to stay calm and strong.

"Hello!" The shout came from the trail ahead. Almost blending in with the browns and dark greens of the forest, an Indian stepped away from a large tree. He stood tall in a headdress with three feathers sticking out oddly but he wore only a loincloth. As he walked toward her a soft clinking of beads sounded like the baby rattle she had given to William. In spite of herself, she smiled.

"Hello, madam." The Indian's voice was low and pleasant, almost like a melody coming out of the forest itself. He stopped before her and waited.

Her head was nodding up and down. "How...what are you doing out here in the forest, sir?"

"You not know me?"

His black eyes and gaunt cheeks seemed familiar but she couldn't think where she had seen him. Few Indians came into Butlersburg and those that came to trade or to guide hunting parties into the forest only stayed long enough to attend to their business and get out.

The man pointed to his head but the motion was meaningless to her. With both hands he reached up and clasped his headdress, pulling it away from his bare scalp. She took a couple of steps back as he leaned toward her. She thought he was just putting the headdress on the ground but he remained bent over in front of her. *Whatever is he doing?*

And then she saw it. A jagged scar cut in the shape of a spearhead showed white against his browned skin. This was her Indian. The one she had nursed back from certain death as he lay on the buffalo robe in the cabin those years ago. When he was well enough one day he had just disappeared with nary a word. And here he was in this new land.

"Of course. I remember you! And you look well."

"Your stitching saved me." He stepped back and repositioned his headdress. "Why are you here? In this place?"

For a fleeting moment her breath caught as she thought of the home she and John had abandoned but there was no gain in thinking about that. "We had to leave. Loyalists, you know." And she forced a smile.

The man had changed. Gone was the constant threat in his hooded eyes but he didn't smile as he talked about his own journey to safety here on the British side of the river. His cheekbones were padded with extra flesh, his skin held a luster of its own, not the garish war paints she remembered, and his arms rippled with strength as he picked his tomahawk from the ground.

"You are Black Bear Claw. I remember your necklace."

"And you are Mrs. Garner."

He remembered her name! Oh, this was surely a different man than the silent, belligerent warrior who had just disappeared one day, with no word of goodbye and certainly no thanks to her. The two walked back along the path toward the cabin, both watching for herbs along the forest trail. When they neared the opening in the trees that was her home, Black Bear Claw stopped.

"I leave you now. Maybe see again," he said, and hesitated before adding, "Madam."

Lucy smiled and nodded.

LATER THAT AFTERNOON she worked with Tom in the garden plot they had planted alongside her cabin. At the end of a long line that Lucy had tied to the nearest tree, William hobbled back and forth between the two adults collecting stones and twigs and bits of brightly colored leaves, and clucking over each new piece he found.

"Don't walk on the plants, William," Lucy called for the hundredth time and went back to weeding the peas. Soon they would be ready to eat, as would the spring onions. Tom had taken a few moments away from sawing and building to help in the plot. He was working so close she smelled his sweaty odor but it was a good smell. Men often smelled like that. John certainly had.

"Can you carry on from here, Lucy?" Tom asked.

"Yes, of course. You go on with your building." She flashed a smile and turned back to the peas.

A SHORT DISTANCE AWAY, far enough that he couldn't hear but could see well enough, John watched the scene as he leaned out from behind an old and sturdy maple whose leafy canopy kept him in dark shade. It was true. She had found someone else. Her deep red curls flipped and tossed with every movement in spite of the bonnet she wore. Her back to him, she bent to pull some particularly difficult weed and he flashed back to those days before the war separated them. A tear wet his cheek and a strange sound strangled in his throat.

The little boy—Harper John—ran for his mother and she scooped him up, soothing his tears. He was awfully small for a four-year-old. Maybe he had been sick. Behind the tree again John slid to the ground and leaned against it, his long legs stretched out in the grass before him. Who was this man? His mind filled with all the days and nights of separation, of sorrow, and pain so hurtful he had almost chosen to give up rather than persevere. Never had he considered that she might not wait for him.

When darkness fell he pulled himself up. The light in the cabin shone through the trees. He longed to follow its beckoning brightness to his wife's arms but could not. Another had taken his place. He staggered into the woods for his horse and rode back to the barracks.

IN THE CABIN THE CANDLE HAD BURNED DOWN to the flickering point as had Lucy's strength. Once again Tom had pleaded with her to marry him and let him move into the cabin and, once again, she had put him off. He had stomped out and slammed the door.

She realized she had to face facts. John was not coming back. Tomorrow she would take the wagon into Butlersburg and visit the barrister. He would tell her what her legal rights were.

Chapter Eleven

June, 1784

NO ONE ASKED HIM WHY he was in the barracks; in fact, barely anyone looked his way, let alone spoke to him. John had found out very quickly that his name was hated here. Where once he and Lucy were among their own people, those Loyalists whose backgrounds were so similar to their own, those who had lost more than anyone on this earth should be called upon to lose, he was now shunned. And worse, he had lost Lucy and Harper John. He smoothed the grey coverlet over his thin mattress, flicked a bedbug off onto the dirt floor, and stomped on it.

Around him soldiers shuffled in and out of the barracks, listless and thin in their leggings and trousers. Food was scarce and eyes brightened up whenever the harvest was mentioned or a ship's sails were sighted on the lake to the east. John remembered the under ripe corn he had eaten in a similar situation during the war. Now that hostilities had stopped there should have been more to eat but the land, which had been so badly treated, took as much time to recover as did the broken bodies. And hearts.

He headed for the bright spot that was the doorway out of the barracks. He ought to check in with the Colonel but didn't. The Rangers were disbanded and Butler was safely ensconced in his own home. The man had no more hold over him. Still, perhaps he might find a glimmer of hope there, a way to carry on. Outside, he glanced around the empty parade ground and noted the quiet. Even the cabins that still housed families stood dark and empty as everyone was off in the surrounding forests.

The horse had a mind of its own and headed the same way it had every other day for the past week, toward the path into the forest. Again, John dismounted, tied his horse and quietly crept forward so that he could see. He should get on with his life, he knew, but day after day something drew him to Lucy, even though he knew she was gone from him forever. He peered out from behind his tree.

She was hoeing in the patch just beside the cabin. Alone. Perhaps he could talk to her. As stealthily as he had tracked the enemy not so very long ago, he crept from tree to tree, listening to the birdsong, standing stock still when it stopped, his eyes on Lucy the whole time. Where was the child? And the sergeant? He glanced all around but saw only the cow tethered on a long line to the porch rail and the cabin with its fresh-hewn logs and sacks draped over the opening where one day would be a window, once there was glass to be had here in this land.

So close now that he could hear her labored breathing each time she hacked at a weed, John stopped. Would she want to see him? His empty stomach pitched and rolled as he backed away into the trees once more, never taking his eyes away from her. Auburn curls streamed down her back over the homespun dress that moved slightly in the breeze and with every stroke she took with the hoe. She stopped a moment, drew her left arm across her brow, and turned toward the trees.

"Who is it?" she called.

He didn't move but held his breath.

"Sergeant Crawford? Are you there?" She dropped the hoe and walked toward him. "William, is that you?" Her voice tinkled with that laugh he remembered so well. "It's not nice to tease your mama."

All was silent for a few moments and he took a shallow breath; should he chance a look?

"Aha! Got you!" The voice shouted right into his ear as she grabbed his left arm in a playful grip like a cat that has caught her quarry. She screamed and jumped back, not recognizing him with his long beard and his unkempt hair. The jaunty hat that she had known was long gone. When he reached to calm her, she screamed again.

"Lucy."

Her hand dropped away from her mouth and her eyes widened. A knowing light shone from them and they crinkled at the corners as a smile crept onto her face. He began to hope just a little.

"Is it…is it you?" she whispered.

He reached for her and she stepped into his arms, smelling of soap and sunshine and sweat and sweetness. All he wanted to do was hold her so nothing and no one would ever separate them again and he certainly tried to. But visions of her and the sergeant swept into his mind. *Don't think of it. Of him. Of them. Together.*

He pushed her away, looked into those blue orbs again, and spoke. "Who is he?"

She looked away.

"Who is the soldier I've seen here every single time I've come?" When she edged back, he grabbed her arm. "Who, Lucy?"

"He is no one, John. Just a kind man who has been helping us."

Her hand burned on his arm and he wrenched away. "Don't tell me that. I've seen you smile at him."

"John, you must believe me. He is a friend. And…he helped me so much when Harper John___." She stopped. Her hands covered her face and she turned from him, sobbing.

Women's tears had always repulsed him; thankfully, he had seen few from Lucy. But here she stood, her face in her hands, crying so hard he could not bear it. He reached for her. The soft tendrils of her hair brushed his cheek. "Lucy, what is it?" He pulled her to face him.

"He's dead," she whispered.

He could not understand what she meant. Who was dead? He tried again. "Lucy, who?"

"H...H...Harper John...he, he...fell in the hole...with Peter and James." She struggled to control her shaking voice, "and Nathan." She sniffled and took a deep breath. All was silent a moment and then she let out the breath through her mouth and looked right at him. "Our son, Harper John, is dead."

Of all the thoughts he had had the whole time he was away, never once did he imagine this. His arms dropped to his sides and he sagged to the ground barely catching himself from falling onto a small pile of rocks, a marker of some sort. Lucy sat beside him and quietly told the whole story of Harper John's tragic death, of the boys allowing him to play with them, of her joy that finally they were accepted on this side of the river, and of her vigil over the hole where their wee boy finally died.

When she told of the cave-in after the rain, they held each other there on the forest floor and mourned their first-born, their sad separation, the loss of their hopes and their farm. She told him of wrapping Harper John's wee broken body in the patchwork quilt before she allowed the men to take him. He heard her words but could not believe his son was gone. That he would never see him again.

"But...I saw him." He pushed back to look into her face. "Playing. You had him tied while you worked in the garden."

She sniffed and wiped her eyes with the corner of her apron. "You saw William."

"Who is William?" Did she have a child with this other man? He jumped up and shouted at her. "Who is this William?" Why was she smiling when he felt so angry?

Lucy stood, not too close, but there was something about her body now. What had seemed a mass of prickly parts now was soft curves accentuated by her broad smile. She came closer. Grabbed his hand. And whispered, "He is our second son, John."

That night, time started again for John and Lucy. He held his second son in his arms and saw his own dimpled chin on the child's face. William even had his hairline, a deep dipping vee over his forehead, which sloped back very quickly on both sides of his head. Lucy sat the two of them side by side on the bench and told him William was surely his double. Long after William had fallen asleep in his corner bed, they burned the candle down low telling their tales. Gradually their hands moved closer over the width of the rough hewn table until John placed his over Lucy's, his eyes on her all the while.

The candle guttered and went out. They rose and went to bed as they had so many years ago before the war and the partings and the losses. But long after Lucy's breathing had slowed, he stroked her hair, still sparkling in the dim moonlight, and thought of all he had told her of his journey. He told her of the cold nights and the prickly pine boughs, of his monumental fear and his close calls. He even told her some of the secrets that he had sworn never to tell on pain of his life but he did not mention one thing. He could not bring himself to tell that detail, that one tiny fact, the knowing of which might once again jeopardize his family. She was better not to know.

JOHN AWOKE WITH THE SUN streaming through the bare window space, tickling his nose, and making his head twitch back and forth on the pillow. Not wanting to open his eyes he rolled away from the brightness and against Lucy. Her warmth stole up his arm across his shoulders and down below his waist. He snuggled closer but hesitated for a fraction of a second. He cracked open one eye and looked over Lucy's curls to the other side of the bed. Under a mop of blond hair tugged and tousled by sleep, two hazel eyes stared back at him.

Out of bed and into his trousers, John hurried, as though he had been caught doing something wrong. The child shrunk back against the wall and let out a loud wail.

"William, William," Lucy cried, sitting up in bed, and hurrying to him. "Don't cry. Remember your father from last night?" She picked him up, walked around to where John was standing, smiled and stroked his back, and sat on the edge of the bed. His father sat beside them. As the boy settled, John reached out a finger and touched William's soft arm. "Hello, my son." His voice caught in his throat but his face blossomed into a broad smile. "I must get to know you."

THE MORNING PROGRESSED with much bumping and butting into each other as the three moved about the tiny cabin, straightening and tidying, and getting their breakfast. John noticed William's reluctance to be on the same side of the room as his father and his absolute refusal to leave his mother's side. When Lucy made to go outside to the outhouse, William hollered until she took him with her, but John went, too, and sat outside in the grass with the wee boy to wait. In the distance hoof beats sounded and John jumped to his feet.

Into the yard rode a group of men, dressed in their Sunday best, their whiskers trimmed and their hair tied neatly back. They certainly didn't look as though they were here to work. John looked into their smiling faces and relaxed just a little. Then he noticed one particular man with a bouquet of flowers in his hand and wearing a puzzled look. The man stepped down, took a couple of steps toward John, and stopped.

"What...who are you?" He looked from John's face to William beside him and off toward the cabin. "Is Lucy here?"

John stretched up to his full six feet and his voice boomed across the short distance between them. "You mean Mrs. Garner, don't you...sir?" he added. This was the man he had spied on for the last week. The sergeant. He was all cleaned up and wearing a fresh shirt and slicked down hair but this was definitely the man.

"No. I mean Lucy. Where is she?" He moved closer. "What are you doing with William?"

John's sides stiffened and he sucked in his breath. He mustn't lose his temper. Lucy would not appreciate that. "You look like you're all dressed up to meet the preacher."

"I brought him with me." He pointed to the grey beard who was walking toward them. "LUCY and I are getting married this morning." His chin went up and he held out the daisies.

John didn't even think about it. He smashed those daisies right out of the sergeant's hand. "You're not getting married this morning, at least not to my wife! You can pick up your flowers and march right back to your horse. Get out of here."

"John!"

Her voice came from behind him. He glanced back at Lucy's face, her eyes blazing and her mouth twitching. "Is that any way to treat our guests?" William stood between them, looking from his angry mother to his new father.

Noticing his son's puzzled look, John took a step toward him and Lucy. He stopped. She hadn't told him about this marriage business. In all the talking they did last night no word of this ever came up. How could she keep it from him? Blindly he staggered back to the cabin and slammed the door so that the cups rattled on the table. He glanced at the bed but looked away and grabbed his hat and musket and threw open the door. In the yard he bounded onto his waiting horse and galloped away.

Back to the barracks he rode, back to the dreary and dark existence he had known ever since he crossed the river, back to the hopelessness and the barely stifled hatred from all he met. Perhaps he should have stayed with her, over across the river, with their boy and girl whose faces he saw so clearly in his mind's eye. But he wanted Lucy and he had ridden all this way to reclaim her.

On his bunk, with his face to the wall, he considered his options. Lucy had seemed very glad to see him, he had to admit that, but why didn't she say something? Clearly she had another life now. He wondered if the boy was even his own, whether she had told the truth about that. He should have hit the sergeant himself rather than just his flowers. *The boy does have my chin dimple and his hair grows like mine.* But they were dressed for a wedding. The man clearly had some sign from Lucy that she would marry him. She must have thought he was dead. Now he might as well be.

Chapter Twelve

July, 1784

LUCY SAT BY THE TABLE SHELLING PEAS into the large wooden bowl in her lap, glad for the bounty from her garden, especially when food had been so short the last few months. Her work in the garden was beginning to reap some rewards and she expected those plots in the village and the outlying new farms were as well. Surely this year would bring them all closer to comfort in this new land. Certainly the land itself was rich and fertile. Just look at the garden. And the Indian corn and oats the men had planted around the tree stumps were growing well.

If only John would come back. Stubborn man! Her hands rested in her lap as his stricken face came again into her mind. She ought to have told him that night of her desperate need to marry again. Of course he would have been angry. *I just wanted one night with my husband. Surely that was not so bad? One night without explaining how close I had come to marrying another man.*

William rolled over on his cot and she went back to her task. In the ten days since John had ridden off, Tom had not appeared at all and neither had any of the other men who had been so helpful when she was alone. They probably all thought John was here helping her but he wasn't. She had seen no one and, truth be told, was lonely and tired. The peas shelled, she set the bowl on the table and stepped outside to throw the pods into the pen for the sow that rooted and grunted, snuffling up the bounty in no time.

"Mama, mama!" William called to her from the porch. She ran to him, scooped him up in her arms and took him to the outhouse.

"Quickly now, William," she called. "We're going for a ride."

THE STREETS WERE ACTUALLY LAID OUT NOW, Lucy noticed, as she steered the horse towards the barracks where John must be staying. And buildings were rising along those streets. Homes, actual homes, some of them with two stories, lined the street where not long ago only a well-worn path had stretched from the barracks to the forest beyond.

William sat beside her on the wagon seat hanging on to her skirt and grabbing a little harder each time they hit a rut or the wagon lurched. This was his first time on the wagon without her arms around him but his excitement squashed any apprehension. He gawked in every direction as though he had never seen the village. In truth they had only been on their own land about three months, but a lot had changed.

The hitching rail still stretched in front of the barracks. Lucy drove the horse in tight, tied the lines off and helped William down. The afternoon sun was definitely sliding lower in the sky. Perhaps this was a fool's errand. Why would John want to go back to the barracks when he could be with her and William? The man was impossible to understand.

William tried to run off toward a group of children in front of one of the cabins but she held tight to his hand and marched into the barracks. The smell of death hit her as soon as she stepped over the threshold and into the dark where wraith-like figures inched toward them, bony-fingered hands outstretched in pleading gestures of supplication she would have known anywhere, even in the absence of their feeble cries.

"Food."

"Please, ma'am."

"Bread."

The voices squeaked one over the other. As the men came closer their eyes spoke what their words had suggested. These men were starving. She drew William closer to her and took a step back, her instinct to escape greater than her need to find her husband. She stopped, though, and held her ground. "John Garner. Is he here?" A hand grazed her arm and she recoiled instantly. "Please, tell me. Is he here? Have you seen him?"

At her tone the men seemed to come to their senses. As a body they edged back not taking actual steps but rather gliding away from her, back into the gloom, leaving behind a foul odor. Her hand covered her mouth. Able to see better now, she scanned the area for John but recognized nothing and no one. The light dissipated as suddenly as if someone had blown out a candle. William grabbed her skirts and clung so tightly she couldn't move.

"Stop, child," she soothed. "You're hurting me." He began to whimper and even though she still couldn't see much she bent over to lift him into her arms. "The door just blew shut, that's all." As she soothed him, light streamed over them as someone thwacked the door open again, this time fastening it. She hurried toward the light.

"Lucy. What are you doing in here?"

She looked up from William's tousled hair into John's face. He was the one who had fastened the door. "We came for you," she began but John turned his back and headed back outside. "Wait, John."

In the bright sun his dark hair shone, hatless as he was, and involuntarily she thought of his homecoming night. He led her to a rough table left over from the food lines that used to be so full but had shrunk to almost nothing now that settlers were on their own land providing their own meals as best they could.

He turned slightly, motioned for her to sit on one side, and sat, himself, on the other. William sidled in close to her. Her arm around their son, she studied her husband. *This is a fool's errand.* Now she was here she could not think how to start.

"You came." His voice was barely a whisper.

"Of course I came. We need to settle this." She waited for him to speak but he was silent. "I've done my best with the corn and the wheat, John, but with a little one I just can't do everything." He looked away and she watched his mouth twitching. "Please, come home."

Silent and still they sat, the three of them, baking under the hot sun, until John's hand inched ever so slowly across the bleached wood and touched hers. She raised her eyes to his, his mouth crinkled into a sad semblance of a smile, and he grasped her hand.

"We'll sort it all out, Lucy." He paused. "At home."

"Garner," someone called across the parade ground.

Lucy pulled away from John to watch the Colonel puffing toward them. John hurried to his feet and out of habit saluted the portly man.

"Mrs. Garner. I'm pleased to see you here as well. Pleased," he repeated.

She remembered his strange habit of repeating phrases from the other times they had conversed. "Colonel." She gave a slight nod of her head and pulled William up as well.

Absently the Colonel patted William on the head and turned to John, asking him to visit at his home for a private chat on the morrow. He turned abruptly and lumbered off towards the office he still kept upstairs in the barracks, its entrance at the east side of the large building. John gathered his meager possessions from the barracks while Lucy loaded William up onto the wagon and they rode off in silence, the horse tied behind.

THE NEXT DAY LUCY AGAIN was alone in the cabin as John had hurried through a bare minimum of chores and then rode off to the village to speak to the Colonel. What that could be about she had no idea. She tied William to his long tether, grabbed the hoe, and began to hack at the weeds sprouting between the rows of corn as though her life depended on it.

Much good her visit to town had done. John was back but she was still doing all the work. When would that man return to being the dependable fellow she had married? And he certainly had a bee in his bonnet, hardly speaking to her, and not even noticing William as he sat right beside him eating his porridge. Perhaps she had done wrong to persuade him to come back home. They certainly hadn't settled anything. Why, they hadn't even talked.

Where was the gentle John who had sat across from her and pleaded with his eyes for her to take him back? She reached over and pulled hard on a dandelion whose roots she had exposed with the hoe.

"Mama, mama," William called and she dropped the hoe to mark her spot before hurrying over to him.

"What is it, my child?"

"Potty, mama. Potty," he answered and pointed to the outhouse.

No sooner was she back at her work than John came riding back along the path from the camp. He rode straight to the cabin, tied his horse and stepped up on the porch. With a quick glance at her, he lifted the latch and disappeared inside. Not so much as a hello or a smile had he given her. This was just not her husband. Hacking and hoeing she finished the short row. William played happily in the dirt. She left him there and stepped into the cabin.

He stood at the side of the bed, his back to her as he stooped over, tossing bits of paper, a dark stocking, odds and ends, all in a great hurry. She closed the door softly and watched her husband. What was he looking for? His extra shirt and a pair of crumpled breeches came out on top of the rest. He worked at a fever pitch, his breath coming in short gasps as though someone or some-thing was after him, and his life—or hers—depended on it.

He stood straight a moment before returning to the battered bag and turning it upside down. Nothing else came out. He paused and then suddenly turned the bag upside down and slid his hand inside a hidden pocket. She could hardly see what he was holding but it looked like an engraving. Sitting on the bed now he held the blackened square before him and ran his forefinger over the thing. She wondered again what it was but was soon transfixed by his eyes that had glazed over and, although almost closed, were so intent on the object he held.

"John?" She edged his way. He leapt from the bed, his eyes now wide open glaring at her as the object disappeared behind him. "What is that?" she asked in the smallest voice she could muster. "What have you got behind your back?"

Their eyes stayed locked in a straight line, the shortest distance between two points, as though they were balancing on a thin tight-rope, the least wrong move threatening to plunge them into the abyss. He did not speak. The moment stretched, Lucy's thoughts tumbling together in her brain, each supposition a worse contemplation than the last until she broke the punishing stare and dropped her eyes. She reached for a chair, felt her way into it, and slid up to the table. "You have to talk to me."

From the corner of her eye she saw him pick up the bag and stuff his possessions back inside, attach the belt on the outside, and slide the bag under the bed. His musky male sweat filled the tiny room as she ran her hand absently over the rough hewn pine and flicked a stray crumb from the morning's Johnny cake onto the floor. A rough spot snagged on her finger and slivered off. She jerked her hand away.

Across from her he pulled out the other chair and sat. She glanced up to see dirt and sweat mingling to make wild rivulets on his brow, which dripped down his reddened cheeks and were lost in the shaggy beard he had grown since he left her three years before. He held her in his sight until she looked away and he spoke.

"Lucy...I...I must tell you."

"What, John?" Her voice was a squeak, even to her, but she had to go on. "What must you tell me?"

Slowly and softly he began to tell her of the three years he had been gone. Looking right into her face he spoke of the battles he watched but could not take part in for fear of being found out as a spy. From the branches of pines and maples or around the raw corners of burnt out barns and longhouse skeletons, he had watched his countrymen, friend and enemy, as they were hounded down and butchered in the heat of senseless battle. His voice took on a dead quality and his eyes seemed to be seeing the story happening again as he stared at the knothole where wee William, last week, had pounded out the nubby center and she had scolded him.

"But the fighting has been over for so long, John. Over a year, and the war over, too. What took you so long to come back to us? Didn't you want to?"

"That's just it, Lucy." He reached across the table and clasped her fingers in his.

She held her breath at the look of panic in his eyes and even in his tight gripping of her fingers. "Tell me," she whispered.

And he did. He told her about his whole life the last three years. He had already sketched out the battles, and his battered body he had shown her the first night in the new cabin, but now he looked into those brilliant blue eyes of hers—the ones he had always said he loved—and told her about his other family.

She sat silent and still, her senses battered to corn meal, and felt the thrust of his truth through her hips which had borne his sons, in her legs which had stepped lightly with him through the forest trails, through her shoulders, stooped low now over the table, and in that most secret place where she had sheltered the idea of him throughout this cursed war. This war that was over but went on killing her.

He was still talking, holding tight to her hands, but nothing of what he said made its way into her lonely prison. Now she had him back but he was not the man who had gone off on that final mission. "Children…" she heard and gave her head a shake. "Children? You have other…?"

"Yes, Lucy, I do."

"When? How old?" She could barely speak but had to know.

He let her hands go and drew back in his chair before rising and pacing softly over to the window where William was still playing outside. "They are almost his age." He nodded his head at William. "Twins, a boy and a girl." His words came again. "No, that's wrong. They would be sixteen months now."

Slowly she rose to her feet with the help of the table to lean on and made her way to the door and outside where she sat down in the dirt, grabbed William into her arms, and held him as though her life might depend on it.

That night John sat opposite her again and looked back and forth from his plate to her and occasionally to William. She felt his pain but sunk as she was in her own misery could not think of easing his burden. As she watched her son struggle with forking his food into his mouth, she thought of that other set of children who would soon be doing the same thing. *Why was John suddenly so upset this morning? Even before he had confessed to her?*

"John."

Immediately his eyes were on her, his fork midway to his mouth with a piece of speared venison. At the look of absolute hope on his bearded face, her heart softened ever so slightly and she spoke again. "What was the news? This morning?"

His eyes blurred and stole away from her, as though a sheet of fine muslin had fallen between them. He would rather die than let her see the whole of his pain. His hand reached toward her but could not seem to draw away the curtain and penetrate that widening space; it fell with a thud and lay on the table separating them.

Why did he not speak? She could bear anything but this gnawing silence. Beside her William laid his fork across his empty plate, the small sound clattering like a pile of broken dishes. She tore her gaze away from her husband and focused on the wee boy.

"Mama?" He looked from Lucy to John and back again. When neither answered, his little face crinkled and his mouth opened again. "Mama hurt?"

"No, no, William. Mama is not hurt." Her arm slipped about his shoulders and she squeezed him to her. "Would you like to play in the dirt?" She led him outside and settled down beside him. John came, too, and sat on his other side. Presently he took a stick and began to draw in the dirt and William beamed. Lucy left them and went to do the clearing up while the daylight held.

Later they resumed their places at the table and John cleared his throat. William was fast asleep on his bed in the corner with no cover at all in the hot July night. This time John reached over and grasped her shaking hands. His head erect, his eyes on her, unwavering, he breathed in and opened his mouth.

"I must tell you about my children and their mother."

"Shh, you'll wake William," she whispered, trying to listen but fearing the words that were coming at her.

"You were the one I wanted, Lucy, and I…I wanted to wait. She…her name was…" His voice broke and he looked down at their joined hands. Lucy tried to pull away but he held tight to her sweating fingers. "I…she needed help and I did, too. I didn't think where it would lead. I truly regret it now."

Her head spinning like the buzzing fly overhead, she felt the tears come again, hated them, but wept for her loss of John, their farm, their very lives. When she tugged her hands away, this time John let her go and she brought them to her face to try to cover her pain and her shame. He moved to sit beside her on the bench.

"There is more, Lucy."

She heard his voice and pulled herself up from the depths to focus on his drawn face beside her.

"The Colonel. That is what he wanted to tell me this morning."

He had gone early, she remembered, riding away like a runaway horse. "What…"

"A messenger came yesterday, one of the last spies we had across the river, and he told the Colonel."

His words tumbled out, one after the other, as he held her in his gaze, each word lashing her heart so hard that she just wanted him to finish. "Just tell me, John," she cried. "What did he tell the Colonel?"

"My children. They…they are dead!"

"How? The war's over." Lucy reached to touch his arm and ran her hot hand across his back.

"They were murdered, Lucy. When she learned what I was and knew I was not coming back, she…she…"

"What, John. Tell me."

He dropped his head to the table and Lucy heard a faint whisper drift out from under his shuddering shoulders. Three words. And then three more.

"She smothered them...in their beds.

Chapter Thirteen

August, 1784

FINALLY THE GRINDING WHEELS OF GOVERNMENT, both British and
Native, ramped up and land was purchased from the Mississauga
and Chippawa nations so that real surveys could begin. Those
loyalists who had been waiting for over two years had already
staked tenuous claims to land on their own, Colonel Butler among
them. In gatherings under the linden trees out of the summer sun
and in front of the army stores, pathetic stories came to light as
settlers, hungry for the companionship of their own kind, told
their tales.

Against the backdrop of hogs and cattle being driven from the
boats into temporary stock pens at the top of the hill and the clink,
clink of wagons wheeling early potatoes across to Navy Hall, in
hushed voices men spoke of their children carried off by Indians
or their wives murdered by revolutionaries, the scars of their
guilt red and raw on their faces. Only by talking with those who
had suffered similar stabs to the heart could these men hope to
expunge their pain.

The women swayed and jostled in their own groups not far off,
thankful to have a respite, however short, from the daily grind of
hoeing and weeding, cooking and cleaning, mending and tending
to their multitude of life-giving chores. They could escape their

thoughts for these few moments and joy was on the faces smiling under the wide-brimmed bonnets each wore.

John yanked the horses to a stop at the rail and held the lines while Lucy and wee William climbed down. The boy toddled off immediately to play with a group of children running on the parade ground and Lucy watched him a moment before joining the ladies.

"Mrs. Garner! 'Tis a bra brit thing to see youse." The voice came from her left and Lucy turned to see her friend smiling out from under her black bonnet.

"Mrs. McKie! How are you keeping?" she asked and then noticed the black bonnet and the matching black dress. "Is something…or someone…?"

Mrs. McKie stopped her. "Nae, lassie, 'tis sich a bricht sunny day a washt me dress. 'Tis all I had to coor me nakit bodie!"

It felt so good to laugh with the other women and to share stories about children and gardens both growing under the simmering sun this first warless summer in many a year. Lucy loved listening to the talk brimming with nothing of any importance. She wanted to stay with Mrs. McKie and the other women but John's voice hollering to William forced her to turn from the words and smiles folding her in, and step away. John was lifting William into the wagon as she approached. He climbed up himself, grabbed the lines, and looked down at her.

"Are you finished already, John?" She stood by the wagon.

"There is no more news." His tone told the story.

She climbed up beside her husband and wee son and immediately John edged the horse back away from the rail. Under the searing sun the cold in his heart reached across the child between them. She shivered.

"Mrs. Garner!"

A shout came from the direction of the barracks building. The wagon slowed and Lucy craned behind to see who was hailing them. The uniform was trim, the smile broad, and the waving hand welcoming. She took in a quick breath and glanced at John.

So far he hadn't noticed but the call came again and John shifted in the seat beside her to see who was hailing. He slapped the lines and hollered at the horses; the wagon bounced away at a frightening speed.

"Mama," William cried and she held him tight against her beating heart, her feet wedged against the front of the wagon in a desperate attempt to keep her place. She glanced at her husband pleading with her eyes but he ignored both her and their screaming son. Ahead a feathered Indian jumped out of the way of the speeding horses.

"Garner!" Just ahead, the Colonel stepped into the path of the speeding wagon. "Garner," he called again and jumped aside.

"John! You'll kill us," Lucy yelled. He tried to pull the horses back but they galloped on, maddened beyond all hope of control. From the corner of her eye she glimpsed a flash of red on the left. The sergeant whipped his black horse to pull alongside, ahead, right up even with the charging team. When he leaped, Lucy thought her heart would come right out of her chest, but amazingly he landed on the lead horse.

John put his whole weight on the leads to try to hold the horses and his face contorted into a shocking rictus out of which bulged eyes almost all white, so wide with fear were they. The veins in his neck swelled to hardened ropes of terror. Her own distress sat on her like a crushing millstone which, at the sight of her stricken husband, knocked the wind right out of her and along with it, all sense of smell, of sound, and even of sight, save for a narrow tunnel of vision completely filled with John.

She watched the bluish cords lifting red, mottled skin above the dun of his shirt and felt, finally, John's absolute terror. She smelled his fear, like sweat on a sweltering day that never quite goes away, and, at last, realization of what he had done, had been through, and had suffered all the time she was here in this place, crystallized into a drop of understanding.

She saw the Sergeant yank the harness, not letting up one bit, until the frothing, frenzied animal began to yield. The wagon slowed and John's hands held the horses back but he could not, would not let go. William's screams pierced her thoughts. She held him to her and stroked his head. Her leg muscles eased her away from the hard footboard. Words flew at her like arrows at a target. Her vision widened to show men clambering up to relieve John and lift William and her off the wagon which had so nearly borne them to their deaths.

"You'll be fine, now, ma'am. Just let us get you all down on solid ground." She saw John step down the other side, out of sight, and turned to the wee voice at her side. "Sh, sh," she whispered over and over as a strong arm propelled both her and her son to a spot in the shade.

"Lucinda," the voice said.

She held her son in her lap and soothed him. Gradually his tears subsided, his sobs stopped, and her eyes lifted to those of the sergeant. He smiled ever so slightly but John pushed in beside him. From one to the other she looked back and forth. Onlookers stopped their wagging of tongues and shaking of heads. A fly buzzed around the sergeant's head, lit, and took off to land right on John's nose. He stood still, unflinching. Slowly she reached up and swished the creature away. His green eyes widened and he straightened to his full height beside the sergeant.

Lucy took his outstretched hand. They stood together. She thanked Sergeant Crawford and turned to her husband. William, now in his father's arms, the small family walked away from the crowd.

Part II
The Capital Years

Chapter Fourteen

July, 1792

FAR OFF DOWN THE LAKE the outline of several boats flecked the brilliant blue of Lake Ontario's pristine waters, causing a shout to go up on the green banks of the Niagara River where heads turned and eyes strained to see who was approaching. Under the sheltering mantle of tall oaks, chestnuts and maples that blocked out the searing sun, lines of townsfolk scanned the waters to the east, hoping their long wait was at an end.

Lucy waited with the children while John went off to sell a few bags of new potatoes and bowls of fresh-picked blueberries. She and the children had found bushes in the woods fully laden with plump berries. Despite those eaten by William and his siblings, they had extra to trade here in the village. With luck John would come to meet them carrying needles and thread from the storehouse. Usually she joined him in this trading as much for the chance to see other people as for the trading but, in today's heat, she had chosen to bring the children to catch a breeze from the shore.

"Are they coming, Mama?" William asked. "Can you see?" The ten-year-old stood on tippy toes and strained to see but the crowds gathered in front and he was thwarted. He grabbed at her arm. "Mama! Can you see them?"

"Not yet, the boats are too far away." She held the sleeping baby in her arms while watching closely to make sure the twins didn't go too far. "Where is your father?" she asked of no one in particular. "He's going to miss the landing." She turned around but the crowds behind blocked off her view of the paths to Navy Hall.

People pressed against her and a small tremor shook through her body. "Hang on to my skirt, boys." She didn't want to alarm them. Where was that man? William held her arm in a hot vise-like grip, his fingers wet through her sleeve; his brothers pressed against her other side. She glanced down. Hemmed in as they were, the twins giggled over some secret understood only by five-year-olds and seemed unaffected by the throng surrounding them.

"Lucy."

The raised voice came from behind. She stretched her neck around as John elbowed his way in to stand at her back. He reached for Helen and she passed the child to him, glad of the brief blast of cooler air against her chest where she had been holding the child.

"They're here!"

"I see her."

"Look at her hat."

Shouts sounded all around as Lucy stretched to see the boat glide in to the dock below. Their view now obstructed by the treed hillside, the crowd shuffled down the hill to see the famous visitors.

Lucy and John moved, too, and took turns hoisting the boys up for a look at the elegant lady and gentleman stepping along the planks of the dock. Her hat was tall and seemed excessive for the diminutive form dressed in grey serge with black braiding, a white laced collar just peeking out at her neck. She was slim—surprising after a number of pregnancies—and her feet fairly danced along the dock as though delighted to move after so many days travelling from Quebec City.

"Can we get closer, John? I can't see her face."

"There's the Governor." He nodded toward the robust man striding along the dock beside his wife, a wide smile for the crowd lighting up his face. Much clapping of hands and throaty chuckles, nodding of heads and relieved sighs greeted the couple. They faced the crowd, both grinning. Even under the broad-brimmed bonnet the woman wore, Lucy could see her dazzling smile.

"So that's Mrs. Simcoe," John breathed in her ear. "Just a little bit of a thing. Wonder how she'll fare this winter."

A FEW WEEKS LATER Lucy was in the outhouse when she heard a horse and wagon and the children's shouts. *I hope it's their father, finally back from the village.* She pulled her skirts straight and pushed the squeaking door open to a lively scene. Mrs. McKie stepped down from her wagon, her jovial husband tying the lines off on the wagon before carefully climbing down the other side. The twins rushed over to Mrs. Mckie but William, as usual, hung back a few feet, although the look on his face showed how anxious he was to see what the welcome guests had brought with them this time.

"Welcome, Mrs. McKie. How lovely to see you."

"We had to come as soon as we heard, Mrs. Garner." She clasped Lucy's hands in her own, her concerned gaze scaring Lucy.

"What do you mean?" Lucy pulled her hands away and smiled in spite of the tiny knot forming in her stomach. "Heard what?"

Mr. McKie broke in. "The land grants. We heard about the mix-up."

"I'm sorry but I don't know what you mean. What mix-up?"

A shared glance between the two made her worry even more. She had wondered if life was just too good to be true these last few years with John finally settling down to farming again and the birth of three more children, all well and whole. Their crops had been good and gradually the cabin lost its bare and drab look as they replaced what they had lost in the war. Why, John had even built another room on the west side of the cabin to house their burgeoning family.

Seated on the porch now, the three adults looked back and forth at each other like children in a game wondering whose turn it was. Lucy could hold her tongue no longer.

"Please. Tell me what you know," she said, "even if it's bad news."

"Where's John," asked Mr. McKie in a soft voice. Both of them turned to look at her, stilling their rockers as they waited.

"He's in the village. Something about a meeting. I didn't pay much attention, I'm afraid."

Mr. McKie walked to the railing and stood studying the homestead all around him. "The Governor has been settling land on people and clearing up all the confusing claims." He hesitated, turned, and looked at her. "Someone else has been given the rights to this land, Mrs. Garner. Your name was never entered on the official list."

"That can't be! Colonel Butler gave us this land himself." Now she was out of her chair, nose to nose with Mr. McKie. "You must be wrong!"

But he was not wrong. When John arrived a few moments later he confirmed what Mr. McKie had told her. And even though she struggled to think of a way out of this dilemma, she could not. She and John would have to move. Once again they would have to pack up what they could, leave behind the newly refurbished cabin, the four acres of cleared land laden with corn and wheat, and the large garden just beginning to produce in abundance against the long winter to come. Oh, they had a new parcel of land allotted to them now but would have to start all over again to make it livable.

It was more than she could bear.

THE VERY NEXT MORNING JOHN took the horse and rode off into the trees heading for Bertie Township and the hundred acres of land allotted to them. He wanted to see firsthand exactly what they had in store and told Lucy he hoped to be back the next day or maybe the day following. Truth be told he was somewhat glad of the chance to move on and make a new start although he certainly wouldn't tell that to Lucy. Even though they had settled in well near the village Governor Simcoe now called Newark, still an air of mistrust and disbelief lingered over all they did. The traitor label still followed him and both he and Lucy suffered because of it.

Not to mention his other family. Usually he pushed the past as far down inside him as he could for a very simple reason. He could do nothing about it. The children were gone, their mother had disappeared, and he desperately wanted to keep his place in Lucy's heart. On days like today, though, he had ample time to think as he travelled the road toward Bertie Township and their uncertain future.

As the afternoon waned toward evening, John found the land allotted to him and Lucy. Lot 1, Concession 1 of Bertie Township had only seemed numbers until now. He stopped the horse to study the apron of untamed land framed on two sides by water right where Lake Erie fed into the Niagara River before it began its pell-mell rush to the falls. Nudging the horse with his knees he cantered the length and breadth of the hundred acres and was especially pleased to see the speed of the current in the river. A germ of an idea pushed into his brain.

The farmers here would need a mill, somewhere to grind their grains, and this racing river would always be thus as the lake waters ran at top speed for the magnificent cataract he had witnessed firsthand earlier in the day. There were great stands of timber for building and burning. John jumped off the horse and in true farmer fashion stuck his hand down to pull up a huge clump of grass and check the soil. Dark and rich the clod of dirt was and he held it to his nose. Fresh, moist, with a scent of something new and untouched, the soil crumbled in his fingers. He felt the newness of it in his very marrow. "Hooray!" he shouted and dropped the reins to do a merry, jumping, laughing dance around the startled horse.

"Whoa! Whoa, girl!" He yanked the horse's reins. By now the shadows were so long he felt like he had company here on his new land. He led the animal to drink at the river's edge and listened to its thirsty slurping while all around the horse's submerged mouth the water turned rosy gold as the day shot its last shards of light across the pristine lake.

In the morning John's food was gone, a sad circumstance as the nearest settlement was at Chippawa, a good distance back along the road to Newark. Nevertheless he saddled the horse and set out through the trees, but not before having one last look out across the hundred acres that were his.

At Chippawa Mrs. Oldfield served up a hearty porridge and he set out once again for home, accompanied by the rushing waters of the Niagara River and his turbulent thoughts. For the first time since he and Lucy had escaped across the river from Fort Niagara he smiled, freely and fondly. He was a lucky man.

Since the couple had put so much into the land, and the garden and field crops had barely started to ripen, they received permission to stay until after harvest and until such a time as the roads would freeze and bear the weight of their full wagon. John, his promised land filling his thoughts each and every day, several times rode the twenty miles to gaze on it and make his own plans. He saw just where he would build their home, not a cabin this time, but a real house of boards and planks with several rooms and an honest-to-goodness stairway to the second floor children's bedrooms. There was no telling how many more babies might be coming and he wanted to be prepared.

On a cold but sunny day in January the young family packed up once more and set out for their new home. The twins, Robert and Thomas, rode with William in a niche John had carefully constructed among their assorted belongings to keep the rambunctious boys from falling off. Little Helen, a year old now, sat wedged between her parents, her hands grasping their clothing on either side of her.

John held the lines tight in his hands, unwilling to risk losing so much as a stray cup or spoon from their load. Every so often he glanced at Lucy. Did she share his joy? She faced the road, her winter bonnet meant to control her still unruly curls, but with the bounce and bumps of the wagon, gradually he saw more and more of her lovely auburn hair. The cool wind nipped away at all of them and, more than once, Lucy tucked the buffalo robe around the boys in back and another around the three of them up front. Her cheeks grew red as the sun stretched toward the west but every so often just when he thought she was ready to curse him for taking them from their warm hearth so early in the year, she glanced his way, caught his eye, and smiled. Her eyes spoke warmth to him even if she was silent and cold.

Though he could barely feel his hands, rigid against the pull of the lines, and even if the wind whipped into every crevice of his clothing, her smile flamed his hopes and he pushed on toward their land at Fort Erie. Near midday they stopped by the thundering falls where towering white ice sculptures formed fantastical illusions and, even though the cold spray reached them on the wind, the children forgot their discomfort for a while.

Lucy kept a tight hold on Helen's hand and an eagle eye on the boys lest they stray too close to the edge of the deep gorge. John, too, curbed his sons' enthusiasm with strong words and worried admonishments. Before the hurried fire they warmed the stew and themselves before gulping the food and climbing back on the wagon.

The children slept now, their parents keeping watch, and the sun dipped out from behind the clouds now and then but mostly it hid. At Fort Chippawa John could bear the cold no longer. Hard though it was not to reach their land, he realized they must stop. Mrs. Oldfield remembered him and took them in for the swiftly approaching night.

In the morning they were off again, this time with John singing in his off-key but joyous voice, as he gazed at the horizon hoping to see a ridge of blue in the west. Eventually he did.

"WATER!" WILLIAM CRIED and pointed ahead.

"I see it, too," echoed Lucy and glanced at John, her eyebrows raised.

He nodded. And frozen to the bone as they were, the hope of reaching the land of their father's stories spurred them on.

The wagon creaked over the rough ground to the place John had found on his trips last fall until finally he hauled back on the lines and the heavy load stopped. "Here we are, Lucy." He grinned at her. "Do you like it?"

"We need a fire, John."

They set about making a winter camp. He headed straight for the dead pine, pulled up the lowest spidery branches and hauled kindling to the spot where his fires had flared last fall. The boys carried cut wood from the stacks waiting not far off and Lucy pulled out yet another pot of stew, frozen in its container, and positioned it on a flat rock right in the middle of the fire. As it warmed she helped John stretch the makeshift tent over its poles and spread the oilcloth over the bare ground inside. They would all sleep here until better accommodation was available.

The next morning John had everyone up with the sun. Once they had finished their porridge he and Lucy kept the children choring the whole day long, so anxious were they to build better shelter. Drawn by the smoke from the camp fire, which young William kept blazing, by mid-morning three different wagons had pulled into the clearing and new neighbors cut and sawed one straight pine after another into manageable logs.

Lucy had all she could do to keep the children out of the workers' way. She settled the little ones near the fire and busied them with picking unsavory visitors out of the remaining flour she had left from last year's bountiful crop of wheat, while she mixed bowls of pan bread ready to pour into the heated pots over the fire.

Other women had come with their men, hair tied back in warm scarves, heavy coats over their skirts, and smiles bright as harbor beacons. The odd crow squeaked out its call complaining about the mayhem below. Lucy had all she could do making enough food for this army of workers but as, one by one, the men dropped their tools and moved toward the fire, loaves and meat pies magically appeared to be shared by everyone.

Little by little the building sounds abated and young and old alike all filled their bellies. Lucy's own hunger satisfied, she glanced around the campfire at the three neighbor women who were busily feeding their families. John picked up Helen and laughed at her attempts to chew the bits of meat he offered her. All too soon, he passed Helen to her.

"Time," he said. "That winter sun won't wait and night falls fast here."

She took the child from her husband. One by one the other men went back to work and the peaceful slip of silence in the woods was over. The children started a game of hide-and-seek under the canopy of fir trees but soon were chased out by the men with their saws cutting and chewing through the downed logs. Lucy caught her own four and settled them around the fire, this time peeling bark off outside cuts to be used later as kindling.

Next morning more wagons came but John needed to make a trip to the fort for supplies. Lucy stayed behind, anxious to see the work progress, and everyone continued without John. William took over the managing of the children and Lucy took John's place at one end of the crosscut saw.

John pushed the team as fast as he could along the forest track, hoping to get back with his load early in the afternoon. Thankful for the mild winter so far, he still had to get shelter built as quickly as possible. He cracked the lines over the team.

Neither he nor Lucy had ever been to Fort Erie, a fact that added just a little apprehension to the journey. He had no trouble finding the fort as there was only the one road leading straight to it. The palisade gates were open.

In the store, John rhymed off his instructions to the slender man filling orders. His shirt sleeves held up by armbands, the man reached high and low for the nails, sacking, foodstuffs, and assorted supplies. A woman came from the doorway behind the counter into the store. John's breath caught. His eyes felt as though they had never been open until this day. Her back to him, she busied herself with a bolt of blue fabric. He watched her hips sway, her arms reach for a bolt of grey, and her black braid fixed on top of her head.

Was it her?

Suddenly he realized the man was speaking to him. He tore his eyes away and faced him. "Wha'?" He couldn't speak. Nothing but dry coughs issued from his mouth. She glanced his way, looked back to her work, but jerked around again. She dropped the pillow ticking on the counter, leaned closer, and peered into his eyes.

"John?"

A dozen words filled his mouth but none of them could escape. The shopkeeper looked back and forth between them but spoke not a word. John tried to speak. Gulped and tried again. This time a sound started in his stomach, scratched into his throat—he licked his parched lips—and squeaked out into the still room. "Alice."

Chapter Fifteen

January, 1793

THE SHOPKEEPER LOOKED FROM ONE TO THE OTHER but John and Alice held their peace. So silent were they all that a persistent scratching in the corner behind the sacks of flour stood out like the ticking of the grandfather clock John had bought from a travelling peddler just last year.

Alice spoke first. "John. It is you!"

"You know this man?" the shopkeeper asked.

"Yes," she answered and glanced quickly at the man. "We met during the war. In New York." Her eyes on John's face she added, "There were so many displaced people back then. I took him in."

"What do you mean 'took him in'?" His eyes narrowed as he studied first John and then Alice. Was she his wife?

She glanced again at the bolt of fabric and ran her fingers over it as though at this moment its grainy texture was all she cared about. Her hand was reddened and rough looking and moved across the intricately woven cloth leaving an ever so small ripple in its wake but making no sound at all.

"I'm waiting." The man seemed to growl rather than speak.

She looked at him and whispered. "I gave him a place to sleep."

The shopkeeper nodded his head but looked back and forth between them. John cleared his throat and this time was able to speak. "Alice saved me from the American soldiers combing the woods looking for me." Why was he trying to help her with this lie? After what she had done? He didn't trust himself to look at her; instead, he stared the shopkeeper in the eye and continued. "I am much indebted to your wife, sir."

"My wife! She's no wife of mine," he muttered.

"He's my brother, John, and spent the war holed up in this fort hiding from all need to fight, brave man that he is."

The man grabbed her arm. "You'll be sorry for that, woman."

"There's no call for that, sir," John hollered, and reached over the counter to poke the man's shoulder with his fist. "Do not mistreat the lady."

"Lady! She's no lady. Why I heard tell she killed her children after her fancy man took off and left her to care for them." His hard eyes narrowed and bored into John's own. A spark flashed in his eyes. "Maybe they were your brats!"

His gut wrenched with fear and loathing. It was true, then. She had killed their twins. His legs turned to mush and he grabbed the counter. As though struck from behind John struggled to stay upright against the overwhelming flood of emotion engulfing him. He rocked back and forth against the counter, his two hands gripping so hard they whitened and tightened until he could bear it no more.

Her face was right before him and with a superhuman effort he struggled to keep his senses. In her eyes he read danger and fear, tears and rapid blinks showing her fight against her own demons. He wanted to grab that slim neck of hers and wring the whole story out of her but movement to his left distracted him. The shopkeeper stood a few feet away pointing a rifle right at him.

"Henry!" Alice screamed the name, at the same time pushing at her brother, ruining his aim. John stepped in with a swift hook to the man's jaw. The rifle clattered to the floor and he kicked it out of reach, ducking a wild punch at the same time. He twisted the shopkeeper's arm behind his back and pushed him, face down, on the counter.

....

Like the times he'd experienced during that long ago war, the battle rage was on him and he pushed away everything else until the whining grunts of the man registered in his brain and hands pulled him back. Others had come in to see what the scuffle was. Alice, too, was beside him, her hands ripping at his shirtsleeve as she tried to stop him.

He loosened his grip. The shopkeeper whimpered beneath him. Hands pulled him off the man. Alice stroked his arm, moaning in his ear; she stopped the moment he glared at her. She reached up to touch his face, but her hand stopped in midair. Her hair smelled like rainwater in spring. He shook her off.

The shopkeeper's fearful eyes brought sense back into his head. He stood up straight. Deep breaths. Little by little he calmed and so did his adversary who again stood behind the counter, Alice beside him. The other men had moved off. John looked down at his goods strewn over the counter, scratched his chin in a long moment of struggle, and began to gather the items together. Alice's hands moved the bolt of fabric out of the way but the shopkeeper stood stock-still.

"Here is your money," John said. He held the coins out and waited.

"Henry," said Alice. "Take it." She pointed at the coins John held over the worn counter.

He grabbed the money and turned away.

The trip back to the farm went by in a rush of thoughts and feelings the like of which John had never experienced. She was here, so close, so dangerous to him and Lucy and their settled life. He hoped he could forget that part of his life but he would have to go to the fort, and often. And what's more, Lucy would, too.

As he neared their new place, the spring sun crept into his cold heart and he began to feel better. Here were his friends helping to build their home on this prime land that they had been lucky to get. Young William was stripping bark with a smile on his face and eyes that danced his joy. The other children frolicked in a game of jump rope and Lucy, her hair tied back and her sleeves pushed up over her elbows, stirred a huge pot over the fire. Even though her hands were busy, her shining eyes and that grin that covered her whole face welcomed him better than a marching band with high-flying banners.

A FEW NIGHTS LATER they slept in the cabin for the first time. Heavy snow had come that day, giving them even more cause for celebrating a solid roof over their heads. John sat in the rocker by their stove, the baby on his lap. Only imaginary walls and the placement of the beds marked the individual rooms, but the outside walls and the roof held the storm at bay and he smiled. Lucy sat sewing in the weak light of the candle, her hands reddened and rough, but steady as ever.

"Drat!" She stuck her finger into her mouth and frowned at him. "I pricked myself. And I've broken the needle. Something else we need to replenish at the fort."

He stopped rocking. The baby whimpered until his hands patted her back to sleep.

"When can we go to the fort, John? Tomorrow?"

"I, ah, have so much to do." He licked his lips and added, "Can't it wait a few more days?"

"Well, I guess it can if no one needs any clothes mended or bread to eat. You know we ran out of flour yesterday."

"Hmmm. I see what you mean." He took the child and settled her into the cradle by their bed. Back in the room he pulled out the chair opposite Lucy at the table. "I have something to tell you, Lucinda."

She looked away from her bleeding finger and studied him. His fingers moved restlessly across the table between them and his head sat stiff on his shoulders. A sheen of gray had lightened his once-dark brown hair and she could see the toll these years had taken. More gray streaked his reddish-brown beard. He was almost an old man. In the dim light of the almost spent candle his eyes watered and his dark pupils hid secrets she might never know.

Under her gaze he dropped his glance to the table and she noticed how wrinkled his eyelids seemed. He blinked a few times and raised his head. From his narrow mouth came the story of his journey to the fort and of finding Alice. When his words ceased she did not speak but listened to the baby's snuffling, the candle guttering as it burned down, and the rain dripping on the roof above. For once she was silent.

Just a few inches apart their hands did not touch. She was finally beaten.

"Say something, Lucinda."

"Don't call me that!" She spat out the words and clamped her mouth shut, afraid that once breached the dam of her hurts would burst in a torrent so virulent it would drown them all. Her husband had taken another woman, had babies with her, and had almost not come back after the war. Pushing that pain away had taken practically all she had, especially after losing Harper John, her first-born, her—oh, she couldn't think about it all again. She grabbed a corner of her apron and swiped at her eyes.

John rose and hurried around the table. His hands were like fire on her shoulders and she wrenched away. "Leave me alone."

"Lucy." His fingers burned her hair.

"Don't touch me. Don't!" The chair tipped as she jumped up and away from him. She ran for the bed, bumping the cradle on her way, and fell across the patchwork quilt. The baby cried and the rain pelted their new roof but none of it penetrated the wall of hurt around Lucy.

Sometime in the night the bed creaked and she rolled over. She was covered. John. Half asleep she reached for him but he was under the quilt and she lay on top of it. She could not touch him.

THE WAGON BOUNCED OVER THE RUTTED TRAIL shaking its joints and those of its passengers so forcefully that they must surely break to pieces if they didn't soon arrive at the fort. Lucy was glad to have left the children behind under the care of a neighbor. They might have pitched right out of the wagon. She could hardly bear the ride herself.

She and John had barely spoken the last couple of days while the sun dried up the road enough to make the trip to the fort but, at least, they were talking. Practical as always she realized there was nothing to be done but try to outface this latest setback. As they neared the hitching rail outside the store she hoped she wouldn't have reason to regret her decision. Planning to come and meet this woman, this Alice, was one thing sitting in their cabin, but her pitching stomach and icy fingers showed how different the actual doing might be.

"We're here." John tied the lines and reached for her hand, giving it a squeeze, before jumping down and turning to help her. This was hard for him, too, she thought, and forced a tight smile. His eyes crinkled at the corners and that green spark glittered as, with his two hands, he held her away from him. The first smile she had seen from him in days creased his tired face. He pulled her to him and his thumping heart betrayed his own trepidation.

"We must go in," he whispered.

She drew away, nodding. They had to do this. Together they mounted the porch.

John heaved the heavy door open and she followed him inside. A gust of wind swept her skirts tight against her legs before they got the door closed. For the first time ever, she stood behind John and waited for him to go first. There must be a counter. Dusty sacks of flour and corn seed lined both sides of the narrow path John took. His boots shuffled ahead of her. To her left something bright edged into view and she couldn't resist raising her eyes to have a look. The bolt of cloth was as blue as the sky on a hot summer's day. Her hand moved of its own accord. Crisp and new, the cloth drew Lucy to stroke it and rub it between her finger and thumb in the age-old test of quality.

"Would you like a length, ma'am?"

She jerked her hand back and stammered, "No. I'm only looking. At its bright color." The woman wore a black dress, close fitting and edged with white eyelet, a light shop apron covering the front. Was this Alice? Lucy's heart hammered inside but she stiffened her spine and lifted her chin. John was across the room fingering harness for horses, oblivious to this black-haired woman smiling at Lucy.

When she spoke again, Lucy heard the little catch in her voice. A deep shuddering breath rose from within her. "Are you Alice?"

"Yes, how did you know?" She peered at Lucy. "Have I met you?"

A crash on the other side of the room took the women's attention. John had knocked over a keg of nails and knelt in the mess trying to pick them up again. He swept his bare hands into the nails, scooped out great handfuls and dropped them back into the keg. His fingers moved like lightning. Lucy called over, "Have a care, John." She was too late. He jumped up and ran for the window's light to see his bleeding hand. Alice came with a cloth and wrapped it around, pressing tightly, a look of sheer amazement on her face.

The three of them stood in the light of the window, their eyes all focused on the wound.

"The hand will be fine," John said, nodding his head up and down.

"Yes," Lucy chimed in, and heard Alice agree, but she couldn't look up.

The silence grew like a cough that wants to come, wants to escape, wants to flee, but can't, and no amount of swallowing and harrumphing can make it. John shifted his foot and the nails clinked. Alice's hands slowly withdrew from holding the cloth against the wound. Lucy's arms were stiff with grasping John's hand but she would not let go. Without moving her head one iota, Lucy swept her eyes around her limited viewpoint. The black dress beside her was shimmering in the sunlight but her own brown hung in dutiful folds down to the nail-strewn floor. Finally, she gathered her courage and lifted her eyes.

"I'm Mrs. Garner," she said, "John's wife."

"And I'm Miss Webster," answered the woman in black.

Amid smiles and nodding heads, the three extricated themselves. Alice fetched a broom and dustpan to scoop up the nails while Lucy herded John over to a chair where she could properly wrap his wound.

The storekeeper came in from the back room, scowled at them, and went to the counter to see to a tall Indian who had just come through the door. The wound wrapped, Alice waited on John and Lucy. As soon as they paid for their flour, needles, and other items, they headed outside into the sudden sun. Just as John took the lines in his hands the door opened and Alice stepped out. She hurried over to the wagon.

"I hope we can be friends," she said to Lucy. "And let all that is past be past." The woman's glance was hard yet strangely soft and her dark lashes fluttered again and again. Lucy tried to smile but her face remained frozen. No key to the problem presented itself. As the seconds stretched to minutes the three of them remained locked in a triangular clash and, even though no guns blazed nor swords slashed, battle lines were drawn.

Lucy gripped her clasped hands in her lap. John flicked the lines, the horses found their step and, blessedly, the blur of the trees along the track swept the woman from her mind.

Chapter Sixteen

February, 1793

THE WEATHER TURNED FIERCE again and John missed the neighbors most likely now snug and safe in their own homes with the wind worrying at the chinking. He coaxed the horses back into the temporary shelter against the cabin wall. In the spring they'd start on a barn but until then this lean-to would have to do. He pulled the brush close, a makeshift fence to keep the animals inside at night although they weren't likely to run in this weather. The branches of pine and spruce would keep out the wolves, too, he hoped.

Inside the new cabin he stamped the snow from his boots and hung his wet clothes near the stove. A burst of muffled laughter came from under the buffalo robe thrown over the big rocker. The children played a game known only to them with short silent moments broken every so often by spurts of laughter. Sitting by the candle Lucy hunched over a length of fabric painstakingly putting in one stitch after another. She hated sewing, he knew, and wished he could spare her but they all had to do their part. He wondered how to broach the topic in his mind.

Before the men had left a few days ago the conversation between putting the cedar shakes on the roof and huddling around the bonfire had taken a worrisome turn. Deeds had been the topic. And the granting of land that might already be promised elsewhere. Those little playing card notes of ownership that had failed them so badly back in Newark kept popping into his head. John had paid the cost of their use when no paper was to be found this side of the river.

He needed to go to Newark. He would not lose their land again.

"Drat! I've lost another needle down through the floorboards." Lucy dropped her worn hands to the table. Her eyes just inches from the work, she pulled at the thread before leaning back, taking a breath, and fixing her eyes on him. "You're awfully quiet this cold night," she said.

He nodded his head but said nothing as he bore her scrutiny and tried not to look away. Soon, however, she had it out of him and had agreed that on the morrow he should strike out for Newark. Perhaps he could see the Governor or at the very least the land agent and finally get a copy of a real deed to this new land grant. He relaxed in the chair and again turned his eyes to the children.

THE NEXT AFTERNOON as the cold winter sun edged its way down under the horizon he reached Newark. A golden sheen gilded the snow banked along the open trail and reflected off the smoky windows of Navy Hall where he hoped to find the Governor. His horse snorted through icy bits of bristly hair as he tied her to the railing, and then threw a blanket over her in case the wait was long. His hands stiff with cold, he tried the door and breathed easier when it opened.

Voices rose as he entered and he found himself in the midst of much bustle and hurry. An elegantly dressed man with short-cropped graying hair and the beginnings of a double chin under a broad, well-fed face seemed the center of the scene. His eyes darted from piles of blankets to packets of flour and salt pork and his small but perfectly formed fingers underlined his every word as he barked orders to all and sundry. John closed the door and stood to one side.

"You. What are you waiting for?" the man barked. "Take this pile out to the sleigh." His eyes were on John whose military training kicked in. With nary a word of protest, he grabbed the indicated bundle and followed an Indian, similarly encumbered, out the door. They emptied their arms and headed back inside. John hesitated to interrupt the man for surely this was the famous Governor Simcoe who was ordering the loading of all the supplies, for what reason he could not guess.

When the room was emptied and the sleigh loaded, everyone went their own way; John saw his chance.

"Sir," he called as the Governor turned away and made for the door that led further in to Navy Hall. "Sir," he almost shouted at the retreating figure. "I must speak with you."

"And who are you?" the booming voice called out as Governor Simcoe turned back.

"I am John Garner, late of this township but now of Bertie Township." The governor took a couple of steps toward John. "And what do you need of me at this awkward and extremely inconvenient time, my good man."

"It's the land grants, sir. In Bertie Township."

"Yes, what about them? You have one already, don't you?" He almost shouted, his face so close to John's that his sharp woodsy scent combined with the sweaty smell of a man of action rendered John speechless. He stood a moment, felt his head nodding, and then continued.

"I, I need proof, sir. A proper deed. Of ownership." He stopped and waited. In less time than a heartbeat the Governor turned on his heel and headed for the door. Over his shoulder he hollered, "Come with us tomorrow. We'll talk on the trail."

Where they were going in the morning, John couldn't say, but decided to take the offered chance and tag along. Back at the new cabin he'd be waiting out the winter by the fireside so a few more days away would surely not matter at all. He found lodging, stabled his horse, and ate a hot meal of soup with bits of meat floating amidst nondescript vegetables. His appetite sated he wrote a short message to Lucy and left it with the innkeeper. Into the room full of sleeping men, he crept with his bedroll and stretched out on the floor.

Before there was even a hint of light dawning in the east, the men rose and headed for Navy Hall, their packs on their backs. John rode alongside them. The Governor wore a fur cap, gloves and moccasins but took no great coat, a fact that struck John as quite odd in this freezing cold.

"Why is this horse here?" shouted the Governor. "Horses will only slow us down."

John tried to argue but was not even heard. He trudged back to the stable and left his horse, a sinking feeling creeping along his spine. The men were soldiers with the odd officer sprinkled in, but all wore their own rather than soldiers' clothing. Just a very few hats and the odd redcoat suggested the military. What had he got himself into?

In short order they set out on the trail leading into the interior. John had once traveled some distance on this path with a hunting group but by midday he recognized nothing of his surroundings. Talking was almost impossible on the narrow trail snaking through magnificent oak, elm, and ash trees and banked with so much snow that single file was all they could manage. Nevertheless, the sun streaked through the trees and lit up the white banks with tiny glistening gems. Snow showers caught the men by surprise as the sun melted the snow on the branches overhead just enough to cause an avalanche of white powder. Much stomping and dusting off of hats stopped them for a few moments. Almost immediately the line edged ahead once more.

Two whole days of marching far inland away from his home had him puzzled. He still didn't know just where they were going. Had he been a fool to follow Simcoe's suggestion? The next night John moved around the fire circle to where the Governor sat brushing his boots and drying them in the dim light of the flames. He edged in close to the man determined to get his questions answered.

"Sir?" he said.

The governor glanced up at him and frowned. "What is it, my good man?"

"You said we could talk on the trail if I came with you."

"Beg pardon?" He picked at a particularly resistant spot on his boots before looking up again and studying John. "Ah, yes. I recall now. That evening before we left time flew faster than an eagle after a mouse in the snow." His eyes left the boots and studied John. "Something about land deeds, wasn't it?"

"Yes, sir." He paused. "I have already lost one parcel of land because two men had title. I've had to move my family and start over again."

"Something about a paper shortage, wasn't it?"

"Yes, sir. And I do not have a proper deed for my land in Bertie Township." His backside started to heat up as though he was right in the flames but he went on. "I just want to make sure that no one can take my land again."

The Governor nodded as he looked past John into the flames. "What is your name?" John told him and Simcoe promised to look into the problem. His boots finished he pulled them back on, rose, and called everyone to him. In a deep bass he began singing *God Save the King*. Every man joined in, the woods still and dark, as their loyal notes to their King and country drifted up into the frosty trees.

Lying in his blankets as close as he could get to the fire John considered leaving on the morrow and finding his way back home, but realized how ill prepared he was to take such a journey on unknown trails in this wintry landscape. He would stay with the rest.

Two days later the small party arrived at the Mohawk village where Joseph Brant himself met them. Simcoe was anxious to push on to Detroit but chose to visit the church and take part in a service with their Indian hosts. As the men filed out of the small church John stopped near Brant who looked very much the same as years before. Would the Indian remember him? He stepped into the light and waited while Brant and Simcoe finished their conversation.

"Ah, John Garner, is it not?" Brant's musical voice boomed under the frosted firs edging the doorway.

"Thayendanagea, sir." John dipped his head slightly and smiled, glad that the sad results of the treaty between the British and the Americans had not dampened the personality of the man.

"Are you on this journey as well, my friend?"

"By accident, it seems, but I am pleased to accompany such a distinguished group. This country surely needs good roads." The Governor had mentioned the night before his plans to stretch roads the length and breadth of the province.

Brant glanced at him as though he might speak but kept silent. "Where is your new home?" the man asked and John described its location. Nodding, the Indian turned away.

In the morning the party set off again, but Brant left them. Duty called him back to the Mohawk village. The rest of the Indians guided the Governor's party along the La Tranche River, fully frozen. Boats were impossible; hence, they walked. The adventure had grown on John. Hoping that Lucy had received his scribbled message and was not angry with him, he put his family out of his mind and concentrated on the vast white land they traversed.

Large drops of rain iced off the trees and down John's neck as he trudged behind the over-loaded sleigh. Beneath his feet the packed snow was now covered with water making a slick track where he fell not once but many times. And every time he got up with his clothes more sodden and his feet sloshing about in boots soaked through.

After two terrible days of this, the temperature plummeted and all their wet clothing turned to ice. John slapped his arms across his chest before the evening fire in an effort to bring back some feeling. He felt his fingers once more but his toes were another matter. He daren't sit too near the flames as he might burn them without even knowing it, so bereft were they of any sensation.

Simcoe gave orders to make a more permanent camp and the Indians set to with hatchets and evergreen boughs, lashing small stripling trees together to form a framework. Not nearly as large as a traditional longhouse, the structure nevertheless held everyone and kept the wind from rendering them all permanent ice men. Smoke filtered out of the tiny hole in the roof but the place still reeked with the damp stink of unwashed bodies.

Wakened yet again in the night with the thawing of his frozen ears, John turned onto his back. He lay listening to the hacking and coughing, the constant dripping of snow as it melted into the fire from the hole above, and the odd whimpering of the sleeping men whose nightmares voiced what their waking minds would not.

Lucy was foremost in his thoughts; once again he had left her to bear the brunt of the farm and family. He couldn't help wondering if he had made a mistake coming on this jaunt to Detroit. Even if it was an adventure, he was sure to hear Lucy's opinions later.

Wedged together in the cramped space like logs on the river in springtime, the men breathed a miasma of smoke and their own bodily emanations. Their shifting and turning underlined his mind's meanderings until he rolled onto his stomach and pulled the blanket over his tender ears. His thoughts turned to Alice and the strange coincidence that she should turn up at Fort Erie. A hard knot formed in his stomach. It felt like a rock poking into his gut. Those twins, eyes bright and hands fisting into the air when he last looked at them in the cradle… No, he would not think of them. He dare not. With effort he slowed his breathing, pictured Lucy's red-gold curls flying in the wind in those early days of joy, and smiled into the dank earth beneath his blanket.

Several days later the Governor's party halted their journey before a wide river on the north side of which the chimneys of Detroit sputtered their smoke into the hazy blue sky. John squinted into the afternoon sun on the choppy water, a brisk wind in his face, and the sprawling town filling his view. After a brief pause, boats full of supplies and men set off for the other shore. The open water was full of huge chunks of ice that smashed against the boats most dangerously. The wind whipped stronger as they fought their way across while the sun slipped behind the clouds. This being the narrow point of the river, the group soon reached the other shore where men-at-arms welcomed them into the fort to the sounds of a royal salute firing into the late afternoon sky.

Four days later the Governor had the whole group up at dawn and retracing their steps across the river. His Majesty's ships lying in the harbor fired respectfully to their departing Governor and his company. The day before, the locals had even conducted prayer services in the woods to wish the group safely on their way.

The clear weather held for the journey back to Newark. John picked up a few details about the lackluster attitude of the British towards Fort Detroit. Hostilities with France occupied most of their resources, so the word went among the men. The Governor, on the other hand, lost no opportunity to sing the praises of this land and, at the forks of the La Tranche River, chose a site and drew up plans for a new capital to be called New London. The fine dry plain surrounded by tall oaks and snow-laden evergreens had him smiling and nodding as he tramped its length and breadth. The mighty river where they stopped for the night he renamed the Thames.

As before, the Indians traveled ahead of the main group and set up camp for the night. The aroma of stewing raccoons or porcupines led the weary travelers into camp, the latter tasting a little like pork, John thought.

As they neared Newark his thoughts turned to home, to the building work in the spring, and to his family. Trudging behind a pack-laden Indian, he hardly saw the frozen snow underfoot nor the blue sky above, a fine backdrop to the latticework of bare branches overhead. The man ahead stepped up onto a fallen tree lying across a deep gorge slicing fifteen feet into the earth. Barely noting the trickle of water below where mostly ice lay, John followed with nary a pause.

A crack rent the air. He felt the slightest shift under his feet. The tree shuddered beneath him and he had a sense of the man ahead sliding toward him. He glanced at the opposite bank but it was too far. Another crack. This time he fell, grabbing, reaching, holding onto a short nub of a broken branch. The Indian slammed against him with his pack but John held on as the man went down.

For long still moments his breath stopped and his hearing failed. Suspended in the air he was powerless, waiting, as if all the waiting he had ever done in his life came together in this one time of utter and total helplessness. A thousand thoughts of jobs he might have done better, people he could have treated more kindly, and words he wished he had said flashed through his mind.

Thwack. His hip took the brunt of the slam into the rocky hill-side but he held tight to the branch. His feet found footing and he wedged himself into the snowy outcropping. The branch bit and tore his hands until he realized he must let it go or follow the whole tree to the creek bed below. Thick tufts of icy grass held him there, his cheek wedged into the hillside, as though it had hands and could keep him from falling the rest of the way down.

He began to slip.

Just as he thought he could hold no longer something grazed his other cheek. He almost shrugged it off before realizing what it was. A rope. From above. Willing his hand to grab hold on the first try he reached for it. And felt its cold hard coils within his grasp.

As he lay wrapped in his blanket that night he sifted through the events of the day. As before the Indians had built a shelter from the wind and prepared food for them all. Tomorrow they would reach the Indian village and leave Brant's band behind. He would say prayers of thanks again but this time his life would be among the items he listed. The Indian who had died was not so fortunate. And in the days to come, he would consider the new plan that had come to his mind.

Chapter Seventeen

March, 1793-February, 1794

"YOU KNOW I WENT TO NEWARK about the deed, Lucy."

"So you said." Lifting her shoulders and expanding her chest in an exaggerated movement, she sighed. The sigh came, as much from relief as anything but, judging by John's face, he didn't take it that way. Hands on his hips he faced her. She could see the frustration in his narrowed eyes and his nodding head. He stepped forward and jerked at the saddlebag on the table, laying it open in a trice, and pulling out a packet.

"There!" He laid the paper on the table and smoothed its slight creases. "Now, no one will ever take our land again. Surely that was worth a five-week trip in the woods with the Governor of this province?"

Her hand went to his arm, to the fuzzy bits of red-gold hair so soft at her touch. "Of course it was, but could you not have said how long you'd be gone?" She would not tell him of her nervous nights and anxious days fearing he had left again, or worse, was struck down and needed her help. With a shake of her head she banished all such thoughts and forced a smile.

And was rewarded. Turning over the hand she stroked, he grasped hers and brought it to his lips to brush a tender kiss on the work-worn fingers. She leaned against his chest as his arms wrapped her into that safe place she had missed so much.

And then he was speaking again and she pulled back out of the safety of his embrace to hear.

"Lucy, I did a lot of thinking on that march."

His voice flowed with excitement. Her breath caught. She tried to match his mood and asked, "About what, my dear?"

"About this land and what we can do with it."

"We'll farm it." What was he thinking? "Of course, we'll farm it, John."

But John's idea was different. They were so close to the raging river and the land for miles around was turning into tidy farms with growing fields of grain. All those grains would need milling. He was just the man to do it. He pulled her to the table where they sat facing each other. "I'm tired of farming, Lucy. We could do well running a mill. I've already decided where the channel off the main river needs to be and I can start immediately. With a good summer's work we can be up and running by fall, just in time for harvest."

He sat back and smiled that grin which had won her over when he asked for her hand those many years ago. She had said yes then.

"How can we clear the land, plant crops for the winter, and build a grist mill? There just isn't time." She shook her head. "Or money."

"But I haven't told you the best part. We'll sell most of the land, keep a little for a good garden and the gristmill, and use the profits to finance the mill. And to live on for the summer." Again he grinned that cat-that-swallowed-the-canary grin.

IN SPITE OF HIS HIP INJURED on the return trip from Detroit, John spent time for the next few days measuring off the section of land he meant to keep and writing copious notes of description. By the week's end he was off on horseback to Newark and the land office for a formal separation. Afterward, papers in hand, he stopped at the Angel Tavern, the local meeting place.

Seated in the corner before his midday meal he listened to the conversations around him and in no time honed in on two gentlemen looking for land. They had come across the river with hopes of settling in the area but were not eligible for the free land grants given to loyalists. John picked up his mug, moved to their table, and in the space of an hour sold the land. Money in hand he stopped at the hardware store and bought two pick axes and two shovels before heading for home and Lucy.

Over the next days and weeks the sun melted the snow and ice from the river as John laid out and began to dig a trench from near the river to his proposed mill site. Underneath the foot or so of lovely fresh earth he struck bedrock making the work impossible until he found someone who knew how to use explosives to blast the rock out of the way. The path of the sluice moved along much faster at that point and John held a neighborhood barn raising to put up the mill with the promise of reduced milling rates for all who helped on the project.

MEANWHILE LUCY AND WILLIAM and even the younger children planted the newly dug garden, tended the animals, gathered berries and herbs in the woods and got on with the business of living. On a fine day in August Robert and Thomas were gathering blueberries along the river's edge with strict instructions about just how close to the water they might go. They left off their task and ran to their mother so excited they could hardly get the words out.

"A ship, mama, a ship!" Robert shouted as he ran toward her. His red hair was swept back from his forehead and his eyes were popping.

"Look, mama, look!" Not to be outdone Thomas poked his bare arm toward the water. "It's coming right for us!"

"John! Look down the river!" she shouted but, by then, hers was not the only voice. John ran from the mill, she scooped up Helen out of the dirt in the garden, William dropped his basket half full of beans and they all ran for the water's edge.

"Our mill stones, I'll wager." John's smile filled his face but soon creases furrowed his sunburned brow.

"What is it, John?" Lucy stood beside him, the water churning at their feet.

"How are we ever going to get them to the mill?"

"You'll figure it out." She squeezed his arm before reaching down to get a better hold on Helen's hand.

And figure it out he did, along with the help of the men on the boat, two teams of oxen from the neighbors, and a lot of pushing and pulling, coaxing and coddling. By nightfall the millstones were set in place, the ship had continued on its journey out into the lake, and John had new bruises, bumps, and scrapes for Lucy to poultice before crawling into bed.

"You did it." She whispered, so as not to wake the children already asleep in their bedrooms, still unwalled, but permeated with a palpable joy covering them all. John did not answer. She stroked his shoulder and smiled. He lay facing her, his eyes shut and his breathing long and languorous.

AS THE DAYS SHORTENED in the heel of that year wagons loaded with corn and wheat and pulled by long-suffering oxen over the rough roads trundled alongside the mill where the unloading could begin. Lucy often took the younger children to watch the water cascade over the flat boards of the turning mill wheel, careful not to stand too near the spray.

Inside the mill the huge stones ground the grain until a fine sheen of pale dust covered the planked floor and wafted up to the floor above. John's wide-brimmed hat was white with flour as he sat over his figures at the rough table. Watching his every move from across the table was a customer whose forehead creased with concentration but who every couple of minutes slowly nodded his head. The figuring done, the men shook hands and clattered down the steps and outdoors.

The farmer pulled his empty wagon away from the loading dock, unhitched it till the morrow, and rode off on his horse. John watched him leave, glad to take in a few breaths of fresh air. Near the cabin William supervised the twins pulling onions in the garden and laying them to dry in the dirt. He glanced back at the river to where Lucy sat by the water's edge, wee Helen by her side. He couldn't see what they were about but was glad Lucy was sitting for the moment.

A large canoe heading into the river caught his eye but he paid it no mind; such sights were common in the water across which lay the country that had once been their own. Before the revolution. Above the dull grind of the millstone and the water rushing over the mill wheel, he thought he heard shots and jerked his head up. Lucy ran toward him, Helen in her arms.

He pushed them into the mill before him and ran for his rifle upstairs by the desk. Shouting at his man to stop the mill wheel, John ran back outside. Two of the men paddled furiously in the surging water but the other two aimed their rifles at the mill and him.

The canoe was almost at the spot where Lucy and Helen had been sitting. Even as he watched they jumped out and hauled it onto the shore. Behind him the three boys clattered up the steps onto the loading dock. Lucy came from the mill, her rifle in hand, and the mill hand, too, although with only a musket.

"Boys, get inside. Look to your sister." He chanced a glance back at their startled faces. William's excitement turned to alarm and he pushed his brothers ahead of him into the safety of the mill. "We're ready now," John said in a low voice as the strangers advanced toward them their own rifles at the ready. At thirty paces away the motley dressed intruders halted.

"What do you want?" John shouted.

"Grain. We need grain." The tallest of the four took a step forward. "You seem to have plenty to share."

Even with the rifle hiding the man's face, John caught the smile in his tone. Was he friendly or was he mocking? "This grain belongs to farmers here, not to me. It isn't mine to give."

"Four of us against you, a useless musket, and a woman," he sneered. John felt the determination in the hard crust of the man's words.

"You don't know what a crack shot this woman is. And the musket makes three against four. Who wants to take the chance he's the lucky one?" He watched as the men looked back and forth from one to the other.

"We have money. Would you sell us a bag of flour?" He lowered his rifle a little.

John considered. This was one way to get rid of the intruders and surely his customer would appreciate the coin. "Yes, one bag. Put down your weapons and one of you come here." John sent the mill hand for a sack while he and Lucy kept their rifles trained on the men. In a few moments the transaction was completed, the strangers back in their canoe paddling across the river.

"The children." Lucy whispered as she dropped her rifle and ran inside.

He lowered his own gun but watched the canoe until it was but a speck heading down the other side of the lake. At last he took a deep breath. William had stolen out to stand beside him and he ruffled the boy's hair. "All over now, son."

That night all the sacks of grain were again inside the mill and the back door bolted and locked. The front door, easily seen from the cabin window, was latched and blocked with wood piled as high as John's head. No one would get inside without making a racket, John was certain.

That night he heard every rustling of the children in their beds and crept to the window more than once. All was well. The animals in the lean-to against the cabin made nary a sound, the moon floated peacefully across the inky sky, and an owl hooted once in the night. As daylight finally seeped into the cabin, John relaxed into a deep sleep, all too soon ended by the sweet sounds of his children laughing and Lucy shushing them.

The days went by and farmers came and went, their grain the source of John's growing cache of notes and silver. Lucy harvested the rest of her herb garden, hanging cattails, choke cherries and fresh mint from the rafters for use over the coming winter. Apple and pear rings drying on long cords stretched across the beams gave a festive look to their home.

Milling stopped as winter approached and John lodged the animals more securely inside the lean-to for protection from the approaching winter. More trees were cut and trimmed to build the interior walls, a job that occupied John on the cold days that winter. Christmas came and went and it looked as if the couple had finally rebuilt their lives with every prospect of good years to come.

Periodically neighbors dropped in to while away the time before the stove, sipping cider and swapping tales. And John and Lucy did their share of visiting as well, hitching up the horse to the two-seater sleigh he had bought at the fort's supply store and setting off in the wintry whiteness, the children's squeals like joyous bells in the crisp air.

On one such day in early February they met up with another sleigh and almost collided on the narrow trail. John maneuvered his vehicle alongside the other and realized that the woman under a beaver hat and layers of clothing topped off with a buffalo robe was none other than Alice. Her whole face was reddened but, whether with the cold or agitation, he couldn't tell.

He glanced at Lucy's raised eyebrows.

"John! Mr. Garner, I mean," Alice yelled. She held the lines tight in her bare hands and leaned far back against the seat as her spooked horse pitched and pulled against the bit. Alice's eyes shone white and wild.

John glanced around but saw no danger. He sat up straighter and handed the lines to Lucy. She took them without a word.

"What is it?" He really didn't want to get involved but could do no less. He reached across and took hold of her lines, his hand closing around hers. "Hold that horse still, Alice. And tell us what is the trouble."

"Is he still following me?" She jerked her head around to look behind.

John glanced back along the snowy trail from which she had come, his eyes squinting against the sun glinting through the black poles of trees that suddenly seemed like sentinels all around them. He jerked around to check the children but they were still snug under their robes even if their eyes shone wide as they studied the strange woman.

"Is who following you, Miss Potter?" Lucy's voice was almost a whisper beside him. Her face was taut but her lips were slightly open with a hint of a smile softening her look.

"Why, my brother, of course." She hesitated. "He flew at me in such a rage, I ran up to my room and locked myself in. When he was busy with a customer I took the back stairs and, with my satchel, escaped to the stable."

John pulled his muffler closer about his neck against the rising wind and again glanced at Lucy. She had her hands full lifting Helen from the back seat on to her lap and settling the boys down again. "We can't stay here. Lead on back to the mill and we'll follow. You can get warm there." And with not another word he flicked the lines and the horse jerked ahead.

"I'M SORRY, MRS. GARNER, I had nowhere else to turn. I hope you believe me." The woman had stripped off her coat and hat and hung them where Lucy indicated. John was busy outside with not one horse but two and Lucy wondered where he would find room to shelter yet another animal in their crowded lean-to stable. Perhaps this summer he would find the time to put up a proper barn and they could get a cow again.

But just now what was she to do with this woman? And how long would she stay? William had glanced from the stranger to his mother and taken the little ones to his room. Their voices drifted out to fill up the long silences in the main cabin.

"Would you care for a hot drink?" She forced herself to look into Alice's eyes. "Tea?"

Alice nodded but said nothing. Lucy tried to stop her fingers from shaking as she prepared the tea. She clattered the cups and spoons from the shelf to the table, added a bowl of the last bit of sugar in the house, and prayed she wouldn't spill the kettle as she filled the teapot. Outside she could hear John with the horses, mumbling and shuffling about, probably not in any hurry to come inside and face the two women. Well, he created this nightmare. He had best come inside to deal with it.

Chapter Eighteen

March, 1794

THREE WEEKS. *That woman has been here three full weeks. Seems more like three years.* Lucy fumed as she swept up the floorboards around the buffalo robe in the corner where Alice seemed to have taken up permanent residence. Just now the woman was outside in the privy and Lucy hoped she would take a good long time to go about her business.

It was not that she was unpleasant; in fact, the opposite. Alice tried to help so much that Lucy was a stranger in her own house. And the children. From being shy and standoffish they had become comfortable and even asked the woman to play games with them. Except William. He was old enough to feel the strain when they all sat squeezed in at the table for meals where the main course was usually tension sliced so thick Lucy thought she would choke.

At night she should have been able to talk to John but they were both all too aware that just a few feet away, on the other side of the curtain across their bedroom door, lay the woman who had borne him two children. As they lay in the bed, John's arm holding her to him, she knew he was trying to use that arm to speak for him, but the weight of it crushed her. She appreciated his concern for her. She really did. But day after day and night after night she could feel herself shrinking inside. In the same way, had he lain with that woman?

John had visited the fort the week before but he came back with little to report. With a room full of customers, Alice's brother had no time for chitchat or for belligerence, for that matter, and not a word had been said about her absence. He did look a little harried, John said, sweeping his hand through greasy hair whenever he didn't know where to find a small iron pot or lace edgings shipped from England, but no one would know he had not always been alone serving customers.

The door opened with an immediate draft blowing through to the bedroom where Lucy yanked the corners of the quilt tight and smoothed the wrinkles. When she swept back into the main room, Alice was rocking in John's chair, her arms around wee Helen, but her eyes lost in a stony stare. Lucy reached for the child's hand. "Come along, Helen. Help me tidy the beds." In her drab smock, the fine-boned little girl smiled and took her mother's hand.

Alice said nothing.

Later that day William and the twins clattered into the house dripping wet snow and holding thick icicles in their mittened hands. "Mama." They thrust their treasures into her face in between licking the icicles with rosy tongues.

"Take those back outside, boys, or you'll have my floors a mess."

"Oh, let them have their fun, Mrs. Garner. It's only a little water." The voice was low and flat.

Lucy's throat went dry and her back stiffened. The boys looked at her with hopeful eyes. She dipped her head, took a deep breath, and motioned the boys outside. Helen sat at the table making piles of dried corn bits, lost in her own little world. The rocking chair tipped back and forth, wooden rockers on wooden floor, marking the time it took for Lucy to control her anger. She strode to the dry sink and reached for the knife. She hacked at the eyes of the supper potatoes.

The tension in the air at supper cast a cold cloud over the whole room. John took his place at the end of the table, bowed his head, and droned the grace in a monotone voice. Seated between the twins William took furtive glances at his parents until Lucy placed his bowl in front of him and he slurped the stew. Even the twins sat with their heads down picking at their food.

"Ow!" Helen's voice cut the silence. She shrieked and then settled to a whimper, sliding closer to her mother, never taking her stricken eyes off Alice, to her right.

"Whatever is the matter, child?" asked Lucy, and John joined in, but Helen just shook her head. Throughout the rest of the even more silent meal, Helen refused to eat and only succumbed when Lucy held the spoon and fed her.

A few days later Lucy, William, and the twins were outside helping John gather the syrup pails and tip them into the large cauldron for boiling down. Spring smells and sounds filled the air but the family had little time to stop and breathe it all in. The track from tree to tree was almost mush, and mud, mixed with the melting snow, slopped over their boots and trickled down inside. Lucy wanted to get the job done and get inside to dry out. The boys, on the other hand, balled the granular snow in their mittens and threw at every target they could.

John tended the fire and kept the children away but, full of energy, they ran and flung themselves in snow banks, their cheeks red with excitement. Watching her children, Lucy's lips spread in a smile as she spelled John off at the fire. He made his way to the cabin for another muffler as the ends of his had slipped into the sap-filled cauldron and were sopping wet.

As he walked the long path he couldn't help laughing to himself at the children's play. Perhaps Helen had wakened from her nap and would come out to play as well. All was silent as he slipped the latch on the door. She must still be sleeping. But where was Alice? The main room was empty, the only sound water hissing and bubbling from a pot on the stove.

He slipped off his muffler, dropped it over a nearby chair, and removed his boots. He padded across the pine boards to Helen's room and heard his daughter's soft snuffling sleep sounds. He edged back the curtain. Alice leaned over the bed, her long arms above her head, clutching a pillow. For a few seconds his brain tried to make sense of the scene but Alice thrust the pillow downward and he flung himself at her. From behind, he pulled at her arms, and shook loose the pillow, which fell across Helen's body. With a mighty shove John threw the woman away from the bed and snatched the pillow off his daughter.

"Helen, Helen," he called. Her eyes opened wide and she struggled in his arms. There was movement off to his right; he spun around, putting the child behind him, just as Alice rammed her head into him, knocking the breath right out of him. She pushed him aside; he couldn't move. Alice grabbed the child and covered her mouth as she bore her out of the room. He stumbled after the two but fell across the bedpost. For an excruciating moment time stopped along with his breath and he lay across the narrow bed gasping for air, his eyes trained on the sight of Alice dragging Helen towards the stove. *No! Don't!*

Air rushed back into his lungs. He stumbled past the edge of the bed and into the main room. The heat from the stove hit him. She had lifted a lid off the hot surface and stood with Helen in her arms, trying to get hold of the child's hand. Screams filled his head, hotter than the flames escaping through the gaping hole, and certainly every bit as terrifying. Whether they were his or Alice's or Helen's he did not know but they drove him forward. He rammed into the woman at the same time as he closed one arm around Helen and pulled her to him.

Just then Lucy burst through the door and he thrust Helen into her arms before turning back. He wasn't taking any chances this time. He pinioned the mad woman on the floor and rammed her arms behind her back. She let out a terrifying screech and wrenched her head sideways trying to reach his hands with her gnashing teeth. Lucy tossed him her apron from the wall hook and he wound the ties round and round Alice's struggling hands.

When she could move no more he stood up. Lucy sat in the rocker with Helen plastered against her body and holding on for dear life. Wrapped in the grip of her mother's arms, the child sobbed and sobbed. John knelt on the floor and stroked Helen's tousled braids trying to comfort her in the only way he knew. His eyes met Lucy's. Their brilliant blue was dampened to a smoldering steely shade, a shade he had never seen before, and never wanted to see again.

After much soothing, the child quieted. The bound woman lay subdued in the corner, rocking her head back and forth. Her dark hair tumbled over her shoulders in complete disarray and her shawl, which had earlier been so neatly pinned across her chest, now threatened to choke her. A red welt flamed across her cheek. Her eyes, though, whites large as saucers and filled with huge shining black pupils, followed every move in the bleak room. She sucked in air between her gnashing teeth and constantly wrenched her whole body in an effort to free herself from the tight knots of the apron strings John had used to bind her.

When the boys came inside Lucy sent them to their room and urged William to take his sister along with him. John fetched rope from the lean-to. He replaced the apron strings with the rope and this time bound Alice's feet as well. The vision of that pillow, so close to his helpless daughter, filled his mind. He tightened the knots. He had to keep his family safe while he got help from a neighbor. The last knot tied, he leaned back on his haunches a moment. From deep down in his gut, the memory of two other little children came surging out and he stood up and stumbled out the door.

THE QUIET OF THE CABIN in the morning light belied the terror of the night before. Lucy had lain awake listening for any sign that Alice was loose in their cabin, the proximity of her four children to the crazed woman feeding her fears. She had heard the grandfather clock toll each dark hour till daybreak. A short time later John had returned with Mr. McKie and the two had set off for Newark with Alice in the back of the wagon.

Now Helen was down for her afternoon nap and the three boys had escaped outside, tired of Lucy's frequent hugs and pats whenever she was near them. For the fifth time she tiptoed in to gaze at her daughter, her fear of what might have been still raw in her mind. Never again would she ignore her own instincts.

She just hoped that Mr. McKie would be enough help for John as he took Alice to Newark and found someone to take charge of her. She had tried to harm Helen, they knew that, and killed her own two children according to the story. Her wild tantrum had not been the act of a sane person and Lucy did not know just what was to be done with the woman in Newark, only that she couldn't stay among decent folk. And certainly not in their home.

Wee Helen cried out in her cot and Lucy hurried to soothe her back to sleep for just a little while longer. Soon, though, the door opened and the boys tumbled in, wet boots and all, laughing together. She got them into dry clothes and settled with tasks at the table. William was old enough to peel potatoes and the twins counted out the dried peas, the last of those they had saved over the winter. William, always the older brother, took the opportunity to teach his brothers arithmetic. Helen wandered out and she settled the child with a hug and a rag doll. She, herself, took John's chair beside the stove.

The animals in the lean-to began to kick up a fuss. She set her knitting aside and went to the window. In the lengthening shadows cast by the tall trees lining the laneway a horse and rider rode into view. At that distance the man was unrecognizable. She reached for her rifle, cocked it and looked out again. Behind her the room went still.

The man rode right up to their porch, his muffed hat all but hiding his face as he dismounted and looped the horse's reins around the post. In the late afternoon half-light she thought she saw something familiar about him, maybe the slope of his shoulders, but couldn't be sure. She was just trying to figure out what to do when heavy footsteps sounded on the porch and he passed out of her view. She froze.

A gentle knock followed by banging and shouting so loud that the door shuddered on its hinges broke her out of her stupor. The twins stared at her. Helen whimpered. Even William, usually so calm and reasonable, looked from her to the barred door and back again. "Mama. Are you going to open it?" She nodded her head, gripped the rifle in her hands, and took a deep breath.

"Who is it?" Her voice seemed to wear all of her fear in its thin timbre and she called again, this time louder. "Who's there?"

"It's a friend, Mrs. Garner. Open the door."

She hesitated a moment before motioning for William to lift the bar. A cold draft blew in and she shivered but held the rifle poised in her arms, ready. The stranger's head ducked under the lintel and he was inside, his eyes dark pools in the late afternoon gloom. He stood for a moment, glanced around, and smiled.

"You don't know me, do you?" He looked away from her to the hook beside him, and hung his snow-covered hat there. He faced her again. "Is that better?"

A flood of warmth rushed to Lucy's fingers and she almost dropped the rifle. Her lips cracked into a smile. "Sergeant Crawford!"

His dark sideburns were longer now and deep lines ran on both sides of his face. The biggest change was his wrinkled face and the way his eyes crinkled almost shut whenever his loud laugh erupted. The fort was his destination. Stopping along the way from Newark, at Chippawa, he had asked about Lucy and her husband, only to be told he had just missed John riding the other way along the Portage Road.

"No matter," said Lucy as she sat across from him and told him of John's errand. "He would not have been able to stop." And he probably wouldn't want to, she thought. Sergeant Crawford's name never entered their conversations. "What is your purpose, riding all this way to Fort Erie by yourself?"

The sergeant told of the tales that had reached Newark about the storekeeper at Fort Erie who had apparently threatened an Indian carrying pelts. The poor savage was lucky to escape with his life and high-tailed it all the way to Newark to complain about his treatment and the outright theft of his furs.

"But why did you come alone, Sergeant?"

"It's rather a secret, Mrs. Garner." He looked straight at her and dropped his voice. "You, I will tell, though."

"I don't mean to pry," she said, her interest piqued.

He nodded and spoke, "I want to find land. Thought I'd do some scouting down this way."

"But the army. Are you leaving your position?"

"That's it exactly, Mrs. Garner." He went on to tell her of his plans for a land grant and marriage to a certain young woman.

THE NIGHT HAD SETTLED OVER THE CABIN as Lucy sent William out to feed the animals and, herself, finished preparations for their evening meal. Once again they would have a guest sleeping on the buffalo robe in the corner, but from this one they had nothing to fear. And he would leave in the morning. After supper the children played a game of Simon Says until Helen got confused and started to wail at her brothers. "Time for sleep." Lucy took Helen by the hand. "Hurry along now, children."

A short time later she sat in John's rocker and, sliding the candle near, picked up her mending. The room was quiet, too quiet. She stole a glance at the sergeant. He sat across from her, his arms resting on the table, one finger of his right hand drawing circles, over and over. His black hair, shot with grey, hung down both sides of his face. He had untied it. The light of the candle cast a soft glow over the room, reminding her of the painting she had loved in her Boston home all those years ago.

He looked up and caught her staring at him. She pricked her finger. A tiny dot of blood welled up and she thrust the finger into her mouth. Feeling his eyes on her she glanced up again.

He chuckled. After a long moment he stood, paused, and turned to his bag. "Morning will come early. I must sleep." He shifted the furniture to find room to spread out the buffalo robe.

Lucy hurried to her room and pulled the curtain tight behind her. "Goodnight, Mrs. Garner," he called and she mumbled an answer.

THE DAY WAS ALMOST OVER as John drove the wagon along the last part of the road into Newark. His thoughts were ragged and narrow, focused as they were on getting his cargo to Navy Hall and off his hands. The drive had been cold with a wintry wind out of the east buffeting them all the way from the farm. The two men had agreed to push on as quickly as they could, stopping only briefly for food and to allow their charge to relieve herself. In the woods, John had made sure he kept hold of the long rope as she slipped behind a tree or bushes. He was prepared to tug on the rope if she took too long but she had been quiet and cooperative the whole time.

In the wagon box, she lay on a pile of last year's straw with her two arms tied, one to each side of the wagon. He had not trusted her enough to untie her but forcing her to ride the whole day in such discomfort weighed heavily on him. He stole a glance. Her once-lustrous hair hung in loose hanks covered with bits of broken straw. Dirt marked both her gown and her face as though he had plucked her from the streets. What would people say when they saw her state?

The roads were bare as they trundled into Newark, all sane people resting at home warming their hands before their fires. As the wagon pulled up before Navy Hall, John shouted to a passerby pushing along the street, his head tucked into his turned-up collar. "Where can I take a prisoner?" For a moment the man kept going as though he hadn't heard. "Sir!" John shouted louder this time, and the man stopped so abruptly he almost stumbled in the muddy slush. Saying nothing, he pointed to the plain door on the other side of a hitching rail.

As John untied the ropes on the wagon sides, Alice sat still and even allowed him to help her down. He wound the ropes around her, fastening her arms behind her back. The two men flanked her as they tried the door. The heat of a roaring fire welcomed them into an empty room. On the table sat a steaming mug, a shiny fork, and a bone-handled knife. The sweet aroma of hot tea reminded John how long the day had been.

"Hello! Is anyone here?" he hollered.

An interior door flew open to admit a man carrying a tin plate of food, his eyes wide. "What are you doing here?" He shouted the words and slammed the plate onto the small table.

Alice hurled herself across the room and into the path of the soldier, screaming. "They've captured me, sir! Please, make them release me!"

Chapter Nineteen

March, 1794

JOHN SHIFTED AGAIN ON THE HARD BENCH as he watched the logs burn to ash, every crackle and spit of the smoking fire startling him. A soldier had been left to guard the four of them. John strained to hear the raised voices coming from behind the closed office door. To his right Alice sat perfectly still, her tied hands calm in her lap, as though all she was waiting for was a shopkeeper to take her order or for a freshly formed loaf of bread dough to rise for baking.

Mr. McKie sat to the left, his head nodding gently in the heat, and his discarded muffler across his lap. On the other side of the fireplace the scratch of the soldier's ragged quill pen stole into John's thoughts and he glanced at the man. Parted in the middle, his wavy blonde hair hung loose almost to his shoulders. His pink face may have been caused by the fire but John thought it more likely that he was just one of those florid-faced fellows who came along once in a while. He wasn't suffering for lack of food. Pudgy cheeks, a wisping moustache stretched across his miniature mouth, and gold-rimmed spectacles gave him quite a harmless appearance.

"What are you staring at, sir?" The man glared at John.

"Nothing, sir," John replied. He forced his eyes toward the sound coming from behind the closed door. Footsteps pounded on the wooden floor. John jumped to his feet. The door slammed open. Alice rose as well; he was immediately wary, not knowing what she might do or say. Mr. McKie moved to her other side.

"Well, Garner, we meet again." Governor Simcoe stood before them, his dark brown eyes wide with pleasure for the briefest of moments. His features hardened, though, as his glance included Alice. "What is all of this about?"

John outlined the incidents at his farm, stressing the fact that he had narrowly missed losing his youngest child on account of Alice's mad actions. He stressed her lack of stability and her propensity for losing her temper and, indeed, all control at the least suggestion that did not please her. When the governor suggested there must be more to the story, John agreed that there was and asked for privacy. Leaving Alice and Mr. McKie with the soldier, he followed Governor Simcoe into the back room.

Seated in the straight-backed chair that Simcoe had indicated, John took a deep breath. "She tried to smother my daughter, sir."

"Do you have proof of that?" The governor's eyes bore into his own as he leaned forward across the desk, his gouty hands clasped together and so misshapen John could hardly keep from staring at them.

"I saw her, sir."

"But surely you must be mistaken. The woman out there is extremely calm, especially given that she's been hauled here tied up in a wagon on a journey of at least a day." His dark eyebrows arched as his forehead wrinkled in an obvious question.

John's hands twisted and turned in his lap as he tried to think how he could convince the Governor of the truth of his story. He struggled to remember every detail of seeing Alice standing over wee Helen. "I came in just as she held the pillow in the air. It flashed down on top of my girl. Alice's arms pushed down. Helen's feet kicked the quilt." His chest heaved. He gasped for air. "I threw her off! And pulled the pillow away. Thank the Lord I was in time."

In the jagged pattern of the floorboards he saw again his daughter's wide eyes as she looked from him to Alice. And he told the rest of the story of having the breath knocked out of him, of helplessly watching Alice take the child to the fire, of Lucy coming in and of his final subduing of the crazed woman.

The governor sat silent but nodding, his wide eyes full of compassion. John could see the man believed him. He sank back in the spindle-backed chair and waited.

"We will take over now, Garner."

The next day Mr. McKie and John left Newark and Alice, with a promise from the governor that justice would be done. She was locked up in the guardroom of Navy Hall for the moment until a decision could be made where to hold her separate from any male prisoners who might come in. John would be notified of the trial, as his testimony and Lucy's, too, were crucial to obtaining a conviction.

THE TRIP HOME PROVED UNEVENTFUL even if the muddy road was one pitfall after another until John thought he would almost prefer one of the horse's legs breaking just so they could stop. As it was he was aware of every bone in his body. Through the whole journey he kept wondering why he had never put a padded seat on the wagon. If he made it home in one piece, that seat would be one of his first chores. Mr. McKie had gone from being taciturn at the best of times to completely silent except for a series of moans and grunts that corresponded with John's own.

After dropping off his friend and thanking him profusely he soon turned the wagon up his own laneway. The moon lit the ground through the trees in such a clear and beautiful light that he felt more relaxed than he had for weeks, ever since he'd allowed Alice to stay with them. He regretted that he had never asked her about their twins and that omission weighed heavily on him now. Perhaps he didn't want to know if the rumors of their deaths were true, and of Alice's part in whatever happened. Lucy had urged him to find out but he hadn't. How he regretted that decision.

The familiar knot formed in his belly. He flicked the lines urging the horses towards the cabin where the chimney spewed a thin line of white smoke against the darkening sky. A faint glow showed at the window but no faces appeared. The horses unhitched and tended, he made his way to the door, pausing to bang the mud and icy slop off his boots. Still no one appeared to welcome him home but laughter seeped out into the night. He pushed the door. It was locked. A faint frustration crept across his forehead. Why did they not hear him? And rush out in welcome? He banged his fist on the wooden door.

Silence. John called out. The bar lifted. The door swung back to reveal lamp-lit faces with wide eyes and smiles of joy. He smiled, too, until he saw the man standing so close to his wife.

They got the door closed and John's wet and muddy things hung by the fire. The children all talked at once, so anxious were they to see their father. Robert and Thomas pushed in close and little Helen pulled at his leg trying to get his attention. William stood back a few steps but even he seemed full of excitement, whether at seeing his father or because of the earlier hilarity in the cabin John couldn't guess.

"Children, let your father get his breath," Lucy said, her eyes soft and apologetic. "Sit, John. We're just about to eat."

"And I see you have a guest." He measured each word like a dose of bad-tasting medicine. The small room went silent.

"Mr. Garner. I'm pleased to see you again." The sergeant's words were proper and he did look genuinely pleased. "After all this time," he added, nodding his head.

John dipped his head slightly and sat to eat. The children slid into their chairs and noisily pulled them to the table. In moments hands were passing plates and a large spoon ladling stew, all of which went far towards mollifying the weary traveler. Everyone settled in to the steaming meal. Even Helen, squeezed onto her mother's lap in order to make room, chewed at a half slice of bread in between tastes from Lucy's spoon.

IN THE WEE SMALL HOURS OF THE NIGHT John lay, exhausted yet sleepless, listening to the silence of his home. Lucy's back was to him but her breathing rose and fell in a comforting rhythm interrupted periodically by a tiny cough or a slight rustle of bedclothes until she lapsed back into silence. From the rest of the cabin he heard nothing, not even from that damnable sergeant who was sleeping mere feet outside their door.

The sergeant had explained his presence to John's satisfaction, although not why he had stayed over an extra day. Much as he wanted to, John could find no blame. The man had once planned to marry Lucy, though. And she, him. Doubts niggled at him and he shifted away from Lucy although he could still feel her warmth against his back.

What about himself? He had betrayed Lucy by living with Alice during the war and having children with her. He shuddered at the vision of that woman standing over his wee daughter with murder in her mind and wondered how he could ever have cared for her. And what would happen in Newark? The Governor was trustworthy, he knew, but still, she was full of trickery.

Helen called out. He listened to see if she wakened but all was silent. He rolled over again trying not to disturb Lucy and edged his arm around her slight frame. She snuggled into him and he was comforted. All would be right in the morning. He felt himself sliding into that dreamy state before sleep. He let it all go. All, that is, except the man in the next room.

THE NEXT DAY JOHN FOUND HIMSELF on the way to Fort Erie and riding right next to Sergeant Crawford, a situation he continually berated himself for causing. He had questioned the sergeant's motives for coming to the fort and to see Lucy, not in so many words, but by suggestive glances at the man and Lucy and saying nothing for most of the morning. Even with just the two of them, when the sergeant had insisted on helping to tend the animals, John's mouth had remained set in a thin line, no matter what was said to him.

At the noon meal he sat, head down, eyes studying the motion of his spoon as he lifted each morsel of stew to his mouth, and never once looked up. Finally Lucy lost patience with him and his mood. Plates clattered onto the table, silverware slammed alongside, and the children sat silent and scared at the words spewing from their mother's lips.

Shortly thereafter the two men escaped on their horses, preferring any company, even each other's, to that of the shrew they had left slamming and banging as she tidied up.

John broke the silence. "So now you can tell me. Why exactly are you heading for Fort Erie, alone?"

The sergeant glanced over and pulled his horse up short. John stopped as well and watched his companion's changing face, as he seemed to decide just what he might divulge. After a moment the man spoke.

"What I told your wife is true." He ran his tongue over his lips. "It's just not the whole story."

"I thought as much. Tell me."

"My superiors are worried, that's all."

"About what?" John had a sudden thought. "Do you mean the British? Or those in charge here?"

"Those back in England have their hands full fighting the French. On the continent. No time for us." He spat in the mud. Grabbing John's arm he leaned over close. "We're in real trouble. So many Americans want land. We're the closest place to find it."

"But we're a British---"

"Don't you see? We're nothing next to the war with France. The King has all he can do to hold on to the seas. He doesn't need this frozen wasteland."

"Surely you're wrong." John's voice weakened even as he spoke. "What about the Americans? How will we hold out against their armies?" He lapsed into silence, remembering the scene at his mill the previous year.

"That's just it," he said. Both men listened to the heavy breathing of their horses.

"Let's go. I've got to sort out this mess with the storekeeper."

As the two approached the fort near the mouth of the river the water ran high and carried with it huge ice floes which crashed and smashed against each other on their frenzied race downriver. The pier along the water's edge tipped away from the wind and looked ready to break loose at any moment. And if the pier went, the narrow strip of flooded land before the fort's walls would soon follow.

For the moment, though, all seemed secure and the men made their way into the fort. While the sergeant completed his session with the commander, John waited outside and thought how glad he was to have escaped the soldier's life. But he might have to fight again. Maybe he wasn't as free as he thought. Just as his mind took him down that rocky road the sergeant reentered the anteroom, lines creasing his forehead. He pushed by John muttering, "Let's get your business done."

The company store had changed since the last time John and Lucy had visited for supplies. Once-neat tables piled high with orderly stacks of merchandise and clean bolts of muslin and hanks of wool had given way to absolute mayhem. Open sacks of corn and flour tipped into the aisles. Furs had fallen out of their packs. A haze of dust stirred in the foul-smelling air. The counter at the back was so piled with merchandise John could hardly see the storekeeper standing in the gloom behind it.

"What're ya' lookin' at?" The man's gravelly voice suited the messy shop.

Carefully stepping through the chaos, John led the sergeant to the back and began to ask Henry about Alice. He hoped to learn more about her history and even what might have happened to their twins.

"I thought I recognized ya. You was with her, wasn't ya?" His gnarled finger pointed into John's face. "And she's prob'ly livin' with ya now, eh?" He leaned far over the counter until his face was inches away.

John stood firm. The man's breath fouled the air; if his jabbing finger wouldn't hurt John, the smell might. Slowly he reached for the finger, grabbed hold of it, and forced it away from his face.

The sergeant stood to his right, breathing heavily, ready. "Do you want to know where she is, sir?" he asked.

"Who're you? What would you know of it?" He snarled almost by reflex but a glint in his eye showed Henry's interest. He nodded ever so slightly. "Tell me. I'll kill the bitch."

Choosing his words with the utmost care John told the man where Alice was and why. Henry moved nary a muscle throughout. Only his mouth twitched from time to time and, once, he glared at the sergeant's added words. John, however, carried on speaking so calmly onlookers would never suspect the story was about his own family. Finally the room was silent and John dared to broach that other, more dangerous question.

"What happened to her children?"

"Children! They were just babes, they were."

"Yes, they were. Do you know?" He watched the man making up his mind just what to say. "Where are they?"

"Why'd you wanna know? Nothin' to you, are they?" He came around the edge of the counter and stopped, his face inches from John's. "Unless they are! You the father, then?" he shouted.

The sergeant pushed in closer. John held his place in front of the storekeeper but averted his head and tried not to breathe. Should he tell? Of the twins and their parentage? What would the man do with that information? Beside him the sergeant edged his rifle closer to Henry, forcing him to back off. He certainly didn't want the sergeant to know his dark secret. Questions and more questions filled John's brain as his heart pounded against his ribcage, so loud surely they could hear it.

But the two men stood firm, oblivious to John's inner struggles. Henry might turn wild if John confessed but maybe he already knew what had happened. John's breathing slowed, his head nodded slightly, and he raised his hands in front of him as though to ward off blows. "I am their father."

The sergeant sucked in air. Henry didn't move a muscle. For a long moment he stared into John's eyes. The hate in the man's eyes grew and John tensed himself against the attack he knew was coming. He saw the moment Henry realized he was facing not one man but two, and his flickering eyelids as he lowered his head. All the fight went out of him; he hurried back around the counter.

"Why'd ya leave them babes with her? Didn't ya know what she'd do?"

"I...I...had to come back," John sputtered. "My family...the Colonel, those damnable Americans." It all came rushing into his mind again.

"Shoulda brought her, too. And the babes." He banged his fist on the counter. "When the new babe was born she drowned it in the stream. Did ya know that, my man?"

John staggered back a step. Not only had she killed the twins, she'd had another and murdered it, too.

"Ah, ya didn't know about that, did ya?"

One last thing he had to know, even if it killed him. "How?"

"How'd ya think?" Henry knew exactly what John was asking. "With a pillow. One at a time. They was sleepin'." He turned away, his shoulders heaving.

John's hands hung at his sides. He was still breathing but he knew now what the dead must feel lying in the stone cold earth. Nothing. Absolutely nothing. All the goodness and love and hurt and heart had been kicked out of him.

He backed out the door.

Chapter Twenty

April, 1794

NEWARK HAD ALL THE MARKS of a real town now with hard-packed streets, carefully built houses under freshly budding branches, and people scurrying this way and that to avoid horses and wagons clip-clopping towards merchant row. Before each shop wooden-planked walkways kept customers out of the mud as they stepped from tinsmith to general store and candle maker to livery stable, although this last had no walkway before it. Evenly spaced hitching rails on both sides of the wide street held fast the triple-wrapped lines of riderless horses and quite a number of buggies and wagons.

The town breathed excitement. Before the newly built courthouse whose columns rose tall and stately, bustling bodies pushed through the wide open doors, everyone hoping for a good seat. Today was the trial whose story had run through the kitchens and cabins of Niagara faster than sap on a sunny day in March.

Young William had been most insistent that he come, but John and Lucinda had refused and ignored his long face on the way to the McKie's who had promised to take care of the children. For the first time in years they were alone as they rumbled over the rough roads toward an event they both knew would be difficult no matter how it turned out. John had hardly spoken and she didn't want to press him. Her fingers twisted in her lap as she looked down the street at the throngs of people.

As John edged the horses up to the rail, Lucy felt a hundred eyes on her. She forced a smile to her lips even though those staring were all strangers. Had everyone she ever knew left? And how did these strangers recognize her and John? She took his arm and concentrated on missing the mud underfoot until they were on the boardwalk. As if by magic, braies, boots, swishing skirts, and one set of moccasins slipped to either side, clearing a pathway. John's footsteps echoed as he walked. She stumbled. Immediately his arm tightened on her elbow, a warm pressure guiding her into the building.

Once the trial began Lucy surreptitiously studied Alice where she sat a few rows ahead on the other side of the tall-ceilinged room. She wore the same gown as the day John had taken her away and for a fleeting moment Lucy wondered where the woman's other clothes had gone. As though she felt the heat of Lucy's eyes on her, Alice slowly turned. Her eyes roamed a moment until she spied John. Such a look of hate flooded her features that Lucy shivered and inched closer to her husband. For a second Alice's eyes held her own until her lawyer nudged her.

"Not guilty," she said.

The jury of twelve men was sworn in, the bespectacled judge stared down upon the courtroom, and a tallish man struggling to keep his white wig on his head began to talk. Lucy scanned the rows of gawkers leaning forward on the benches to follow the story of one witness after another. When John rose to take his seat at the front a collective holding of breath was so infectious that Lucy found herself joining in. This was the testimony they had come to hear.

She looked at the wide planks of the dusty floor. Strong and well cut they were, but already worn with the passing of muddy boots and dusty shoes over the last year of trials for relatively minor offences. Stolen horses, a fistfight which had ended up with a table broken, countless disputes over land titles, and any number of minor disturbances had kept the court busy since its inception. Today, however, was the first trial for attempted murder. Today all of these people would hear how Alice had tried to smother Helen.

She wished she had been able to stay behind with the children but John had insisted her testimony was crucial. He was probably right. She felt someone was watching her and raised her eyes to John but he seemed intent on the object in his hands. Seated beside the judge's box on a raised platform a little lower than that of the judge, her husband twisted his hat in his hands and followed the wandering steps of the lawyer with steady eyes. As he drew out the story of Helen's near death, she felt herself again rush into the cabin, discover John struggling with the woman, and hear her wee Helen sobbing her heart out.

An elbow dug into her ribs. She glared back at the haughty glance of the offending woman but, looking up, realized everyone was staring at her. John stood in the aisle waiting for her to get out before he sat down. She had to testify.

The questions came at her like a volley of buckshot, some missing, some grazing her with minor stings, and some piercing her heart. She told of Alice's crazed actions, of the woman's complete loss of control, and, finally, after the defending lawyer started in on her, of something she had hoped to keep hidden from this cold group of strangers.

"Mrs. Garner. Please respond. I asked you if your husband was faithful to you."

"I…I don't see…"

"You don't have to see, Mrs. Garner." As he leaned her way his wig shifted forward. He grabbed it and, with both hands, patted it into place. "Just give the court your answer."

"He was a soldier. Under Colonel Butler." She looked at the judge beside her. "We all had to do things…during the war, sir."

"Answer my question, ma'am." The strident tones of the man forced her to look at him. A gleam shone from his tawny eyes that bore into her and jumbled her thoughts. He took a step forward.

"Ma'am?" She struggled to remember his question. His lips spewed the words forth again. "Was your husband faithful to you?"

"No."

"What's that? Speak up, woman."

His tone struck her; she rose up to sit high in the chair and glanced around the room. Behind John three feathers rose above the heads. Who was the Indian back there? She excised the thought, looked back at the prosecutor, and forced out the words. "He was a spy for the British, sir, doing his duty." The room buzzed and her persecutor stepped back a pace. Louder, so as to be heard over the din, she continued. "Part of that was pretending to be married to an American woman. So that he could get information, send it to Colonel Butler." The room quieted. No one wanted to miss a word but hearing was no problem as Lucy fairly shouted out her next words. "John was faithful to his king and his country."

Again voices rose from the watchers and this time the judge rapped smartly with his gavel. "I'll have the whole lot of you thrown out if you don't keep silent!"

Lucy's hands covered her ears but the room quieted and she composed herself once more.

"You haven't answered my question, Mrs. Garner." He stood beside her and leaned so close she smelled his tobacco breath. "Was he faithful to you?"

"No," she whispered.

The man went on to force Lucy to reveal that the woman was Alice, that Alice came to live at Fort Erie with her brother, and that she and John had taken Alice into their home a few weeks ago. His sniffing manner made her feel like she was in the wrong and that John and Alice were continuing their relationship right under her nose. The stern faces before her held nary a soft glance nor sympathetic look.

The lawyer pecked at her again and again. Her answers came out of their own accord and once or twice the judge admonished her to speak up. She tried to sit tall but her spine seemed to have melted and as she studied the dark trousers of her persecutor the room seemed to hold only the two of them; his words beat upon her in a merciless, never-ending flogging. From the deepest part of her being she heard the final humiliation and was stirred.

"Did your husband have children with her?"

The room came back into focus. Alice's eyes bore into her and a slight smile crossed her nodding face but Lucy escaped the devilish pull of those eyes and scanned the rows of scowling men and women for one face. John sat alone. His shoulders shifted back and forth as he stared at her, his look of hurt and shame covering his face so thoroughly she was not surprised to see his tears, lit by the light hanging from the ceiling. She looked back at the man.

"Yes. He had children with her. A better question, sir, would be what happened to those children?"

The lawyer looked at her and at the nodding judge before glancing around the room. "As you wish, ma'am. What happened to those children?"

"After my husband came back to Colonel Butler, she...she killed them."

Once more the court erupted with shouts and catcalls. Lucy wasn't sure if they were for her or for Alice. The judge banged and banged, adding his own voice to the mayhem, until finally he stood and crashed his gavel on the table so hard it split in two. The head rolled off onto the floor in front of Lucy. People sat back down and gradually the room quieted.

"This woman also had another child of which my husband had no knowledge."

"Explain why that is so, ma'am." The man spoke deferentially to Lucy.

"The child was born months after he reported back to the Colonel. She never told him." Lucy paused and waited but the lawyer didn't speak. "We learned about that child from her brother just a few weeks ago." She cleared her throat and took a deep breath. "By her own account to her brother, she drowned that newborn in the river."

"You're lying, you witch!" Alice screamed. "You won't get away with it." She jumped to her feet, her bound hands struggling above her head in a vain attempt to get free. Completely out of control she wailed and flailed and the bailiffs ran to subdue her. Like a stuck pig with no way to escape, the red-faced Alice howled her fury. After much kicking and smacking on both sides the bailiff got her gagged and tied to the chair. Her eyes, however, still flared wild and white, bright spots of hellish fire.

Gradually she calmed. The shock in the courtroom was palpable. No one moved or spoke or even breathed, it seemed, until the judge directed the lawyer to continue. He asked a few clarifying questions and established that neither John nor Lucy had ever seen this child and had no first-hand knowledge of it. Finally he excused Lucy and she sat down. The prosecuting attorney rose to say he had no more questions and all eyes focused on the judge.

The sunlight coming through the tall windows all but blinded Lucy as she glanced behind. The feathered headdress was gone. She turned back and nudged closer to John. His hand held hers for a brief moment but he stared straight ahead. On the back of the chair ahead one of last year's flies, fat and dopey, lifted off toward the window where its hopeless struggle to escape was the only sound in the room. The judge lifted his eyes from his papers and scanned the onlookers. He cleared his throat in that time-honored manner of getting the attention of all and sundry and began to speak.

A sudden crash at the back of the room made Lucy swing around in her seat. Framed in the doorway stood someone who should have been there for the whole proceeding. Beside her, John tensed as the man strode past him and right up to the railing where the bailiff's services were again needed in order to restrain him.

"What is the meaning of this, sir?" demanded the crimson-faced judge.

"What're ya doin' here?" The man jabbed his finger like a knife, right at the judge. "That's my sister tied up there." His finger poked toward Alice.

Once again pandemonium took over the court. The judge rammed his fist down over and over, but neither that nor his strident calls for order could quell the racket in the room. People were on their feet, pushing and shouting at their neighbors, but just what they wanted was lost in the melee. Suddenly the sharp crack of a pistol sounded and bits of plaster fell from the ceiling. Turning heads and questioning eyes reined over the now quiet room. Once more the judge banged his fist and one by one people sat. The red-faced bailiff lowered his pistol but fixed the crowd with a stern look.

In the next few moments the judge agreed to hear Henry's testimony. He told of his sister coming across the river at Niagara and finding him at Fort Erie. The fire had gone out of him, though, and his voice softened.

"Speak up, man!" roared the judge.

"Continue with your story," the lawyer said.

And Henry did. He told about her children, the first two, which she had smothered, and her reasons for this. They were sick, she said, full of red spots oozing with pus. They were hours from dying anyway, she said. The pillows just shortened their pain.

A gasp erupted from the room at large. The lawyer stepped closer to Henry. "And what about the newborn?"

Henry dropped his head and was silent. The whole room sat, motionless, on the edge of its seat, waiting. He lifted his head as though it were a great weight and looked past the lawyer straight at Alice. His words were slow but clear. "She drowned it," he whispered.

"Louder, man!"

Henry glared at the judge. "She drowned it!"

THE JURY HAD RETIRED TO ANOTHER ROOM, the stern admonishments of the judge warning them to consider well their verdict. John had pulled himself together and his face was calm, his voice calmer as he quietly spoke to the man beside him. Lucy didn't know who he was but was glad of the distraction for her husband. A soft thrum enveloped the room. Women whispered and men shifted in their seats. The sun had all but disappeared. If the jury did not come back soon the banks of candles wedged into wall sconces would have to be lit.

Lucy had wanted to start for home when her testimony was done but John needed to see Alice punished. More than that, he needed to know his own family was safe from her. With that Lucy could agree. A slight hubbub from the back of the courtroom announced the arrival of the two lawyers and the clerk. The doors on either side of the judge's bench opened. The judge came in one side and a long line of jurors filed through the other. Watching the floor the men tramped to their chairs and waited for the judge to sit.

"Have you reached a verdict?" The stern tones of the judge filled the darkening room and a hush penetrated its shadows. Lucy held her breath. John had told her few prisoners were actually found guilty here in Newark. People didn't like condemning their own. And while Alice was not from Newark, she was a woman and an attractive one at that. One of the jurors glanced around and rose to his feet. The paper in his hand shook.

"We have, your Honor."

"What say you?"

The man paused for a few seconds before raising his eyes to take in the whole room. "We find the defendant…Not guilty!" His voice rang out with the words.

Lucy clutched at John. He slipped down in his chair. Shouts and threats echoed all around. The judge was speaking but all she heard was the pounding of his mangled gavel and the side door smashing open as he escaped. The crowd thronged up the aisle past John and Lucy. Henry looked their way, gave a slight shake of his head, and took his sister's arm. John stared straight ahead as the two came down the aisle but Lucy saw Alice's broad grin and cringed. The two swept by.

For long moments she and John stayed rooted to their chairs. He seemed incapable of speech but she watched as his face cracked and a tear escaped. He swiped at it. Stunned herself, Lucy gripped his arm until he finally dropped his head and turned her way.

"Let's go home," he whispered.

They clung to each other all the way out of the courthouse, along the crowded boardwalk, through the suddenly silent groups of people, to their horses and wagon. Even though darkness was minutes away, they hitched up and headed for home. A few moments later, however, John pulled up the horses right in the middle of the deserted road and turned to Lucy. "We must find somewhere to stay."

She instantly agreed.

"I still have a few coins left. Perhaps the Angel Inn has room." He turned the wagon around and headed back to the Inn they had passed a few moments earlier. Luckily they got a room. John took off his boots and stretched out on the bed. Lucy gave him a long look before going down to the smoky kitchen to see about food. John had had enough of people that day, and they could both do with some privacy.

Lucy slipped back into the stale-smelling room, a kitchen maid close behind her. John sat on the edge of the bed. His shoulders slumped forward and his head hung down so far it seemed in danger of falling off. She shooed the girl out, took John's hand and led him to the tiny square table. Fried salt pork and gray potatoes in grayer grease along with dripping toast cake were hardly enough to tempt them; nevertheless, they each took a spoon and ate.

In the night raucous calls and bawdy laughter from the taproom below kept them awake. Long before their tiny shuttered window admitted any slivers of light, the pair were up and on their way, anxious to get home and rid themselves of the fleas and bedbugs along for the ride. Lucy thought of Alice. The woman was unpredictable. What might she do now? She glanced at John's set features and chose not to speak of it.

Chapter Twenty-One

July, 1794

LUCY'S HAIR STILL TANTALIZED JOHN even eighteen years after he had first fallen for her all that time ago in Boston. Just off the porch she bent over little Helen who was swiping at her teary eyes. The sun lit those curls as it always had even if their red-gold was now tinged with grey. Still he thought of those early days and smiled from his seat on the porch where he held a cup of cool water in his hand.

He had put it off as long as he could, making do with other bits when he needed string, taking the children berry picking and dandelion hunting to augment their food supply. Last night he had even suggested to Lucy she make dandelion tea rather than make a trip to the storehouse at the fort for the real thing. But she had insisted. And today he would go. Alone, though. At least he had won on that.

Was Alice there? That was what had kept him away for so long. They had heard nothing and had not been back to Newark since the trial so had no way of knowing where she had gone. Any vestiges of regret he had felt over her had long been expunged. Now he worried what she might do to get even. And how Henry might react to him in the store. Would the man even serve him? But he must go. He was torn between going alone and taking someone with him. Maybe Mr. McKie would accompany him, although he cringed at the thought of exposing his friend to Henry or Alice.

Helen ran across the yard. "Father!" He slammed his empty cup onto the wide arm of the chair seconds before her tiny body crashed into him but it still went crashing to the porch floor. "May I come to the fort? Please, please?" "Whoa, my girl," he said, laughing in spite of himself. "Not so fast." He lifted her to his knee, ignoring the cup, and prepared himself for the disappointment he would soon see on her face. As Lucy came up the steps, he broke the news to his daughter but promised to bring her some little thing from the store. At Lucy's bidding she slipped off his lap and went inside.

"Are you sure you would not like me to go?" Her words were stiff, unusually so.

"No. I need you here." He looked away from her gaze. "I won't be long. And you can enjoy shelling the peas in the cool shade while I'm choking on dust from the road." He stood and gave her a hug, her errant curls brushing his face.

To carry the two kegs of flour he might sell at the store, John hitched up the team and the wagon soon rumbled out of the yard. Mr. McKie had declined his invitation and John hoped he wouldn't rue his decision to come alone. Nevertheless, he put it all out of his thoughts as the wagon bounced over the rutted road toward the fort. The creation of the new District Land Board should mean better roads very soon; he certainly hoped so as these rough and untended paths crisscrossing farmers' lands meant lots of delays and even some injured horses. McKie had lost a mare when she stepped into a deep sinkhole in the middle of the road. Her leg splintered into bits. McKie had no choice but to shoot her on the spot.

John shuddered. McKie had ridden over and asked for his help. As they approached the spot just a half-mile or so from the grist mill, he had seen the wagon pitched to one side, spilling supplies onto the ground, the wagon tongue cracked enough to be useless for pulling again. Both his and McKie's horses sent up such a loud neighing that controlling them had been almost impossible. Their tossing, tugging heads sprayed foam on every turn.

Lying half on the roadway and half among the weeds lay the dusty black horse, the right foreleg twisted and broken. It hung in conjoined bits over the naturally positioned left leg. Blood spattered both legs. The eyes were open but not by any effort of the horse. Dull whites surrounded brown irises that would stare no more.

He shook his shoulders and his head, forcing his thoughts back to the present and the tall gates of the fort. In just a few moments he tied the lines at the hitching rail. An Indian leaned against the wall just between the door and the wide windows of the store. His arms were crossed and his head tipped forward making his three feathers almost point at John. He made no sound as John stepped by him and entered the store.

John edged into the gloom. A dank and musky smell assailed his senses. He barely breathed. His hand reached to touch the shining glow of a beaver pelt caught in the sunlight streaking from the window. Soft. Another step. Still no sound. He fingered the musket in his other hand and brought it to rest across his chest, his left hand cradling its cool barrel.

Behind him the door creaked open but when he turned to look he saw only the cast iron pans hanging there. He hardly had a chance to breathe before a pile of fabric bolts carried by a woman's straining hands came at him. Her leather apron over a brown skirt hung below the load as she charged toward the counter. Her long fingers were white with the effort of holding such a load.

She dumped the cloth onto the counter before him but was so busy keeping the bolts from falling she didn't look up. It was Alice. Shining black hair tied back in a bun framed her reddened face and for a split second he remembered how she was in New York; his memories threatened to flood his brain but he pushed them back with the memory of Alice holding a pillow over Helen. He coughed and she jerked her head up. Her eyes went from fright to flight. She backed away.

He hardly knew what to say as he watched this woman for whom he had once had such feelings. He laid the musket on the counter, its clunk looming large in the stillness. She watched him, her hands on the counter edge, her eyes black slits. She spoke not a word.

"I have a list." His voice was a whisper.

Still she was silent but her eyes went to his empty hands. "Where?" she asked.

He said the words and she moved to find the needles and tea and other items, dropping each on the counter in front of him but never once looking at him. The Indian appeared beside him but said nothing and neither did John. "I have flour. If Henry wants it." She flashed a glare his way and went back to collecting and tying up his purchases.

"I'll ask him." She turned her back and disappeared once more through the inner door. He glanced at the Indian standing motionless beside him. "Hot day," he said but there was no answer.

JOHN HURRIED THE HORSES along the last bit of road to the mill, his head swimming but his heart happier than it had been in a long while. Lucy was in the garden and all three boys were lying in the grass nearby studying the sky. Cloud shapes, he supposed. Helen must be napping. At his call they all turned and waved, the boys jumping to their feet and running alongside the wagon. Lucy's broad smile welcomed him like nothing else could and he hurried to tie the team and take her in his arms.

"All went well?" she whispered and he murmured into her hair. That night when the children were in bed and he lay beside her, uncovered in the hot August stillness, he recounted the day's news. He was calm and even excited as he told her about Alice and the Indian, who had ridden part way along the trail with him, and of talking with Henry. This last was the reason for his light step every since he came home. Alice was leaving the country. She was going back across the river to marry a man who had come to the fort. So she said. And Henry had seemed glad to be rid of her as well. "Of course, he'll miss her in the store."

"But not for long," Lucy whispered. "Maybe he'll find a wife." With that she rolled over and in spite of the heat John lay next to her, his arm holding her to him.

Part Three
Border Wars

Chapter Twenty-Two

August, 1808

THE DAY AFTER THE WEDDING John and Lucy took their children and headed for home. William had chosen to start his new life with Catherine's family and leaving a hole in Lucy's heart, which existed right along beside the certain satisfaction that they had done well by the boy. Well, he was no longer a boy and had certainly waited long enough to marry and start his own life. Still, the evenings would be longer now without his pleasant smile at the table and his easy hand on his brothers and sister.

"He's a calm man, isn't he, John?" When there was no answer, she leaned over and nudged him out of his reverie.

"Yes, Lucy. Yes."

"You don't even know who I'm talking about, do you?"

He flipped the lines to hurry the horses. "Of course I do. You've been thinking about William all day, my dear. As have I."

"Will you miss him, John?" She turned to see him squinting into the sun as they headed south towards home. Still clean-shaven after the wedding his chin dimple reminded her of their own day in Boston so many years ago but, inside and out, they both wore the scars of the hard years since. When he didn't answer she leaned back on the seat and watched as his strong hands kept the horses on the road for home.

In the back of the wagon Robert and Thomas pestered their sister as usual and Helen's ire was quick to rise, but there was no William to settle them all and soon the three gave up of their own accord. They, too, missed their brother. The twins would be looking for wives, too, and, at seventeen, Helen had taken to arguing with her mother over every little thing they did. All of their chicks would soon be winging away. She wiped a tear from her cheek and John reached over to pat her skirts.

Catherine came from a good family and even though Lucy found her somewhat quiet and morose she liked her new daughter-in-law. Her father's name was John, too, so that naming the first-born son wouldn't be troublesome. Lucy smiled. She shouldn't rush things. Look how long it had taken before Harper John came along. Sweet boy. She still missed him and John did as well but to the other children he was just another fairy tale told by their parents. She turned to see why the children were laughing.

As the sun slipped behind gathering clouds in the western sky they began to recognize points on the trail. None too soon, Lucy thought. The darkness deepened under clouds racing to form a blackened wall before them. John hurried the horses. Glimpses of churning lake water reflected the angry sky and before her eyes the sun sank behind the approaching wall of storm.

"We're almost there," John said.

And indeed they were. Against the smoldering sky three buildings rose up: the stalwart stone mill, its roof newly shingled; their snug board and batten barn just big enough to house the animals and the wagon; and their home. John had been as good as his word. For several years now they had lived in this actual house with plastered walls, smooth pine floors, and hinged doors on all the rooms. A split rail fence encircled the garden, green and golden with its ripening produce. Indeed, the whole place spoke prosperity and peace.

The pink lady skirts of hollyhocks lined the stone walkway to the house; the plants now towered over Lucy and she had only been gone six days. They carried their bags into the house. John went straight to the mill as though the audible grinding and the faint powder of flour in the air hollered his name.

A wagon and team waited in the heat but no one was on the dock. He bounded up the steps, still spry in spite of the toll of years, and stepped into the gloom. It took a few moments for his eyes to adjust but he heard voices in the milling room below. Down the steps he went. Mr. McKie oversaw the grinding of the millstones while chatting with another neighbor off to his left, a regular customer. The Indian hovered nearby.

They all looked up as John entered but Mr. McKie kept the millstones grinding. All seemed to be in good order: the stones themselves, the flour sacks in a pyramid near the door, and the chute clear of weeds and chaff, ready for the next dump of grain. John smiled and nodded at them all but signalled for the grinding to stop.

"There's rain coming in minutes. Best finish this lot and stop."

Immediately Mr. McKie started up again. The Indian glanced out the window at the sky before turning back to his work. The customer hurried up to the main floor with John, made arrangements to come back the next day for his order, and ran for his wagon and home. Below, the milling stopped. Feet sounded on the steps and Mr. McKie's head poked up out of the stairwell.

"Come. Sit," John said. "Tell me about the mill." He swept his hand around the fog-filled room. Across the small desk Mr. McKie sat, took off his hat and shook it near the floor. "Been good, John. Lot of grain. But it's just now startin'."

"Any problems, Stuart?"

"Well, not really." He hesitated a moment.

"Go on."

"Ah, it's nothing, John." He stooped to brush flour off his pant legs.

"Stuart, I've known you long enough to see something's not right." He raised his voice. "Out with it, man."

With a final brush at his dusty trousers, Mr. McKie started talking. A few days earlier another group of Americans had rowed across the river with mischief and mayhem in their minds. Their boat tied at the end of John's dock, the two men had sauntered over to the mill, walked inside, down the steps to the mill stones, and out to watch the water wheel, all the while saying little and answering none of Mr. McKie's questions. Finished, they took their boat, a small affair with a couple of slatted seats and room for maybe four people, and pushed off into the river again, but not before slamming against the dock a few times. Were they trying to knock it down? He didn't know but he had seen their eyes and had kept a watch each night since then.

"No wonder you look so tired, Stuart."

"I just don't trust them, John. This mill stands all alone against hundreds, maybe thousands looking for a free handout."

"Tonight you can get a good night's sleep. And thank you, my friend." He rose and patted Mr. McKie's shoulder as they moved to the door. Outside the sky had let loose. "You'd best come inside, Stuart." The two of them ran for the house.

After a hot meal the twins and Helen sat at the kitchen table playing checkers. Lucy joined John and Mr. McKie in the parlour with mugs of small beer brought back from the wedding. She worried about the Indian in the mill getting soaked but John reminded her of the new roof. "Besides, he'd rather be out there on his own than cooped up in here."

"I suppose you're right." She flexed her fingers a couple of times and rubbed her hands. The men began to talk of the continuing mess of the road system. Some places farmers had sectioned off allowances for the road and just counted them as their contribution to the new land. Other owners had not been so forthcoming. Travellers had to pay to cross their land or were even barred from trespassing. Mr. McKie related yet another story of people having to run from crazed land owners.

After an hour or so of this talk, John suddenly stood. Lucy shook her head in an effort to rouse herself. "What?" she asked, and stood up, too.

"I'm going to Niagara!"

"Now? We just got home." She could not read the look on his face.

Mr. McKie remained seated but looked from one to the other as though not knowing which to watch or what would happen next. Lucy realized how they must seem. She reached out and grabbed John's arm. "Please, John. What do you mean?"

"I mean I'm going to Niagara and get some answers on the roads once and for all."

"But surely you're needed here, John." She led him back to the settee.

No amount of talking could change John's mind and Lucy had to admit there was some sense to his plan. Mr. McKie would be here with the Indian to run the mill.

In the morning, the rain had stopped enough for John to take his horse and head out. As Lucy put her house back in order, Helen pitching in, too, Robert and Thomas lent a hand in the mill. The constant flow of water over the turning water wheel and the regular run of wagon wheels and horses by the house signalled that harvest season was well underway. In a small corner of her brain, Lucy cursed John for leaving them, but she supposed the roads were important and he was a good one to send to move the project along. Many a settler had taken advantage of his writing and legal skills to assert their rights.

By afternoon the sun had shone long enough that she could walk the garden rows without sinking into mud. She cajoled Helen into helping her pull the onions and leave them drying in the rows. Pumpkins and squash had overrun much of the garden but she left them to grow until after the first frost. Into her apron pocket she stuffed a few carrots for supper and headed for the late-planted row of peas.

Lost in her thoughts, at first she didn't realize the mill wheel had stopped. Only the shouting and Robert running toward her registered in her mind. His red face and wild eyes caused another alarm bell to sound in her head. Mr. McKie had fallen down the stairs. They needed her. She hurried to the house, tore off her apron full of carrots, and grabbed her medicine box. "Your hands, mama!" shouted Robert from the doorway and she plunged them right into the soaking dishtowels to wash off the dirt.

On a fine powder of freshly milled flour at the bottom of the stairs lay Mr. McKie. Her eyes went first to the awkward angle of his leg and then to the blood beneath it. Tears came as she rushed down the stairs remembering her father's broken leg; she struggled to keep her thoughts on this day and this man. She had mended her father's leg and she would mend this one.

"It's not so bad, Mrs. Garner," said Mr. McKie.

She made a quick swipe at her eyes. "No, it's not." She steadied her voice. "I...it reminded me of my father is all." With a few deft movements and the help of the onlookers, Robert, Thomas, the Indian, and by this time, Helen, as well, she soon had the leg splinted and bound. When Mr. McKie was drowsy from the laudanum, she sent Thomas off to the next farm to bring back Mrs. McKie. Before nightfall Dorothea, having satisfied herself her husband could ride back to their farm, had struck out with him lying on a bed of straw in the wagon. Robert and Thomas rode along and would return on the morrow.

The house creaked and groaned in the night as Lucy lay alone in her bed. She and Helen had sat and talked after everyone left. She had no heart for mending and her daughter was delighted not to have to sew. As the darkness fell, they lit one candle but soon doused it and retired, their words having come full stop like the mill wheel outside.

She supposed it was the unusual silence that kept her from sleeping. And John's and the boys' absence. The chickens' squawking woke her once or twice but finally she was able to ignore them and fall into a deep sleep. Blood trickled down William's cheek and Catherine sopped at it with her hair; John stood to one side laughing with the Indian. Lucy tried hard to lift the flour sacks at first but then they flew right out of her hands, one after another. An owl hooted so loud and so often it seemed to be laughing, then whispering, "Mama, Mama!" Hands held her arms. "Wake up, Mama! Someone's outside!"

"Helen, you're hurting me." The girl released her. "What's the matter?"

"Don't you hear it, Mama?" she whispered.

Out of bed, she ran to the window, pulled back the curtain just enough to peer into the darkness in the direction of the mill. A slight misty rain smeared the window but she could still see figures on the loading dock. They lugged sacks to the sluice and seemed to drop them in. Wait. They had a small boat there. Lightning flashed just as one man dropped his load into the boat heaped higher than its sides with John's flour.

"Come on," she whispered and grabbed her rifle. "Get the musket." She pointed to the cupboard from which she had just taken her rifle. She hoped the hours she and John had spent teaching all of their children to shoot would pay off.

They ran for the mill, the two of them, nightgowns flapping against their legs and a fine mist slicking their gun hands. Lucy could not guess what Helen's thoughts were but she, herself, was furious. Thieves floated the overloaded boat towards the river, one man in the boat and three more running alongside it.

"Stop, you thieves!" she yelled as she neared them but the men just ran faster and Lucy noticed now the rope attached to the boat. She stopped, aimed and shot and Helen did, too, but both missed. At the river's edge the men kept right on running in the shallows until the water seemed to swallow them up but still they swam and the boat floated behind them. Thunder and lightning struck high overhead as the women stood on the shore and watched the thieves reach their ship.

"I hope the grain's soaked," Helen said and Lucy took her arm.

"Come." They headed toward the mill. "Wait." She stopped for a moment and then took off running.

"What is it, Mama?" Helen shouted.

"The Indian. Where is he?"

They rushed up onto the dock and paused before the dark pit of the open door. Lucy pushed Helen behind her and edged into the blackness. "Where are you? Are you hurt?" Nothing came back but the utter stillness of the space. She stumbled against something on the floor. "We need the lantern," she said and ran her hands over the wall beside her. When she found the lantern she sent Helen to the house to light it from the stove. Hopefully the cooking fire from supper had not gone out completely.

She could see better now and moved along the moonlit strips crossing the floor in her search for the Indian. What was his name? She didn't know it, nor where he was from. He had followed John home from the fort and she had barely seen him let alone spoken to him. Never would he come into the house to eat and John had taken him food. Or one of the twins. She didn't even know where he slept. He wasn't on this floor. She inched back to the stairs leading up to the top storey.

Light glowed in the doorway as Helen returned holding the lantern high. "Good," Lucy whispered and took the light to lead up the stairs. Barefoot in the fine film of dust, they searched John's office and the huge storeroom but found nothing. Lucy hurried back down and crossed over to the steps leading to the millstones. "Hurry," she whispered, but Helen was right behind her.

The contrast between the tiny yellow flame and the shut-up room created a darkness so deep Lucy stopped a moment and reached back for her daughter. Helen's hand on her waist, she lifted the lantern higher. She took a step. And another. The millstones loomed in the blackness but she forced herself to keep looking. Methodically the two women made their way around the perimeter of the room, Lucy grasping the lantern and Helen pulling on her mother's nightdress. "Let go, my dear. You're choking me," she whispered.

And then she heard it. A moan so low that Lucy stopped. "Did you hear?"

"Yes," said her daughter.

"Are you there?" Lucy called, just as Helen gasped beside her. Farther away from the light she had seen what Lucy could not. She held the light higher and edged closer to the sound. In a tangled heap of hair and leather and bare legs, one streaming blood from a black gash in the thigh, they found him. In a flash Lucy was kneeling over him, checking his wound and then ripping a wide swath off the bottom of her nightdress. With it she bound the leg in hopes of stopping the bleeding.

"Is he...going to live?" Helen's voice came with a teary edge to it.

She reached back to grab the girl's hand. "Yes, I think so." She tried to give her words a confidence she really didn't feel. "Hold the lantern higher, Helen." She checked the Indian's whole body, rolling him over and back, and running her fingers through his black tangled hair where her fingers came upon a rigid scar in an L shape. She jerked away, almost knocking over the lantern that, fortunately, Helen steadied.

"What is it, mama?"

She leaned forward and again put her hands into his hair, then held the light as close as she could to the man's upper body. He wore no bear claw necklace but he had the same strong jaw line she had watched over before. A smile came to her face and she nodded her head over and over. She knew him. From long ago. Only now he had a full head of hair and no war paint. Lines seamed his weathered face but she recognized those high cheekbones and thin lips.

"Mama. Tell me."

"I know him, Helen."

"Of course you do. He's worked with father here for years."

"Yes. But I know him from long before you were born." She checked the bandage and looked again at her daughter. "I saved his life."

Lucy felt a bit of a draft and realized she was almost naked. She sent Helen for another nightgown. They cleaned up the Indian and the room around him as much as they could. They brought him a buffalo robe to lie on. They took turns swabbing his brow, although he didn't seem to have a fever. The man groaned at times but mostly he slept. At his side mother and daughter talked the night through.

Lucy told of the time when she and John had lived in New York State and she had been left to tend the farm. Helen was shocked that her father would have left like that and Lucy did her best to describe the times and their helplessness. She told Helen of her fear when the Indians left this man with her, of her crude stitching of his wounded scalp and, ultimately, of birthing her first child alone in that wee cabin.

She wrapped her arm around her daughter as she whispered the story of Harper John's death, the night suddenly seeming cold and cruel. Helen in turn held her mother and they sat together in their thoughts until streaks of daylight pulled them into the present once more.

Lucy released herself from Helen's embrace and slid over to check on the Indian. Now that it was daylight she could see the extent of the wound. Once more she sent Helen, awake now, to the house for supplies. She felt like she had done all of this before and smiled when the thought came again that, of course, she had. And as she bustled around tidying and touching and studying the leg, that sense of having company overtook her. She looked up. Two black eyes stared at her but this time she smiled a warm, broad grin and without hesitation he smiled back.

That morning she had plenty of time alone with the Indian as Helen went back and forth with food and blankets and the good house broom and whatever else Lucy decided she needed as the day wore on. The Indian, Black Bear Claw, could not get up on his own and helping him was all the two women could do. When would those twins return? When she took the man a bowl of stew for his supper, she sat on John's chair which she had brought down from the office and studied him.

He was a far cry from the healthy man she had seen in the woods near their first farm just outside Newark. Then he had stood tall under his three-feathered headdress, his whole body shining with muscled strength and good health. She watched him eat. He wore only one feather now but had insisted on putting it back on, even while lying here on the floor. He lifted the spoon awkwardly with his right hand; two fingers were missing.

Even though she now recognized him, something still wasn't quite right. He hardly made a bump in the light sheet covering him. And then she had it. He seemed to have shrunk. How old must he be? Probably not as old as she was but he looked ten years older. Brown pockmarked skin stretched over sharp cheekbones and deep lines crisscrossed his forehead, broken on one side by an angry scar.

The tinkling sound of his spoon laid to rest in the empty bowl interrupted her thoughts. She stood up and took the bowl but then sat again and began talking. At first Black Bear Claw just watched her but, when she mentioned his facial scar, he reached up with one thin hand and briefly touched it, as though awakening a shadow that passed over his whole being.

"I will tell you," he said. "But only you." He tried to sit up but settled for leaning on one elbow, looking at her, his face more animated than she had seen it in a great while.

"I went back. To my old lands."

"Do you mean to the United States?"

"Yes. My woman was there. And my sons." His voice echoed his pride and she thought of the man she had known. Black Bear Claw's words came out softly, at first, as he told Lucy things she already knew about the revolution but soon the voice took on a bereft and barren sound. He told of the savagely reduced numbers of Indians. Their rights and lands had been devastated. The war over, a whole new wave of land-hungry settlers had pushed toward the western reaches of the former colonies, this time with the support of the new states, many of whom could not see beyond their own need for land to the rights of those who had lived there for centuries.

The British were no better. Many of the Five Nations tribes had fought for the British in hopes of being on the winning side and keeping their lands but they were forsaken in the treaty negotiations. Their lands were ceded to the Americans. When Black Bear

Claw finally found his people there was no peace for him in that land. He and his brothers and sisters tried to keep their traditions and their ways but instead were bribed with trinkets and alcohol until their old ways were no more.

Black Bear Claw stared beyond Lucy to some imaginary window into the past. She had no words. Presently, under the unbroken glare of the slanting sun and perhaps the kindness in her eyes, he stretched up to sit as tall as he could. "My sons are dead," he said. "And all of my people."

"But you came back here," she whispered.

"I remembered a time...when a white woman," he looked at her and continued, "when a white woman was kind." His voice broke. Immediately he lay down again and looked away.

Her tongue felt dry and she definitely needed to visit the outhouse but Lucy sat on and on, replaying the horror of his story in her mind. His breath came in short gasps as did her own. She had no words. Did each person in that war and all other wars have a similar tale? The pain pushed at her ribs until she held her breath so long she thought she might just die, but a sob burst forth and she felt the tears.

"Do not cry, madam," the Indian, her Indian, said.

"No. I won't."

"Mama, mama." Helen's sunshiny voice came through the open window. "The boys are home." Lucy heard her daughter's feet on the loading dock outside and her running footsteps across the floor above. Down the steps she came, her flying skirts stirring up the still air. "They're coming to help us, Mama."

Chapter Twenty-Three

HELEN PREPARED A BED for Black Bear Claw in the house and her brothers helped him hobble inside. Over the next few days his leg mended considerably and John, who had returned the day after the boys, took over the mill work but also began building a room for the Indian right inside the mill.

His experiences in Newark and, indeed, his news from that bustling town took a back seat to what had happened in his absence. After a few days, he sent Robert to check on Mr. McKie. Good news came back in a couple of hours with Robert racing the horse right to the mill where his father was working. "He says he'd come back tomorrow but Mrs. McKie might have something to say about that." He grinned at his father, waiting.

"Get your horse stabled. I need you." John smiled at the bounce in Robert's retreating step.

As September's work evened off and the first breath of cooler air blew across the lake, John opened his door one morning to a young stranger. "The mill was locked up, sir," the man said by way of explanation. "Where did you come from? I never heard a thing," John said. "Come in, come in, while I finish my plate."

Immediately Lucy pulled out a chair at the table and pointed. Spoon in mid-air, John looked across at the youth. "Will you join us, Mr...?"

"Greenstone, sir." Passing his hat from one hand to the other, he spoke quickly and kept glancing toward the window. Helen came in to the kitchen, grabbed her oatmeal and sat next to the stranger, who shifted his chair to give her room.

"Are you in a hurry, then, sir," the girl asked.

"Well, yes." He glanced at John and then at Helen who held his look. John watched from the corner of his eye. As Lucy set a plate of thick-sliced pork and two eggs before the stranger, he dropped his hat on the floor and laid into the food. John sat silent, waiting for the young man to finish. He didn't have long to wait. When the young man pushed his chair away from the table, Lucy offered him more, and he accepted with a lop-sided grin full of glistening teeth.

"Where are you from, Mr. Greenstone?" Helen's voice surprised John. She was grinning at the stranger and paying no attention at all to her father's glare.

"I, uh, I'm from along the river," the young man managed to spit out between bites, but he kept his eyes on his food.

"Which way?" Helen asked.

"Helen, let the poor man eat," said Lucy. Helen carried her dish to the dry sink and turned toward the table again.

John watched his daughter's face as he lifted his jacket from the hook. He would learn more about this surprise guest.

THE NEXT DAY young Mr. Greenstone was back again but this time he came directly to the mill. John had sent his sons to the fort with a wagonload of flour, so was down in the mill room alone as the lad—Timothy, he had said his name was—took the stairs as fast as humanly possible. "What's the hurry, Mr. Greenstone?"

"I have a..." he started, but immediately jerked off his hat and began again. "I have a question, Mr. Garner," he said. John glanced up from the stones which were grinding away and noticed how red the boy's face was and how he stepped back and forth from one foot to the other as if finding the outhouse might have been more appropriate. "Well?" he asked. "What is it?"

He took a deep breath, looked at his feet, and promptly right into John's eyes. "I want to court her. Your daughter. Helen, I mean."

John took his time. He was not at all surprised by the request. "Thing is, son, I don't know anything about you."

"What do you need to know, sir?"

"Where did you come from? Who are your people? Where do you live?" He paused and watched the young man's darting eyes. Something made him hesitate before he spoke again in a much softer voice. "I need to know you, son."

Young Mr. Greenstone's eyes still ran scared. What was he hiding? "Why don't you come to supper this night? Not to see Helen," he added, "but so you and I might have a long chat afterwards."

Nodding, Mr. Greenstone backed away, turned, and took the stairs by twos. His boots clomped across the floor overhead and out the door. John checked the grinding as if by rote, his thoughts full of the little girl Helen used to be. Some time later Lucy touched his arm as he bent over the stones to brush out every last speck of the newly ground flour.

"Lucy!" he said, turning around. "You caught me."

She clapped her hands together and smiled. "I just wondered, are you ever coming for dinner?"

He brushed his hands against his britches and followed her up the steps. Inside the kitchen she set his plate on the table and sat opposite him as he ate. Her fidgeting made him look up. Sitting for once, her hands folded on the table before her, she seemed to be making a study of him. But she wasn't still. The faint tapping of her toe belied her calmness and he had the sense there was a dam about to break. He raised his eyebrows but she said nothing. The toe-tapping, however, stopped.

A few more mouthfuls and he was finished. He put his fork on the plate and settled his hands in his lap, staring at her. "Well?"

"We've a letter, John. A letter from William." She pulled it out of her apron pocket. "And Catherine, too, of course." Quickly she read the short note to him telling their son's news about the crops and the animals and how many bushels of grain he and his father-in-law had harvested but nothing there could account for the glow on Lucy's face.

"What is it, Lucy?" He struggled to keep his voice down. Why didn't she just tell him?

"Catherine has written a post script at the end." Again she paused, but seeing John's face, hurriedly added, "They are coming to visit us." She ran around the table. John jerked his chair back just in time for her to sit on his lap like a newlywed and kiss him. She didn't stay long, though. Almost immediately she leapt up and began pacing the floor, thinking out loud and planning where everyone would sleep and what they would eat and wondering just what day they would arrive until John quietly slipped out the door to go back to his work.

That evening six adults sat down to supper at the table covered with a freshly ironed linen cloth and even a bouquet of daisies and purple thistles. John looked at Lucy on his right and she raised her eyes in answer to his questioning glance. Both of them looked down the table to Helen whose freckled cheeks were glowing. Beside her was their guest.

As soon as the squash and fresh ham were passed the twins started asking Helen just why all the fuss. They hadn't used a tablecloth in months. Was there something she wanted to tell them? Normally able to give as good as she got, the girl seemed tongue-tied. Her colour rose with each jibe until her father could stand it no longer. "What are you doing in this part of the country, Mr. Greenstone?" he asked.

The young man looked up from his plate. John caught the hesitation in his voice and the fear in his eyes. "I'm looking for a place to settle, sir." Again he lowered his head as if the ham on his plate was the most interesting thing in the room. Robert nudged Thomas as though they were twelve-year-olds and John glared at them.

"Where are your folks, Mr. Greenstone?" asked Lucy.

"I haven't any...I mean they are no longer with us, ma'am."

Lucy rose to clear the plates and Helen jumped up to help. No one spoke. John was at a loss as to what to say. He didn't want to cause the young man pain but needed to know about his parents. A lot more questions would need answering before this infatuation between the two young people could continue. The women served the pan cake at the table and finally the meal ended.

Robert asked Mr. Greenstone to join him and Thomas in a game of Trump and nodded for Helen to join in as well, but John interrupted and took their visitor out onto the porch. Lucy sat on the settee, her knitting needles across her lap with a hank of newly carded wool all spun and ready for the sweater she was starting for Helen. Maybe this would be the last thing she'd knit for her daughter. The girl would soon be on her own and so would the twins. She could see a lot of baby bonnets and sweaters in the future and even though she wasn't ready for her children to leave, the idea of grandchildren caught her fancy.

The game progressed at the table with laughing and a certain amount of name-calling but it was all in fun. Not a sound came in from outside but every so often Helen rose from her chair and peeked out. The girl was definitely interested, that was for certain, and Lucy couldn't blame her. Mr. Greenstone was a looker, tall and lean, with muscles filling out his shirt when he moved and tidy dark hair combed to one side. The only thing was his evasive manner. Why, she couldn't say what colour his eyes were as she'd barely seen them!

Without warning, the door crashed open and John strode in, followed a few seconds later by Mr. Greenwood who stopped just over the threshold.

"Mrs. Garner." His voice was a whisper but he cleared his throat, "Mrs. Garner." She stood up, waiting. "Ma'am, thank you for dinner." She began to speak but, like a ghost caught by a candle in the night, he vanished.

"Father, what did you do?" Helen ran past her father out the door into the darkness calling the young man's name.

Lucy and the twins all turned to John. He said nothing but walked past them and along the hall into the bedroom. In a very few moments Helen was back, her disappointment and sheer anger driving her past them and into her room. Silence filled the house more completely than ever a shouting match could have done. After a few moments Lucy slipped by her sons, patted each absently on the shoulders, and barred the door.

"HE'S NOT WHAT YOU THINK, LUCY."

"And what do I think?" She turned to face him in bed. His face was still red and from the look of his eyes blinking and darting in the moonlight, she could see that sleep was a long way off. "Are you reading my mind now?" She laid her hand across his chest and fingered the fuzzy hair at his neck.

She could feel him trying to settle himself and wondered again just what the young man had said which so infuriated her husband. "Helen is certainly taken with him and from all I could see he's a good possibility. She's seventeen, John. You can't blame her for wanting someone."

Turning toward her, he raised up on one elbow. "I can blame her for this one."

"Why, John?"

"He's a soldier, Lucy." When she didn't respond, he added, "an American soldier. And I'll not have her wedding an American!"

"Shhh. Keep your voice down." She was silent a moment. "You're right, of course. But what if she still wants him? And he, her?"

"We'll find someone else for her. I'll not have her mixed up with a bloody American."

Lucy shushed him again. They lay side by side, their bodies comfortably fitting together with the practice of years but their thoughts their own. Long after John's grip had slackened on her waist and his breathing calmed to almost nothing, Lucy felt the catch of trouble in her heart and mind and even started up at a creaking sound out in the hall, but it never came again. She thought once more of her daughter until she, too, slept.

Helen slept late the next morning but Lucy didn't bother her until she had the breakfast all cleared away. The men had gone. Only Lucy's shoes sounded on the floor as she approached Helen's closed door. She rapped gently, heard nothing, and rapped again. "Helen," she called and pushed open the door. "Time to rise, my dear."

She opened the lace-edged curtains and turned to the form in the bed. "Wake up." She nudged the girl's shoulder. Helen rolled over and sat up straight, eying Lucy with hooded eyelids. When Lucy sat on the bed beside her, Helen scooted to the other side, jumped up, and stormed out of the room.

The rest of the day was a blur of gathering the last pumpkins from the garden and feeding the men two heavy meals, all with the dubious help of her silent daughter who had suddenly forgotten everything she knew about housework and certainly about talking. A few grunts were all Lucy got from the girl, and at mealtimes, John and the twins did no better. After the midday meal she had disappeared completely for the better part of the afternoon and the break from her mood was such a relief, Lucy didn't look for her.

But that night John followed Helen to her room and loud voices soon blared out to the kitchen. Lucy asked her sons to take some supper to Black Bear Claw in the mill and to finish off the building of the man's room. Alone, she cleared the table and washed up, all the while wishing the argument would stop. And stop it did. Soon afterwards John was back in the kitchen but only to pass through. Out the door he went, shutting it a little more forcefully than was absolutely necessary, she thought, and disappearing into the dark.

After three more days of the same stiff anger in the house, Lucy could stand it no longer. She left her recalcitrant daughter peeling potatoes and marched to the mill. John was at his desk staring at a paper. Probably another legal document from one of the settlers who needed his help. He looked up as she climbed the stairs and a smile broke upon his face.

It didn't stay long. She sat before him on the edge of a chair and broached the subject of their daughter. When she asked him to make up with the girl, John stood up and turned his back to her before the window. Lucy held her peace and waited but John didn't answer. Confound the man; couldn't he see her point? The girl needed to be married, that was all there was to it, and, after all, they had themselves been Americans until just a few years ago. What was John's problem with the young man?

Still he stared out the window, moving to the right to get a better view past the trees. Curious, she moved to his side. Out on the river, boats full of soldiers glided past them, rowers working hard to make headway in the strong current. She took his arm. "Where...who are they?" she whispered.

He put his arm around her and held tight. "Americans," he answered in a flat voice totally bereft of feeling. She glanced up to see tears shining in his eyes. He made no attempt to hide them.

The next morning Helen was gone. Lucy found the bed rumpled but empty. No clothes hung from the bare wooden pegs on the wall, nor comb, nor tiny mirror by the water pitcher. It was as if no one had ever breathed there. She smoothed the bed with practised hands that lingered over the red ties of the comforter. Helen loved that red yarn but had left her favorite cover behind. Lucy went to find John.

Chapter Twenty-Four

Fall, 1808

"WELL, I THINK WE SHOULD GO AFTER HER." Robert's hazel eyes looked around the table and settled on his father. "We know where she's gone."

"And where is that?" asked John who looked like Atlas shouldering the world.

"With that young fellow who was here. You know that, father."

"I don't know that."

"We have to do something, don't we?" Thomas looked from one to the other. His wide eyes bored into Lucy. "Don't we?"

She covered her ears against the tumult of male voices. One by one their sounds stilled and she felt their stares. Her men. All here but William. And that one other...she forced her thoughts back to the present. Her hands fell away from her face and her chair scraped back from the table. She stood.

They had all failed Helen one way or another but mostly she, herself, had not spoken up. And as a result, Helen was gone. She knew not where or when or if she would ever see her sweet girl again. A sob threatened but she grabbed the edge of the table and held it down, pressing into the pine as though its hard strength might be transmitted up her arms and into her whole person.

"I want my daughter," she whispered, her eyes boring into John's. He flinched. "I want my daughter," she repeated, this time louder, "and we must find her now before it's too late."

THE MILL WAS SILENT that day and the next, with only the splashing of the water over the wheel running round and round in a circle with no break and no flour grinding. The neighbours had arrived in twos and threes soon after the twins had spread the word, all anxious to help one of their own in need. Black Bear Claw had even hobbled out of the mill, his limp slowing but not stopping him as he joined the group. Mr. McKie helped organize everyone and he and John rode off at their head.

By the end of the second day of disappointment, Lucy knew there was no hope. The girl was gone and of her own accord. They sent their neighbors home with instructions to keep an eye out but everyone suspected the search was futile. No one had seen Helen. Not a broken twig nor a footstep in the mud had been found. Dorothea, who had stayed with Lucy for most of the time, gathered her few things together and gave Lucy a long hug before following Mr. McKie out the door.

John and Lucy both tried to go on. Even the twins did their best to be jolly but the heart had gone out of their banter. Without Helen to tease, their jokes just fell into the air and soon they gave up trying. John took to riding out every day along the trails, talking to those he met and returning taut and tired.

Most afternoons Lucy stood by the shore and watched the water as though her daughter might just glide along in a canoe and, on seeing her mother, paddle in to shore. Lots of boats traveled the waterway up and down the lake and a few even ventured into the river, but those were the brave ones. The current was so strong as the river rushed toward the falls that paddling or rowing against it took much strength and many arms. Sometimes a man would wave at her but usually no one could afford the time to risk a wave.

When November's cold winds began to blow across the water, she gave up her vigil, instead listening and watching at the window whenever she had a moment. John had been in the mill all day, not even coming in for dinner, and the twins had taken a plate out to him. His paperwork for the mill and for his neighbours was becoming burdensome and he liked to do it in the daylight hours; his eyes were not what they used to be. A clattering of wagon wheels in the distance brought Lucy running to the window.

Her insides clenched and she struggled to quench her fear of bad news. A man and a woman sat close together on the seat of the wagon. She leaned against the windowpane trying to see through the blurry glass. Suddenly she ran to the door, threw it open, and raced down the steps to meet the visitors. The oncoming team veered away ever so slightly but then came on as before.

"William!" she shouted. The horses shied again. "Catherine, hello, hello!"

Her son pulled the team up and climbed down the far side. Catherine grinned as William lifted her down and Lucy thought she might just fly away with joy.

"I hoped you were still coming." Lucy pulled Catherine into the house while William tended the horses. In the bustle of coats and cases and a pretty parcel that Catherine pressed into her hands, Lucy forgot the weight they had all carried for weeks. She thought of calling John from the mill but voices carried in from outside and she knew they were already helping William. In a very few moments the four men tramped inside, John with his sons, all grinning and sporting the same chin dimple.

She put more wood in the stove and went to work, with Catherine's help, adding carrots and potatoes to the pot simmering on the stove. That done they set out plates and cutlery on the table. Catherine cut the loaf of bread she had brought and reached over William to put it in the center of the table. He squeezed her waist and she smiled. In no time the table was set, the plates were full and the grace was said. Amidst the hubbub William raised his voice. "Where's Helen?"

He looked from one silent face to another but no one answered. Finally his eyes settled on Lucy. "Where's my sister, Mama?"

Her spoon halfway to her open mouth, she felt the familiar ache spread through her whole body like a creeping sickness that threatened to overtake and destroy her. She replaced the spoon on her plate, the stew untouched. "We don't know." She looked into her son's eyes and watched their lustre fade as John and the twins pieced together the story. Catherine, sitting beside her, put her hand on Lucy's arm and kept it there. The story told, everyone began to eat and gradually the conversation started up again. For Lucy, however, the pall settled again over the family, this time including William and Catherine.

The young people took Helen's room and Lucy was glad to see it used again. She did her best to be happy. Catherine marvelled at the strings of threaded apples and herbs hanging high over the stove and Lucy offered lemon sage for her daughter-in-law to take back with her. Having another woman in the house pleased Lucy no end. She hadn't realized how much she had missed that.

As the days passed when the men were out and about all day preparing for winter, Lucy and Catherine spent their time doing the same. Pigs were killed and the meat salted, tallow candles were hung to dry in the cosy kitchen, and straw was piled around the foundation of the house to forestall the winter winds. The two talked as they worked, the warmth in the room not totally due to the fire in the stove.

"I have something to say, Mother," Catherine began one day and Lucy immediately looked up from her chopping board.

"I wasn't going to say yet," she began, "but I thought..." She shook her head and straightened her shoulders.

A faint suspicion formed in Lucy's mind but she kept quiet and grabbed another carrot. She raised her head again and smiled.

"You know what I'm going to say, don't you?" The grin on her face was infectious.

"Tell me," Lucy said, her voice as encouraging as she could make it.

"We...I...a baby!"

Lucy dropped the knife and carrot, wiped her hands on her apron, and reached across the table for Catherine's hands. "Wonderful!" The girl's hazel eyes lit up and that wide smile full of beautiful teeth covered her face. "When?" she whispered.

The baby was coming probably in early summer and the two women spent the rest of the afternoon laughing and planning. Although Lucy still hated to sew, she promised to knit sweaters and booties. What with the efforts of Catherine's mother as well, this child would certainly be well dressed.

When the men returned that evening the women kept the news to themselves. Catherine didn't want to tell William about the baby until she was certain. Lucy couldn't help her sudden lightness of step and, that night, just winked at John when he asked why she was so happy.

In the morning the young couple packed up for their long trip back. The wind had come up and swept stray flakes of snow against the windows. "Are you sure you'll be able to get home alright?" Lucy asked for the third time. William took her by the arms and held her before him. "Yes," he whispered, and smiled at her concern. "We will be snug in our own bed tonight, Mama. Don't you worry." He led Catherine out to the wagon, handed her up, and turned to his gathered family. "We thank you, all of you." His eyes were bright as he turned and strode to the other side, stepped up and loosed the lines.

John put his arm around her and she rested her head against his shoulder. The wagon rumbled out the lane, Catherine waving all the way. The twins went inside out of the cold but John and Lucy stood, watching and listening. The wind carried William's final good-bye, faint but clear, as they disappeared into the trees. Lucy glanced toward the river, ever hopeful of a sign from her other wandering bird, but John took her hand and led her inside.

Chapter Twenty-Five

Spring, 1809

"MOTHER, WHERE ARE YOU?" Robert called.

His feet pounded up the porch steps and into the kitchen. "Stop," she hollered from the bedroom, "your boots!" But it was too late. He had marched halfway across the kitchen to find her and only stopped at the look on her face. "Robert, the snow." What was he waving? She reached up to grab the paper. Her tall son had other plans and held what she could now see was a letter far out of her reach.

John hurried in the door to see what the ruckus was about. She jumped for the letter and then stopped, put on her stern look, and rested her hands on her hips. "Robert. Give it to me. Now."

And he did.

"Do you see her name, Mother?" He pointed to the corner of the homemade envelope.

She ran her finger over the letters and showed John. *Mrs. T. Greenstone*, it read, in a fine hand she recognized immediately.

"Open it, Lucy," John said.

With trembling hands Lucy folded back the flap and pulled out a single sheet of rough paper and began to read aloud.

Dear Mama and Daddy:

I pray this letter finds you well and will ease your mind. Timothy and I are in Buffalo Creek where we fled together. Someone in his regiment married us immediately, you will be relieved to know. As Daddy learned that awful night, he is an American soldier and had been sent to spy on our, now your, side of the border. It is painful for me to say this but I am glad. If not, we would never have met.

Timothy warned me not to go with him, but I insisted and he has smiled every day since. I hope that you can forgive me. Ever your loving daughter, Helen.

"SHE ACTUALLY MARRIED THE MAN," Robert said.

"We can be glad of that much, at least," answered Lucy. Though the news gladdened her heart in that the young couple were safe and married, it was far from joy she was feeling just at this moment. John said nothing. Nor did he move from his spot looking over her shoulder. His head was nodding ever so slightly but his face was a mask.

Robert backed toward the door. "I'll tell Thomas she is safe."

Lucy turned again to John. "What are your thoughts, my dear?" He stood a moment longer, shook his head, and followed Robert out the door.

BY FALL THE FAMILY HAD HEARD no more from Helen and her new husband and their hopes of Helen returning with her husband dimmed as the river started to freeze. Boats still crashed their way through the thin ice along the shore even though, daily, the temperature dipped. One morning the snow started. Lucy hurried to the mill to ask John if he could spare the twins to help her lift the salted pork into the root cellar before it was completely snowed over.

"They're not here, Lucy. I thought you had waylaid them already."

"No," she said, glancing around at the stacks of grain lining the walls. "Are you sure they're not here somewhere?"

"Ask Black Bear Claw." He pointed to the room in the far corner.

She knocked on the door but got no answer. Puzzled, she searched the milling room and even pulled her shawl close around her head to walk out along the mill race but found no one. "John," she called, as she stepped back inside out of the wind. "I can't find any of them."

He met her on the stairs. "I'll check the barn." He rushed out into the cold. She followed but her attention was taken by another boat on the river and she worried for their safety, whoever they might be.

"Lucy!"

She turned back into the wind and headed for the house. John ran toward her and they met half way. The twins' horses were gone. He hollered the words even as he wrapped his arm around her and pulled her toward the house. Snow covered the porch already. They ran inside and slammed the door behind them. John put another log into the stove and they stood side by side rubbing their hands over its top.

"I saw a boat on the river, John," she began. "You don't think..." She couldn't finish.

"No, I don't. What would they have done with the horses?"

"Sold them?" She grabbed his arm. "Have they gone after Helen?"

FOR THREE DAYS AND NIGHTS the storm raged outside and John raged inside. For long hours he stared out the window and Lucy could do or say nothing to ease his fears. She finally stopped trying. They were grown men, her twins, and she trusted them to keep safe. If John had not been so furious she might have worried more but one of them in that state was enough.

Black Bear Claw had disappeared, too. Was he with her boys? She hoped so, but in her heart of hearts she knew he could do little. The third night, the winds calmed and she and John woke to sunlight streaming in the icy window and heavy pounding on the door. John hurried to open it. Wrapped in a blanket covered with shards of ice and pellets of snow, the Indian shivered before him on the doorstep.

"Come in, come in." John dragged the man over the threshold. He stood still while John and Lucy peeled his frozen clothing away and hung it near the stove. His eyebrows were white with ice; he sat wrapped in a quilt while Lucy picked it away, his hands holding a hot mug of tea. He didn't take a sip, only held it.

"Where were you, my friend," Lucy asked. At first he didn't answer but sat still as an icicle on the eaves. She finished her task. Still he hadn't spoken. John turned his chair from the table to face them.

"Black Bear Claw, where have you been?"

The Indian raised his head and his words came out soft but measured. Lucy sat beside John. Black Bear Claw spoke, his voice low and sometimes hardly audible to Lucy, even though she sat barely three feet away. Robert and Thomas had taken Black Bear Claw with them. His tired eyes lifted to Lucy. "I am sorry, missus. I should have tried to stop them." He shook his head.

The boys had gone first to Fort Erie following the trail of their sister and her new husband. No one there had seen them, of course, as the last place Timothy would have gone was to a British fort. A long boat docked at the landing outside the old fort was loaded and ready to go. Her sons arranged passage but could not convince Black Bear Claw to return to America.

"Why didn't you go with them?" Lucy asked, but the Indian just shook his head. After a few moments, his voice wavering and his eyes on the floor, he described the scene. In the falling snow he had stayed on the dock and watched the widening black patch of water as the boat carrying her sons put out into the current and disappeared across the water.

His eyes shifted ever so slightly until he looked into her own, but no more words came from his thin lips.

"Where have you been since then?" she asked and he told them his reluctance to take the horses back in such a storm. He had stabled the animals at the fort and grabbed a corner in the barn himself. The horses were still there as he dared not risk them on the icy roads.

"But you risked yourself," John said.

"Yes. I had to tell missus where sons gone." He looked from John to Lucy where his glance remained.

"Thank you, Black Bear Claw." She reached across and touched his bony hand.

With the house all but empty and the cold of winter settling in on them, Lucy insisted that Black Bear Claw sleep in one of the boys' beds. There was no heat to speak of in the mill and plowing through the drifts for meals was pointless. When the Indian recovered from his long cold walk, he and John went one clear day to fetch the horses back home. After that the three of them settled in for the winter.

SPRING BREAKUP CAME LATE THAT YEAR adding to the agitation of both John and Lucy. Even Black Bear Claw, who had moved back to the mill with the first crack in the ice, stood for hours with his arms crossed and his blanket wrapped around him, staring across at the other shore. The water was open far from shore and he seemed to yearn for that patch to widen.

Eventually the sun and the wind had their way and boats put out into the waves carrying goods and people. Black Bear Claw disappeared again but this time he told Lucy his destination. He planned to help in the ongoing building of the new fort up on the high ground at Fort Erie. That way he would be near if the twins came back.

As the new season began John faced the work alone. Only Lucy was left and neither of them had the strength or the energy they once had. Though he carried on as before, Lucy saw him rubbing his wrists and holding the papers farther and farther away. She insisted he take the vile tasting cod liver oil she had obtained from a traveling peddler, to help his joints and even dosed herself as well.

As April ended and May began its warm dance the couple had almost reconciled themselves to their childless state. After all, John told her, "This was bound to happen." With a slow nodding of her head, she had agreed.

Bent double, her fingers wrestling with the season's early dandelions, she realised those sounds were not just the blood rushing to her head but someone hollering. She pulled herself upright and turned to the road, careful not to step on the early peas. Black Bear Claw. And someone behind him on the other horse. She squinted into the afternoon sun.

"Thomas!" She trampled the rows in a headlong rush toward her son.

John hobbled from the mill. "Welcome, my boy!" He clasped the two of them in a warm embrace.

Lucy jerked back to look into her son's face. "But where's your brother?"

Black Bear Claw disappeared in the direction of the mill and presently, over a cool cup of water, the three sat around the kitchen table. Thomas made a great show of noticing the new embroidered hanging over the settee.

"This long, lonely winter I had ample time for such foolishness."

John's cup clattered to the table. "Enough of this. Tell us about your brother."

Thomas pushed up closer to the table, set his cup down, and raised his head. He glanced at John before reaching for her hands. "He didn't come with me, Mama. I'm sorry."

"But why? Is he sick? Or, no! Is he in jail?" Dozens of possibilities crowded her mind. "Tell me, Thomas!"

"He's found a woman, Mama."

Chapter Twenty-Six

October 13, 1812

Home of William and Catherine Garner in Stamford Township

"GARNER! WAKE UP. WE NEED YOU!" The pounding hammered the door, the baby cried in the crib and Catherine immediately rose. William was right behind her, trying to pull on his trousers as he staggered to the window. He recognized the five horsemen below and threw up the window, letting in the cold night air. The rain that had hammered the area for the past two days had somewhat abated.

"What is it, Nichol?" he called, although in his gut he knew.

"Brock's ordered us out. Now!"

William slammed the window down again and lit a candle. As he pulled on the rest of his clothes, Catherine soothed the baby against her breast but her own eyes were anything but calm. He pursed his lips into not quite a smile, looked away, and headed into the hall.

"What is it?" Thomas whispered coming along the hall, but he needn't have worried about waking the household. Catherine and the baby followed William. Across the hall young Will's door opened. Out he came in his striped nightshirt, eyes round in the dim light, followed by wee John whose diaper hung to his knees. "Mama," the younger one wailed and Catherine grabbed him with her other hand. William patted the boys' heads and pushed by, running down the steps two at a time.

"I'm coming!" shouted Thomas.

"Hurry." William's words were almost lost as the bar crashed to the floor and slammed the door open.

"You'll need your horse," said Nichol.

"Wait for Thomas." William ran for the barn. In just a moment the two brothers had saddled their horses and galloped after the other men into the night.

Since the summer, feelings had run high when word came from another part of Upper Canada. American shells had pummelled the village of Sandwich from right across the river in Detroit. Closely following that disturbing news, those in the Niagara area had learned that the Americans were at war with Britain. And that meant they were, too. Movements of regular troops up and down the Portage Road and upgraded training sessions of the militia had kept the whole area on tenterhooks.

Of course there were those who wanted the Americans to come but William was not one of them and neither were any of the Garner family. Well, except Helen and her husband, he supposed, and Robert, who had started his own family in Buffalo. No one had even met his wife, so dangerous had the crossing between the two countries become. Letters were few and William felt sorely the loss of his brother and sister. With this present escalation of hostilities, who knew when they would see each other again?

The men riding together in the night were joined by others as they proceeded towards Queenstown, but the only sounds were the snorting horses, the jingle of harness as the animals balked at their double loads, and the beating rhythm of the hurrying hooves. Thirty of them rode into the little village with its straight streets and tidy peach orchards. Lights flickered from the windows as they rode by the neat houses and stopped at the stone barracks.

Before William had time to dismount, artillery shells screamed out of the black night, one after another, sending the militiamen scurrying for cover inside the barracks, their wild horses running into the night. The men received their orders and dashed out into the darkness, hoping to reach the redoubts along the river's high banks and repel whatever attack might be coming from the American side of the river.

Like a lightning storm gone wild all over the sky, the shells fell with the rain, landing indiscriminately beside, behind, and between the men, felling some but missing others until most of the men reached the redoubts and crammed behind them. William pushed Thomas against the stone wall and felt what little protection it offered against the murderous onslaught coming across the river.

Regular soldiers posted in the huts above manned an eighteen-pounder and a mortar, firing off deafening shots over their heads. William feared the Americans might be launching an all-out attack from across the river. He yelled to his brother to watch for boats and, sure enough, as the black of the night eased into the wet grey of morning they sighted movement on the other side. Boats loaded with men and even one with a mounted eighteen-pounder put out from shore towards them.

Thomas poked William and pointed downstream where the current had swept one of the American boats. William nodded. He hoped the same had happened to all of their boats but just as that idea shot through his brain, a shout went up along the redoubt. Enemy soldiers were climbing the slope below and coming right for them. Shots rang above and beside William. As the uniformed figures poked up into view, marksmen picked them off one by one until soon no more came.

But the boats were still crossing. William could imagine how many enemy soldiers must be massing there under the outcroppings, ready to climb the cliffs. Suddenly a roaring cheer came from above and he turned to see what was happening but he couldn't. The huts and the hill conspired to cut off his view. He turned back to the water where the eighteen-pounder cannon from his redoubt cut into the boats, ripping both men and boats to shreds.

Beside him, Thomas suddenly stood right up and got off a shot to the side, just below the redoubt. A few enemy soldiers had made their way up the cliff, one fewer after Thomas' shot. Thomas was down again and a few seconds went by before William realized he was no longer shooting. He glanced at his brother. Still holding his rifle in one hand, Thomas held his other up to his head where, in the full daylight now, William could see the blood streaming through his fingers.

Thomas' gun dropped and his hand lay, exposed, beside him. William dropped, too. He sat on the hard paving stones and cradled Thomas in his arms. His own reflection darkened his brother's eyes and he saw all of them swimming the millrace, and him teaching Tommy and Robert to shoot, separating the two twins yet again, crying, laughing, and throwing snowballs. The mirror dimmed and broke. Alone in the mayhem, he clutched his bloody brother to him while all around shells fell and cheers and cries mixed and mingled as the sun came out of its hiding place.

ROBERT JUMPED INTO THE NEAREST BOAT right along with the rest of his militia troupe all the while cursing his brother-in-law. Left to his own devices, he never would have volunteered to fight along-side the Americans. His reasons should have been obvious to Timothy who had tricked him into joining up. And now, here he was. If they made it to shore without getting blown out of the water, they had to scale that huge cliff while fire rained down on them from above.

Behind them three more boats had set out but one had veered off towards the falls far to the south and another was hit by enemy fire. It began sinking almost immediately, its thirty men tossing guns and supplies into the roiling water before jumping in them-selves and trying to outswim the current back to shore. Only one other continued on to their target, following Robert's boat.

Holding their rifles high above their heads, the men, many of whom were no more than boys, splashed the last few feet to shore. Robert just wanted to get under that overhang and hoped the cover would be enough for all of them. His sergeant, however, ordered them out of the shelter and up over the overhang into the open where the steady fire from above hacked into the Americans, laying them out on the cliff side like bundles of castoff clothing, albeit bloodied and torn. They drove upwards, stepping over their wounded in their rush for the top.

Suddenly Robert noticed men and boys running back down the embankment and, without a second thought, turned to follow. He tripped over bodies, heads facing up the cliff and down, but he didn't stop. At the bottom he leaped the overhang and landed badly on his right ankle but immediately dragged himself under, away from the steady stream of fire. Packed tightly, like candles in a carton and just as sticky, the soldiers looked only to themselves, checking their parts to be sure they were whole and safe.

Some found wounds but most had survived unscathed. What would happen now was anyone's guess. From his spot about twenty feet higher than the water Robert could see the Lewiston side of the river. No more boats were coming. What's more, where a short while ago densely packed rows of soldiers and militia had stood, ranks thinned even as he watched, men going not to the waiting boats but slinking back into the trees.

A young man beside him watched as avidly as Robert did. "We should be doing that, too."

"Running away?" Robert asked. "I'd rather die." But would he?

"The militia doesn't have to fight on enemy soil." The man grabbed Robert's arm. "This is not the United States."

And he was absolutely right, Robert realized, a great knot releasing inside him. If only he had realized sooner. He didn't think. And now he'd most likely get killed for his stupidity. More Americans crowded in to their narrow wedge of safety, bloodied and beaten, both soldiers and militia. Another boat made the trip across to fight alongside them. In a few moments a captain ran up the hill and into safety. He took one look at the hundreds of men packed into the space and turned to his sergeant.

The officer ordered them to resume the attack up the cliff. The enlisted men rose and prepared to march out again but the others, those who were not regulars but rather militia and volunteers, stayed where they were.

"I gave you an order," shouted the officer. No one moved. "Fall in, men!"

"We don't fight on foreign soil," someone shouted. "Sir!" The officer raised his rifle but a hubbub rose among the militia.

"Fall in!" screamed the officer aiming his rifle at first one man and then another for what seemed an eternity until Robert was staring right into its barrel. He froze. The officer's hair came loose and fell over his good eye but still he held the rifle tight and Robert felt the fury of the man and knew he was going to die.

But he didn't. As quick as a breath the gun swerved to the man beside him and exploded. Robert jumped away but not soon enough to avoid the blood spatter all down his own left side.

As one body they finally rose. Except for one who would rise no more. Robert reached down to pull the man's hat over his eyes before shouldering his rifle and following the others up the hill into hell.

Rather than take the men the same way they had gone before, this officer led them around the main assault out of sight of the enemy above and up the hill a few hundred yards away. He directed them to spread out along the ridge, taking advantage of the dense thickets and the scarcity of defenders at this spot. Robert heard the constant barrage of guns off to his left as, alone, he stepped out of the thicket at the top of the hill, but all seemed quiet here. He crept along, hunched over, his hands gripping his rifle, barely breathing.

Suddenly voices sounded ahead of him and he clenched his weapon. Not fifty feet away a tall red-jacketed officer wearing a brightly coloured sash and a hat decked out with gold braid and a white ostrich feather broke out of the trees and ran toward him. Robert dug in his feet and with shaking hands fired his weapon. Back into the thicket he flew, the falling white-haired officer filling his mind as he tore down the path to the shelter below. His chest heaved and his heart threatened to leap out of it both for the running and for his fear, which grew and grew. He thought he recognized the man he had felled.

THE AMERICAN CHARGE FORCED THE MILITIA BACK, right along with the few regulars trying to hold the redoubts against the onslaught, but they were beset by guns across the river, by enemy soldiers coming up the cliff, and, most telling, by a large company who had circled around the hill. These last drove right in on their flank and William's group fled through Queenstown to safety near Vrooman's Point, where stood their only gun still firing on the Americans.

He collapsed on the sodden grass alongside the rest of their paltry group. They had failed, all of them. The Americans held the cliffs all along the escarpment, except for the area surrounding Vrooman's Point. And Thomas. They held the redoubt where his brother's body lay; that was the deepest cut of all. He had failed his brother. And they had lost General Brock, their flamboyant commander. Others had stepped up to take his place but failed. *I'll die before I let those murderers away with it.* He sat up and prepared his kit for battle.

In a very few moments, the call came to regroup. William's militia group were detailed to protect a house in nearby Queenstown, part of which was overrun with Americans whooping it up with their looting of houses. Only one man in William's group questioned their assignment and he was silenced with a broad swipe of an officer's rifle butt across his face. Inside was the body of General Brock and his men would do anything to keep the Americans from defiling it.

More and more Americans replaced sections of the British lines on the cliff top as the morning wore on. The battle seemed almost lost; nevertheless, William held his post until welcome reinforcements arrived from Fort George and Fort Chippawa. Two six-pounder guns moved into Queenstown village, trundling right by William to a firing position overlooking the river. Immediately the soldiers opened fire across the river and once again crossing was perilous for the Americans.

At almost the same time Mohawks arrived and with British regulars climbed the heights to set upon the invaders. The Mohawk war cries were so loud and so chilling they filled even their allies with terror. William's insides heaved and he thanked the Lord he hadn't had any food that day. He couldn't see clearly but he thought the Americans were running; for a second he didn't blame them.

BY EVENING THE BATTLE WAS OVER. The Americans had been defeated, although by the most unlikely stroke of luck. From the hundreds of prisoners taken, word began to filter out that many more enemy militia refused to cross the river and fight, leaving their leaders unable to push through and finish the battle. If the militia had fought, the results would have been much different.

William recovered his brother's body and planned to take him home to his parents at the mill even if it took him all night to ride there. His horse was in the stable at the untouched barracks. He lifted Thomas across its haunches and swung up himself, hoping the weight on the horse was lighter than the weight in his heart.

Cantering along the street in the twilight he stopped at the crossroads to allow the column of prisoners to pass ahead of him. Heads down, they wore a motley assortment of blue and grey uniforms, all of them drab. A few militiamen wore vests and coats, most bloodied and torn like the men themselves.

He watched their faces and imagined how he would feel were he in their shoes. Suddenly he sat up straighter in the saddle. That taller one, behind the portly fellow. Was it...? "Robert!" The man kept marching. William hadn't even thought of Robert fighting on the opposite side. He called again and moved his horse along beside the line. The man was looking, but in the dimming light William couldn't see clearly enough. Suddenly the man stopped and those behind trudged right into him.

"Get moving there," the officer shouted from behind. And he did but not before those brilliant blue eyes flashed in the lantern light and a tired smile lit the face of his brother. William followed the procession a few feet further to the barracks and found the prisoners were to be penned up together in the open for the night. In the morning they would most likely be exchanged and go home.

He tried to get Robert released but with tensions riding so high after General Brock's death, no officer would condone such leniency. Finally, he found Robert pushed up against the fence, a black shadow in the complete darkness of the cloudy night. He reached through the fence and clasped his brother's cold hand. For a few moments they did not speak. William felt the hand warm under his touch and dreaded what he must say.

The horse nuzzled up against him pushing him to move on and finish his dread duty.

"I'm sorry, Robert." His voice was barely audible even to himself.

"You? Why are you sorry?" Robert asked. "I'm the one who should apologize." He reached his other hand through the fence and clasped William's shoulder.

William couldn't speak. His eyes were full, his heart empty. From somewhere deep within, his voice rose up and out into the open where Robert could hear. "It's Thomas," he croaked. Robert's arm dropped from his shoulder. "He's dead. Shot." He daren't speak again. He'd never get the tears stopped, if once he let them loose.

Robert had squeezed his eyes shut. Now they flew open and he grabbed at William's extended arm so hard the wire cut a painful yet somehow welcome line across his muscle. The horse shuffled behind him and Robert seemed to sense the truth. He leaned to the right just a little. "Is that him?" he asked.

William nodded. "I'm taking him home, to Mama and Daddy." He hadn't called his father that in years but somehow it just slipped out.

Robert nodded, squeezed his hand, and stepped back. "Best be going, then."

William stood a moment longer, torn between his twin brothers, until the horse pushed against him once more. "If I don't take him now, he'll be buried somewhere here." He stopped, tears filling his eyes again. "Mama will want him home."

"Yes...and I'll be glad to know he's with family...even if I___"

"Don't, Robert. Please don't say it. You've only done your duty, we know that." Both his arms through the fence, he held on to his brother's shirt for a moment before Robert pushed him away.

"Go," he whispered. "God bless you all."

William mounted, took one long look at his brother, and trotted away into the night.

Chapter Twenty-Seven

October, 1812

MUCH AS WILLIAM YEARNED to take the road to Catherine and the children, his duty forced him south through Chippawa, past its dark fort looming out of the wet night. The last time he and Catherine had travelled to visit his parents they had noticed many changes. July, it was. The mill was not yet busy but he had helped his father with his preparations for the coming harvest as though this were a normal year.

But it was not. Soon word had come that war was upon them. He had tried to persuade his parents to move in with him and Catherine but they would have none of it. The danger was not as bad as it seemed, they insisted, and their farmers would need the mill. When he reminded them of all their troubles living on the Portage Road extension with its marchers and fleeing feet, they had smiled. His mother's eyes clouded over. "This is our home," she had said, and he knew she was thinking of two other homes they had been forced to leave.

She had wiped her eyes and he gave up, not wishing to be the cause of more heartbreak. Fifty-three she was now, and his father, fifty-seven. Their years showed in his mother's frequent rubbing of her hands as though she could erase the aching joints that plagued her, and in his father's slow step and slight limp as he went back and forth to the mill. Both of their heads were white but his father's hair had thinned so much his reddened scalp showed right through. He kept his hat on when he could. Lines creased his mother's cheeks but her blue eyes still blazed with her love of life and, more often than not, she smiled her way through the days.

How he could take this dreadful burden to them, he knew not, but take it he must. He ought to have hired a wagon. The horse was tiring and so was he. A couple of times they stopped for water and a few minutes' respite but, driven by his duty, he urged the horse on again until light streaks etched the grey of the night and his father's stone mill rose against the dawning daylight. He longed to weep in their arms but knew they would need his strength and he concentrated on gathering it as he hurried to the home of his childhood.

As he turned into the lane, a red glow grew ahead of him making the house, the barn, and the mill back behind, all jet black as they stood out in relief upon the shore. Streaks of yellow rippled across the water and ran right up to the house. First one figure, then another taller one stepped onto the porch and into the yard. The sun broke above the horizon and the figures began to hurry toward him, bathed in a golden glow.

For a second he was happy and pushed his knees into the horse. And then they stopped, first his father and a second later his mother. Their hands crept up to their shadowed faces and their feet ran again, right up to him and his dreadful burden. In the glowing thread of dawning day no one moved or spoke or even breathed.

He slipped off the horse, careful not to disturb his load, and gathered his frail parents into his arms. His father helped him lift Thomas off the horse and lay him gently on the ground. His mother dropped beside Thomas and gathered him into her arms, rocking and soothing, and saying all manner of nonsensical mother-child things, and sounding for all the world as though she thought he would answer.

They watched, his father and he, standing apart, not touching. Finally, they looked at each other and moved, his father to slowly lean down and touch Thomas' face before taking her arm and persuading her to stand, and he to shoulder his brother once more and carry him into the house. He sat with them and told the story, leaving out nothing, and they slowly turned their eyes to him as they tried to listen.

But he was not finished with hurting them. When he rose to go, telling them he dare not stay longer as the danger was too great, they sank back into their chairs. She took his kiss on her forehead without moving a muscle but when he shook his father's hand and stood to go, she let out a strangled cry. "Be safe, William."

He grabbed the door handle and escaped, trading his horse for his father's in the barn, and riding as fast and as well as he could with tears streaming down his face. The road was long but William welcomed its loneliness. This time when he reached Stamford Township and the turnoff to his own farm, he took it, so great was his need for Catherine and his boys.

TWO DAYS LATER, frost iced the long grasses and browned leaves by the road and the cold air found its way right up under William's coat. Thanks to the ministrations of Catherine and his children, he now had enough space in his mind to acknowledge their victory and to ponder what might have happened after Brock was killed if the Americans had pushed home their advantage.

Thomas' last leap up to shoot kept coming back to him. Why had he not pulled his brother down out of the line of fire? He agonized over that while the horse picked its way through great gashes in the road that promised to be much worse come spring. His mother's haggard face stole into his mind once more and, again, he forced it away. He counted the trees still dripping ice, in an attempt to keep his mind occupied for the long ride back to Queenstown.

At least today no cannon fire marred the silence as he neared the small village, but broken down roofs and burned houses attested to the battle that had so recently taken place. The stone barracks was intact. William supposed that was where he should go. He gripped the reins just a little tighter and wondered what his reception would be. After all, he had left without the permission of his superior officer. In the mayhem and personal devastation he had thought only of his brother and his parents. Even if he was just a volunteer militiaman he feared reprisals for his actions.

Near the barracks, he pulled up at the fenced-in area where last he had seen Robert. Completely in the open, men huddled together around meagre bonfires, fed from piles of torn and broken boards but obviously giving off very little heat. He hadn't realized how many prisoners they had taken. Talking to Robert in the dark that night, he just hadn't noticed. Here, however, in the full light of a frosty day, the frozen breath of hundreds of men amazed him. And they were still here.

Staggering toward him, his arms clutching his body, his shoulders scrunched in, and his head bent like a turtle trying to retreat into his shell, was Robert. William jumped off his horse and pressed up against the fence, his hands reaching through toward his brother. As soon as they touched, though, William let go and reached back to his horse for his blanket. Robert's eyes flickered. William threw the blanket over the fence and his satchel of food as well.

"I'll be back," he said and led his horse to the hitching rail before rushing inside.

Though he was only a lowly private in the militia and not even a regular soldier, William strode into the building. He stood a moment until his eyes grew accustomed to the dim light coming from a single candle on a desk by the wall. Behind it sat a red-coated captain who paid no attention to him but carried on with his paperwork.

"Who's in charge here, sir?" William could not wait.

The man wrote on, his quill scratching against the paper at a furious pace, interrupted only by frequent dips into the inkwell.

William cleared his throat and the captain threw up his hand to stop him but kept writing. William shifted and shuffled as he looked around the room. He had not been inside the barracks before, having only done drills outside in the milder weather. This place was cold and dark and drafty but it was a palace compared to the frozen pen outside. His brother was out there.

"Sir," he said, "I need to speak with you...about an urgent matter."

The captain blotted his paper, rolled it up and tied it into a small, neat scroll. Finally he looked up at William, who could see the lines in the man's face and winced under the stare of his blood-shot eyes. He had not realized how old the man was but grey hair and a greyer face told the tale.

"What is it, young man?" The voice was crisp but tired as though its owner wanted never again to have to speak and certainly not to this young man.

William calmed himself and told his story of Robert and the other prisoners out in the freezing weather. As he spoke the captain's eyes grew troubled and his voice came out considerably softened. "Who are you? Do I know you?"

William spoke his name, his full name, and the man's face broke into a smile. "Is...is your mother Lucinda?...Mrs. Lucinda Garner?"

How did he know her? William slowly nodded and the captain jumped up, knocking over the chair in his haste. He grabbed William's hand and shook it vigorously, talking all the while.

"Finally! Some good news," he said. "Don't you remember me, son?"

William's mind swam but he had not a thought of who this could be.

"I helped your mother get started. On her, their, farm near Newark." He stopped a moment waiting for William to respond. "Before your father came back after the war." He nodded into William's face but William couldn't speak. "And I visited your farm near Fort Erie. I'm Captain Crawford."

A faint glimmer of light seeped into William's head. Perhaps he did remember someone. But it was so long ago. Still, he nodded his head and the captain took his arm, his grip warm and strong.

"Wait here, son. I'll be right back." He grabbed the scroll on his desk and hurried out the door. William wondered if the captain was even thinking about Robert or if all the haste was connected only to the message in his hand. In no time at all, though, the door slammed open again and Captain Crawford poked his head inside.

"Come," he said. William hustled out the door behind him.

With not a glance at the hundreds of men in the enclosure along which they strode, the captain led with such a pace, long-legged William was hard-pressed to keep up. Across the street, into one of the few cottages still standing, the two hurried, ignoring the soldiers on either side of the door. Inside they came to an abrupt stop at the crossed rifles barring their way to Major Scheaffe's inner office.

The captain explained his mission and the rifles slowly retreated. A private stepped in front of them, though, staring at them until they backed off to allow him space. He slipped into the narrow opening and pulled the door closed behind him. In a moment he ushered them inside.

"What do you want, Crawford?" The man's gravelly voice and hooded eyes, which only half looked at them, held no warmth. "Don't you see I am over my head with work?" He spread both his hands over the piles of papers and books and fresh parchment, ready for orders at a moment's notice. "I'd think someone in your position would realize the grave position we're in, even though we supposedly won the battle two days ago."

Captain Crawford didn't answer but remained standing at attention as did William.

"Well, do you want something or do you not, Captain?" shouted the Major as he stood up and leaned over the desk toward them. "Speak up, man!"

The captain blurted out the story of the prisoners freezing in the freak autumn weather outside and, more pointedly, of the relationships between some prisoners and those on this side of the border. Major Scheaffe's brows furrowed as he listened. Standing up straight he stroked his hand over his unshaven chin and studied the piles on his desk. His head nodded every so often.

"Well, sir. What can we do about these men?" asked Captain Crawford.

"Did you send that last message as I requested?"

William almost spoke up himself, so surprised was he that the Major didn't seem to have even listened to Crawford; soon, however, he learned the connection.

"We are exchanging prisoners this very afternoon. As far as one of them being a brother to this man, I can do nothing about that. He will be transported across the river, as will the others."

"But, sir..." William started to say.

"You will keep your silence, soldier, and be glad of the opportunity. What does His Majesty the King care about your family relationships?" He waved them away and sat again at his desk. Captain Crawford turned and ushered William from the room.

The prisoners were exchanged that very afternoon. As small boats from Lewiston emptied British prisoners at the landing below the Heights, long lines of Americans waited to embark back to safety. And Robert went with them. William had been unable to have even a moment with his brother. High up on the bluff he lined up with the regulars overlooking the great Niagara River below. His gun cold in his hands he searched the bedraggled prisoners as they shuffled on board but he couldn't pick out his brother.

That evening he accepted the captain's surprising invitation to dinner. A small voice niggled at the back of his brain, making him just a little uneasy but he looked forward to sharing a pint with the man who had been kind to him—and Robert—that morning.

CAPTAIN CRAWFORD HAD GONE LOOKING FOR HER, those few years back, because he finally admitted to himself she was the reason he had never married. And he had to know how her life had turned out. Seeing Lucy—Mrs. Garner—so settled and secure, as though she had a perfect life, he had moved on. He had dropped all his plans, reneged on the engagement he had mentioned to Lucy, spent his savings on a captain's rank, and remained to serve the King.

And now her son was sitting across from him and her eyes looked into his, waiting for his answer. What had the boy asked? Oh, yes, how did he know his mother?

"I almost married her," he said. Her son's face contorted but he didn't speak. "Before your father came back from the revolution." The thing had been so close, him riding out with the preacher and his friends, all of them spiffed up in their best uniforms, only to see the man they all assumed was dead had returned. He had missed his chance and the wound still burned in his gut. "Do you remember me, from back then?"

"No." The young man's voice was low and he dropped his gaze. "I...I don't remember at all. Nor____"

"Of course, you wouldn't." He stopped talking and stared into the single burning candle of the table between them. The flickering flame reminded him of her unruly curls that summer. A chair scraped the floor but he resisted the tug back to the present. When she faded from his vision he was alone. As usual.

THE GARRISON AT QUEENSTOWN slipped back into a state of order and regular duties, both for the soldiers and for the militia. William found time to go home to Catherine and tend to his farm. A certain amount of normalcy carried them through Christmas. They did not visit his parents, though, for the continuing danger on the roads and the particularly bitter weather that settled in that year. By the time the New Year dawned Catherine's aging parents had left their home near Niagara for safety's sake and now lived with him and Catherine. After all, the house had ample room and Catherine, their only child, could better care for them here.

One fine day in January, William sat in his chair dandling wee Eva on his knee and watching out the window as the birds fluttered about looking for seeds in the sparkling snow. He had just noticed that Catherine was knitting yet another pair of booties and suddenly understood another baby was on the way. Wee Eva was only eight months old and though he loved all his children with a fierce passion, they just didn't need another. Not at this time. Not so soon.

From the other side of the stove came the soft snore of his mother-in-law. Her knitting had fallen from her hands and now lay, idle, over her crisp white apron. That morning Catherine's father had finally taken to his bed with the slight cough and rheumy eyes he had wiped countless times at the breakfast table. For the first time in days no one was actually overhearing his and Catherine's conversation.

He turned to her. "I'm going to Lundy's Lane   t o m o r r o w. To the store." Catherine's eyebrows arched and her forehead wrinkled but she said nothing. Instead she dropped her knitting and wrote a short list of supplies she needed, among them small buttons and yarn if he could find it.

Mrs. Smithers, widowed now, still carried on with the small store she and her husband had set up and it was there that William took the sleigh over the snow-covered roads. He had left off the sleigh bells this time not wanting to give any stray Americans notice of his presence but, actually, the chance of that was slim. The bitter winter kept soldiers and officers alike at home or snug and secure in winter quarters. He was surprised, therefore, to reign in his horse beside several rigs. Perhaps he was not the only one with a bit of an itch this day.

The horse shied as he threw the blanket over her but she'd be frozen and finished if he didn't protect her sweating body. He fastened the straps, gave her a pat on the nose, and headed inside. Assailed immediately by the aroma of fresh bread, tea, and the buzz of excitement in the crowded room, he took the only empty seat at a table with three other men whom he knew.

"Garner," they chorused. "Welcome."

As soon as he sat, Mrs. Smithers squeezed between her customers to take his order and he smiled as he gave it to her. The moment she was gone, however, his friends looked his way with concern on their faces. They said nothing, at first, but tore their eyes away from his and studied the table. William looked down, too, but couldn't see anything in the stained walnut boards.

"What is it?" he asked.

After a moment of silence, all three spoke at once.

"One at a time, boys." The room became still, the only sound Mrs. Smithers bustling over with his order.

"Your parents, William," the redheaded man on his left said. The others were nodding as William steadied himself. "They're not at the mill. We was through there yesterday. Place is a shambles, deserted. And the mill wheel lying on the ground."

Chapter Twenty-Eight

Angel Inn, Newark
December, 1813

THE AMERICANS NOW HELD FORT GEORGE, which lay on the Niagara River, just a stone's throw from the town Butler had started thirty years before. The townspeople did their best to keep the peace laid out by the Americans earlier in the year but this was not an easy task. The industrious among them found ways to sell food and supplies at the fort and walk the thin line between obedience to an invading army and allegiance to their own king in far-off Britain.

While the Americans' daily comings and goings along the lake to Forty Road kept the villagers on edge, for the most part they lived day by day, longing for the time when this border war would be over. But a certain amount of hard feeling between the two sides was inevitable as families were split and neighbors fought each other.

In their small room above the barroom at the Angel Inn, John and Lucy sat wedged in between the rope-slung bed and small table. They had left all of their possessions behind in their rush to escape the inevitable march of the Americans, fresh from vanquishing the British troops at Fort Erie. John had seen the smoke and rushed Lucy out of the house so quickly she barely had time to pack anything but her clothes, a few hams in the larder and cooking pots full of their winter stores.

Taking the Portage Road had been a risk and more than once John had pulled the horses off into the trees to avoid patrols. From a distance the soldiers, whether friend or foe, all looked alike and certainly they sounded the same. Even in the winter their marching feet pounded into the ground like the constant thrum of a drum echoing through the cold day.

They had planned to go to William's but, at the last, John decided against burdening his son with providing for them and had taken the wagon past the turnoff and through the night to Newark. He found the Angel Inn just as daylight slipped over the horizon. Stiff with cold and sitting so long, the two had staggered to the one available room and collapsed on the bed. The innkeeper kindly took care of their exhausted horses, remembering Lucy from those many years before when she had lived in the cabin waiting for John to return after the revolution.

Almost a year ago they had come, when the British still held Fort George and Newark was obviously a British town. They had remained at the Inn, Lucy helping to serve when needed and John lending a hand wherever he could but most often at the mill of a friend some distance away. This night Lucy had carried their supper up the narrow stairs from the Inn below, careful not to trip on her long skirt with the torn hem. She must get to stitching it.

"Let me help you." John dropped the cloth with which he had been drying his hands and hurried to take the plates.

"Mutton again, I'm afraid," Lucy said but smiled into his drawn face. "But there is a good pudding for a sweet, my dear."

As the two sat and ate their meager meal the noise from the Inn below rose to a raucous yelling of excited voices, so noisy John had to raise his voice to speak. "Even louder than usual tonight."

"I wonder. There was a rowdy group that came in just as I was dishing the mutton."

"Who?"

"Not Americans, that's for certes."

John smiled. "Well, they do come here, you know."

"Yes, but they don't get such a happy reception, do they?"

She smiled and nodded, remembering the smoky air downstairs one night just last week. Four of those soldiers from the Fort sat at the corner table and, gradually, all around them became silent, a rare thing in the Inn. The innkeeper, Aaron, had feared trouble and ordered free drinks for the whole house. The men immediately turned their attention to enjoying themselves rather than starting a brawl or something worse.

John said something else.

"Pardon, my dear? I wasn't listening." She turned his way.

"I'm going down to see what the celebration is all about." He stumbled past the bed and out the door before she could reply. In the space of a half hour he was back.

"We've pushed them back to the edge of Newark. They'll be posting a double guard in the Fort tonight." He removed his shoes and lay on the bed. In his eyes, Lucy saw the first glimmer of hope she'd seen for a long time. She ran the dishes down to the small kitchen and resisted the urge to listen herself to the boisterous celebrations in the main room of the Inn.

They had quite a time getting to sleep that night as the partying went on long after bedtime, so long, in fact, that John threatened to go down and roust out the noisemakers but Lucy persuaded him to wait. Sure enough Aaron's commands filtered up as he sent his patrons out into the cold night, the grumbling and groaning mixed in with the odd guffaw until all was quiet.

The next day John was off to the mill some distance away. It had snowed in the night and the wind swept the snow before it like an angry housewife beating her broom at spiders. He took the horses and wagon to bring back flour for Aaron at the end of the day. If the weather changed he might not make it back until the next day. Lucy, however, had her hands full cleaning up the main room of the Inn as well as the two rooms that had housed revellers overnight.

Late in the afternoon two frazzled women ran inside the doorway of the Inn and shouted for silence. Lucy paused in her scouring of the rough table by the door. She had never seen these women before. And certainly not at the Inn. Aaron came from the back, towelling off his hands.

"What is it, ladies?"

The pair fairly shouted in his face that the American commander at Fort George had ordered the town to be burnt.

"What are you saying?" Aaron shouted, too.

"It's true. We only have one hour to take what we can. Before they burn the town."

"It can't be," Lucy cried to Aaron as the women ran out. "Those drinkers from last night." She gasped for words. "They're just playing a ghastly trick."

"No," he said. "It's those turncoat Canadians."

Sure enough, through the stout door strode two men, grinning and glaring at the same time. "You have one hour," they said. "And then we're burning the town."

"No," screamed Lucy. She threw up her hands to beat the chest of the nearest one but Aaron grabbed her from behind and held her still. "Let me go!" She couldn't let them get away with this. Aaron turned her to face him and, taking her by the shoulders, shook her. He said not a word but just held her until she quieted. She looked into Aaron's black beard and bushy eyebrows and saw his own fear. She was wasting time.

"Let me go, Aaron. I'm fine now." Along with the rest of those who, but a few minutes before, had been enjoying a brief respite in their day, she tried to save what she could, both her and John's things, but also Aaron's tables and benches and cooking pots and even the small stoves from some of the bedrooms. All up and down the street women and children stacked their belongings in the snow. Their piles grew and grew but neither they nor their neighbors had near enough time to rescue all they wanted.

Mothers screamed at children lugging prized pictures and bureaus and even the odd rag doll into the snow. Out of second floor windows shirts and frocks fluttered down in the stiff wind settling wherever the winds took them and the children below had no time to search out their own belongings as more and more of their life's possessions floated down from above.

Lucy was the first to look out the upstairs window and see the flames, just one street over, flicking into the sky through the rooftops. She called out to those below and for a second everyone stopped and gazed at the destruction that was coming not only for their neighbors but also for them. Someone yelled and pointed down their street.

Soldiers ran from one house to the next, their flaming torches setting each and every building alight. The wind blew the flames as they ate up the insides, the roofs, the chimneys, and finally the walls themselves of the little town. Perhaps the cruellest cut of all came with the knowledge of just who was setting the fires. Along with the American militiamen a group of American sympathizers called the Canadian Volunteers tossed torches into their own neighbors' homes.

People howled in the streets. When the torchers reached the house next door they learned that the old woman who lived there was sick and could not leave her bed. The soldier gave the order to carry her, bed and all, outside into the snow where she lay shivering under her blankets as her house burned to the ground. Lucy ran to the bed and heaped her spare blankets on the woman but they gave no comfort to the woman or to Lucy.

As dusk came the flames lit up the night sky and for a while the heat warmed the watchers so that they did not immediately begin to look for shelter. When they did, there was none. The Fort was still held by the Americans and all the buildings in the town were burning. A cry went up as the church tower collapsed with a flaming shower of sparks, most of which landed in the snow and were extinguished. Others, however, fell on the townspeople, and one wee boy's coat was fully flaming before his mother screamed and rolled him in the snow to douse the fire.

JOHN WAS TWO MILES AWAY and longing for his supper and his bed after a gruelling day cutting wood in the cold for the miller and his family. An eerie glow filled the sky to the north. As he watched, it grew. Clouds of smoke hazed over him, wafting up into the darkness high above. He cracked the whip over the already laboring horses, suddenly more alert than he'd been all day. As he raced along, the smoke blew in his face. He coughed and rubbed his eyes, but pushed the horses in a careening drive over the snowy roads.

When he reached the edge of the village, his innards clenched hard as rock and he steeled himself against the sight of so many burning houses. But the screams of his neighbors were a different matter. His eyes filled with tears, which streamed down his cheeks, turning to ice like his heart inside. He pushed on. The horses, maddened by the fire, jerked against the lines until they both stopped and no matter how he whipped them would not go any further.

On foot in the snow, he grabbed the harness and pulled the lead horse by sheer willpower, all the while forcing his fears aside and speaking softly in the encouraging voice that his horses knew so well. He could not leave them here as they would run off and probably right into the few buildings that were still flaming. Most were smoking hulks of blackened timbers, the stiff wind whipping the tails of smoke into the dark sky. If only the cries and moans would disappear in the same way.

John led his team past piles and people and into the street where just this morning the Angel Inn had housed his Lucy and the few belongings they had brought from their home. The belongings mattered little. He had to find Lucy. In the distance he saw her running from the flaming Inn, her arms full of pots and plates. She turned to go back inside but someone held her. "Lucy!" Both of them turned his way. John felt a rush of relief that Aaron had stepped into his place.

She ran into his arms, her curls flying loose and the acrid smell of smoke filling his nostrils. But he didn't care. She was safe and the smoke would wash away. They loaded what they could on the wagon and though Lucy tried to leave her blankets with the woman in the bed, she insisted Lucy take them. By the look of her, John thought, she was not long for this world. In the light of Aaron's lantern, they saw all the fight had gone out of the poor soul.

Minutes later Aaron's hands were full holding his own horses as he supervised the loading of the few possessions he managed to save from the Inn. While Lucy sat in the wagon holding the lines, John lent his back to helping lift a bureau and bed onto Aaron's wagon. The wicked flames gradually died down and with them the eerie sounds of gasping wind and cracking wood. Mothers clutched their wailing children while the few men began to build sorry structures against chimneys using blackened wood scavenged from their once pretty homes.

John took a final glance around and climbed up beside Lucy. They had to get out of the bitter cold but he was at a loss as to where to go. Aaron led off with his wagon filled with possessions and John followed, steeling his nerves against the sight of the huddled forms all along the road. At the barracks, which had miraculously not been torched, dozens of hooded figures clustered together, unable to squeeze into the packed building. After a brief discussion he and Aaron separated, Aaron heading for the Fort and John for William's farm in Stamford Township. He was their only hope.

With tragedy unfolding all around them, John did not at first hear the tramping of feet in the distance. As the sound behind them grew, Lucy clutched his arm while he drove the tired team into the night. The fleeing American soldiers soon overtook their wagon and John pulled off the trail to let them by. In single file they squeezed beside the wagon but none of them gave more than a flickering of their wide eyes toward him and Lucy.

They were fleeing Fort George but couldn't cross the half frozen river and, instead, marched quick time toward Queenstown. As the men ahead rushed into the night, another sound came from behind. Horses. He and Lucy barely had time to think what might be happening before, once again, he had to rein in. British soldiers thundered by, both on horseback and on foot, sending clouds of powdered snow off the hoofs and filling the air with steaming snorts from both men and mounts.

Right along the road John was taking they came, the pursued and the pursuers, the first fearing for their lives, the whites of their eyes shining wide in the cold moonlight, the second, having discovered the travesty visited on the townspeople by the Americans, now bent on vengeance. John and Lucy sat by the side of the narrow road and waited for the trailing British foot soldiers to pass. He held tight to Lucy and she shivered against him.

The soldiers caught up to the enemy's rear guard. John was thankful he and Lucy couldn't see in the darkened night but they could hear. Screams and terror-stricken cries came out of the dark, so close that Lucy turned her face into his neck and he clutched her shaking body. In his mind's eye, he saw the bayonets slicing, the horses riding down the foot soldiers and trampling them, and the awful surprise in the eyes of those whose death was upon them. He was glad to hear the Americans routed but his gut wrenched with guilt. Who among those Americans might have been his friends in the years before this war?

When the battle sounds finally stopped, the moon had slipped across the sky and the soldiers marched the prisoners back past their wagon in the night while John stood guard against any mischief that might have been done. Lucy had crawled into the back of the wagon under the blankets and belongings while John covered the horses. He dared not unhitch them. For a few short hours he, too, took refuge with Lucy.

Before the day had begun to dawn he crawled up on the seat once more and, leaving Lucy snuggled in the back, started the horses on the long road to William and warmth. He passed the scene of the previous night's fighting. Blood streaked the stark snow in all directions but he saw only a couple of bodies, enemy soldiers frozen into ghoulish specters. He pushed on.

The horses settled into the trip and the sun came up on glistening snow, white frothing breath floating up from the animals. John and Lucy squeezed together on the seat, trying to keep warm as the wagon bounced along the rutted road. At Queenstown they stopped for an hour but John insisted they carry on as snow clouds threatened to the west.

DECEMBER TWENTY-FIFTH came and went under William and Catherine's snug roof while the cold outside held the whole of Niagara in thrall. William's period of service with the militia had ended and not a moment too soon in Catherine's opinion. His sleep had settled back to normal for most nights although, from time to time, she wakened in the night to wrap her arms around him in hopes of conquering his demons. She knew he blamed himself for Thomas' death. If his brother had not gone with William that fateful night, he might still be alive. But of course those thoughts were useless and she tried very hard to persuade William the loss was just God's way.

Certainly her father's death had been. The old man had become less and less active until all he did was sit in the chair by the stove carving twigs into soldiers. One day, he had just laid down his knife, closed his eyes, and fallen asleep, never to wake again. She brushed a tear from her eyes and glanced around the room.

William's father sat where her father had. And his mother, sweet woman that she was, hunched over a bowl of potatoes she was peeling for the evening meal. They had told the stories of Newark in halting bits, leaving out the lurid parts until the children were asleep, but she could tell from their faces those events would haunt them for the rest of their days. Both had slowed considerably. Where once John had played piggyback whenever young Will wanted, now he simply held the boy on his knee. And Lucy. Her hands shook as she peeled the potatoes, a job which today seemed to be taking the whole afternoon.

Her own mother stayed more and more in her room and said little when she did come out. Catherine considered what she might do to ease the pain of all three of their parents but no easy answers were forthcoming. Perhaps the New Year would bring better times.

Near the end of December, however, the family woke to what at first they took to be thunder in the distance. William first noticed the sound on the way back from doing chores in the barn and spoke of it at breakfast. John glanced at his son but kept his own counsel. Catherine noticed he was the first to lift his empty plate to the sideboard, though. He threw on his coat and stepped outside.

In a moment he was back inside. "I think it's cannon fire," he said, "but far away. Care to go for a ride, William?"

William finished his own breakfast and joined his father. Little Will rushed to the window and reported on their doings. His father and grandfather rode out, heading east.

They were gone most of the morning. By turn Catherine and Lucy kept watch at the frosted window but Mama Cain hardly moved in her chair by the fire. The children had spoons and cooking pots on the floor and banged away until Catherine caught a glance from Lucy at the window and urged them to stop the noise. Just at that moment, she heard a horse.

Lucy turned back and immediately clapped her hands. "Catherine, they're here." She smiled for the first time that morning and Catherine was glad. The men hurried inside, their faces red from the cold but their eyes holding fear at bay.

"What is it, John?" Lucy took his coat and hung it on the hook by the door.

"Our troops are firing on Buffalo," he answered.

"In retaliation," William added. "For Newark."

Catherine pulled the chair out for her husband and poured hot drinks for the men. "What good will that do?" She stood by the table, her hands clenching the back of the chair before her. She had received a letter a few days earlier that none of them knew about. She had a good mind to gather up the family and find that land she was promised in the wilderness, away from this endless fighting. But first she'd have to tell William and she knew what he would say.

....

Chapter Twenty-Nine

January, 1814

THE FIRST TO SICKEN WAS WILLIAM. He took to his bed as soon as the fever hit and Catherine carried cloths and cool water for the rest of the day, wiping his brow and talking to him in a low, soft voice, the words indistinguishable outside the bedroom. Lucy kept track of the children, even wee baby Catt, and John did his best to keep the soup pot filled and the chores done. By nightfall when Lucy went in to see her son, she hardly recognized him. Gone were the kind eyes and ever-present grin. In their place were a rictus of pain and unseeing eyes pointed at the ceiling as though their owner no longer needed them.

She halted by the door, unable to move closer until Catherine reached for her hand and led her into the stuffy room, lit by only one candle on the night table. William's face shone with sweat, which never completely disappeared even with Catherine's constant wiping of it. John came in behind her, having left the children for just a moment, and rested his hand on her waist. She daren't look at him but focused instead on William's hair, drenched black and pushed away from his face by the frequent swabbing.

"Would you like to sit?" Catherine asked, indicating the straight-backed chair by the bed.

"No, that's your place, my dear." She summoned up a smile. "Unless you want a rest?" She thought how tired Catherine must be.

"No...I mean, yes. Just for a few moments." She touched Lucy's arm as she left the room.

Lucy sat beside her son and took up the cloth, bathing his brow and smoothing his hair. John slipped out and she was alone with William. After wiping his face again, she let the cloth rest in the basin and dried her hands on her skirt. Beside the bed, she knelt on the bare floor, her elbows on the bed and her hands cradling her bowed head. Unlike many of her age, she was not used to prayer, having gotten out of the habit when Harper John died all those years ago.

Now, however, Lucy talked to God about her son and asked that he be spared. Unaccustomed as she was, this prayer was short but from the very depths of her heart. She could not lose another child. She could not. Just as she opened her eyes to look again upon her son, a rustling came behind her. Catherine was back. She took the cloth from Lucy and began again to wipe with a gentle hand and a hoping heart.

Through the night they took shifts and Lucy thought William's forehead was cooler towards morning but she didn't want to give Catherine false hope so said nothing. John insisted she lie down in their room and when he came to get her again there was hope in his eyes. He led her back to the sick room and she saw her son's eyes upon her as she came through the door. Just as she was about to smile and rejoice, she noticed baby Catt in Catherine's arms.

Instead of the fighting fists and sucking mouth she was so used to seeing, Catt's eyes were half closed, her arms hung limp by her sides, and the gasp of her breathing told of the six-month-old's struggle to live.

They kept the other children away from the baby and their father, John taking complete charge of them while Lucy cooked and cleaned and washed clothes. She had checked on Catherine's mother and told her to avoid the others, lest she contract the sickness as well. The woman barely answered her.

On the third day wee Catt died. When Catherine carried her out of their room and placed her in Lucy's arms she almost collapsed herself. Her red eyes shone with tears. "Wrap her in the baby quilt," she whispered to Lucy. She turned and went back to her husband.

Downstairs the children played with John in a makeshift house under the table with blankets draped over the chairs. Lucy heard them laughing as she came down the stairs and opened the door at the bottom. Instantly John was on his feet and staring at her, the question in his eyes. With the barest of nods, she shook her head and watched his head fall before he took her in his arms, baby and all, and held them. The other three children played on.

"Where is Mrs. Cain?" Lucy whispered.

"I haven't seen her." He shook his head and glanced back up the stairs. She must still be in her room. John reached for her burden but Lucy held on, not wanting to risk him, too. She found the baby's quilt and wrapped the child inside covering her, face and all, a sob slipping out as she lay the bundle on the settee in the parlour. "Keep the children out," she whispered to John as she closed the door and turned to go back upstairs.

She heard the weeping coming from William and Catherine's bedroom and told herself they needed her to be strong. At the opposite end of the hall she tapped on Mrs. Cain's door but got no answer. She tapped again, a little louder. Still nothing. The doorknob was cold in her hand as she twisted it open and peeked into the darkened room. "Mrs. Cain?" she whispered. "Are you awake?"

She moved to the bed where the blankets were pulled right up over a small lump in the centre of the narrow bed. She listened, she looked, she leaned over to touch the woman. "Mrs. Cain?" The blanket was scratchy in her hand as she slid it back, listening for a sound, any sound that would tell her the tiny woman heard her, but there was nothing. She pulled a grey strand of hair back off the parched face with its toothless mouth half open. Another death.

William was up the next day, insisting that he help to bury his mother-in-law and his daughter but the deep snow cover and ice-hard ground made digging impossible. Lucy sat with him and Catherine as they held their baby for the last time before John placed her in the small box he had found in the barn. Mrs. Cain's box was not ready yet. A day later John brought it to the house and he and his son placed the woman inside. She, too, was wrapped in a quilt but this was one she had pieced together herself many years before.

They put the boxes high up in the barn away from varmints. While no one said anything, Lucy was sure they all prayed that spring would come soon so that the earth would open up and take back these loved ones. John and William took care that the boxes were not disturbed in the meantime.

As the winter wore on, one of the coldest Lucy could remember, the pallor over the house eased a little because of the state of oblivion in which the children lived. They had hardly known their wee sister and their Nana had spent no time with them in the past year. They were children, with that attention span which lasts only until the next new thing comes along.

Lucy stood by the window and watched Will try to make snowballs to throw at John. Romping with the three children in the snow he looked young and light of heart. They each did their own thing to get through these cursed times but she knew his joints would definitely ache in the night. Meanwhile Lucy leaned on the sill and watched not just them but the road beyond.

William had regained his former good health and his ruddy coloring had replaced the pallor in his cheeks. After the bloody battles in December, the area seemed calm but Lucy had seen the looks pass between John and William and the sudden stopping in mid sentence both of them practised whenever she or Catherine came into the room. As if the women didn't know what they were thinking.

While they all were anxious for spring, a small part of Lucy could not escape her fear of what new atrocities might be committed once hostilities started up again. Catherine, once light on her feet with a quick smile for everyone, now wandered through the days with long looks and silent tears whenever she thought no one was looking. Even the children failed to rouse her. As the weeks went by, Lucy became more and more concerned about her daughter-in-law. The girl had learned first-hand the fleeting quality of life and she could never again rest innocent, thinking all would be well.

CATHERINE SAT ON THE CORNER OF THE BED, the door closed, and studied the words of the letter once more. Perhaps she should tell William. But, no, they had enough change to deal with. She'd wait until after the burials in the spring. And maybe this war with the Americans would be over. Besides, who knew where in the back woods this fool land grant was anyhow? She folded up the letter and placed it in the top drawer of the bureau once more.

"Catherine? Where are you?" William pushed the door open and his smile made the room seem warmer. He reached for her hand. This time she let him hold it a moment before she stole away out the door and down the stairs, hardly making a sound on the treads. If she were to let go, even the slightest bit, she knew she might lose herself forever. She needed more time.

SPRING CAME AND THE BODIES WERE BURIED but the healing did not begin. Instead fighting and fear spread over the fields of young hay and winter wheat. The glorious sun seemed an affront to citizens whose hurts were so deep that they now expected nothing but more pain.

William came back from Lundy's Lane one day with news. Land grants had finally been given to those who had fought in the revolution or, if they were dead, to their progeny. John and Lucy had been given their land years before but Catherine's father's claim had not been settled. William's words came from across the table but Catherine just stared at her cup of half-drunk tea. He spoke again. "This affects you, Catherine."

Everyone was watching. Even the children hushed their chatter. Will looked from one parent to the other. "Mama?" His voice barely a whisper and his eyes filling, he spoke again. "Mama?"

"Mama's fine, Will." Catherine forced out the words. Around her the whole room seemed to sigh. She looked from one face to another but said nothing else. Her hand rested on Will's head.

"Did you hear me, Catherine? About the land, I mean?"

"Yes. I...I got a letter," she began.

"You did? Where is it?" her husband asked.

"When did you get it, Catherine?" Lucy whispered. "Why didn't you tell us?"

She couldn't answer.

William moved behind her and put his arms on her shoulders. "She'll tell us when she's ready, I expect." His hands were warm and strong on her flesh.

Chairs scraped the floor, footsteps both soft and loud sounded on the wood planking, and without speaking again, they left her. Her voice was barely a whisper in the empty space. "I didn't want to leave them behind."

William came back and sat beside her. His hand warmed her arm but she couldn't speak. Even though she had him and the other children, the rest of her family, her mother, father, and baby Catt, now lay in the lonely plot on the hillside. Who would take care of them if she claimed her land in far off Nissouri Township?

JOHN TOOK HIS HAT AND HIS HOE out to the cornfield one day in late June to get an early start hacking out the weeds that threatened to choke the young corn. William was off yet again to catch up on the news on Lundy's Lane and, John suspected, to escape the long faces Lucy and Catherine wore a lot of the time. He had to admit, however, Catherine's pluck was returning. Just last evening she had raced young Will all the way to the barn and back, letting him win and laughing over the way wee John tried to keep up with Will.

He kicked at a stubborn thistle. As he straightened shouts came from over by the house. Horses. Riding fast. Hoe in hand he started running. Who were these men? William was not among them although they had come from the direction of Lundy's Lane. They pulled up by the porch and two of the four jumped off their horses. Lucy and Caroline ran out the door. Lucy had her rifle.

"Whoa!" he shouted, wanting to draw their attention away from the women. "What are you doing?" He hardly had enough wind to speak but ran right up to the two who swung their rifles to point at him. "What do...you...want?" The men were strangers, with none too friendly faces. They looked from one to another before facing John again.

"Better slow down, old-timer. You'll keel right over." The man planted his feet firmly in the dirt and squinted at John. He held his rifle just below his eyes, although it was not exactly aimed.

John felt the threat. "Who are you?" He looked into the man's squinty eyes and did not flinch.

"We're, ah, we're here looking for food. To buy," he added.

"We have nothing to sell you. Too early for the crops." John lifted the hoe. "We have barely enough for ourselves."

"I saw a pig in the pen as we rode in." His voice came out in a whine but there was no humour in the man, nor any attempt at courtesy. His eyes roved back to the women on the porch. Young Will stood by his mother, now.

"Are you hungry?" Catherine asked.

"Yes, that's it. We're hungry." His eyes rested on her just a moment too long. "What do you have for us, little lady?"

John couldn't see what to do but he forced himself to keep calm as he edged toward the porch. "Go inside, Will," he whispered. For once the lad did as he was told.

The men looked at each other and back at the group on the step. To John's left, Lucy had raised the rifle and, though she was not sighting down the barrel, certainly gave every indication she knew exactly how to do just that. A surge of pride went through him but before he could do anything else, Catherine took a step forward.

"Gentlemen." Her voice was as soft and smooth as he had ever heard it. "Would you like a glass of cold tea?"

Though he didn't take his eyes off the men, he knew his daughter-in-law wore a wide smile in the best tradition of the welcoming hostess. The men on foot dropped their eyes and backed up a pace.

"I'm sure we can find some sliced ham to go with it." She took another step forward. "If you'll just give us a moment."

The man who had spoken first stepped toward her. "Yes, ma'am. We...thank you." He gestured to the others who dismounted and tied their horses to the rail. Indicating the well, he spoke again. "May we wash up?"

"Of course you may. And then come inside out of the heat." Catherine turned her back on them and slipped into the house. Lucy handed her rifle to John and followed her. John leaned his hoe against the wall beside the door and, when the men had finished at the well, ushered them inside.

They never did say just who they were or what their business was but after sampling Catherine's hospitality they went on their way, this time with smiles and mayhap even a little shame. When William came back later that afternoon he was regaled with stories about the excitement, all of them tinged with humour and smiles. Young Will added his version at supper that night, but John sat silent and thoughtful and William sought his company on the porch after the meal.

"I don't know, son." He stood by the rail and looked off in the direction the men had taken. "They had mischief in their minds, there's no doubt...Catherine's quick thinking saved us all."

"I should have been here."

"Yes, well, we never know when danger is coming to call, do we?"

"Still, we were lucky today. Another time..." William leaned over the rail, his arms resting on it. "You and Mama came here for safety, but..." He shrugged his shoulders, stood a moment, and moved inside. John heard him helping Catherine put the children to bed but he was back in a very few moments. Lucy and Catherine joined them.

"I didn't tell you in front of the children," William began, "but a couple of weeks ago the Americans attacked in Stoney Creek. They almost won the day."

He told the rest of the story as they sat and watched the darkness descend. Fireflies blinked now and then and John wondered what else was out there in the night. The British victory, which William described, was due in large part to mistake and mishap although whether the stories were true was debatable. John had brought Lucy here for safety but now he wondered. Was any place safe?

Chapter Thirty

July, 1814

AN UNEXPECTED VISITOR to the farm forestalled William's next foray to the inn on Lundy's Lane. He rode in on a spent horse which he led right up to the water trough. As the animal drank and drank, the visitor, one of William's fellow militiamen, leaned against the trough.

Lucy and John had been resting in their room at this hottest part of the day but, as soon as he heard the galloping horse, John lumbered off the bed to the window. Pulling on his trousers, John hollered for William, ignoring the napping children as he stomped along the hall and down the stairs. By the time he got outside with his musket, William was hurrying from the barn, a welcoming smile lighting up his sunburned face.

"Father, this is George Jones. We were together in the militia."

John dropped his musket to his side and smiled at the man. "You look as though you've ridden all the way from Detroit," he said.

"Well, almost, sir. I've come with news." He took off his hat and pushed back a straggling lock of dirty brown hair. "I'd be thankful to get out of the sun, even if only for a few minutes," he said.

John took the horse to the barn before joining the others around the kitchen table. Lucy had come down and she helped Catherine pass around cool water from the well. Jones drank his straight down and asked for another before he began to talk.

"There's been a battle, William." He faced his friend across the table. "The Americans have captured Fort Erie."

William leaned forward. "When?"

"How?" Lucy's voice cut in. "I thought the fort was impregnable."

Jones looked at each of them in turn, ending with John. "You haven't said anything, sir."

"No. And I'm guessing you have more to tell, young man."

The visitor took another gulp of water before he faced John. "Since Moraviantown when the British left Tecumseh to fight and die, we've lost our foothold in this part of Upper Canada. There's talk we settlers are on our own now."

William looked at Catherine's white face. "But we're all still safe here, aren't we?" He eyed George and his father.

"What's the rest of the news that has made you ride all up and down the township in the heat of the day?" asked John.

"You're right, sir. There's more."

"Out with it, George," William urged.

"The whole American army may be headed for Niagara. We have to stop them." He tried to take another drink but the glass was empty.

Lucy slipped over to the pail for more water. A silent message seemed to pass between John and William. For a long moment no one spoke.

"You want men, don't you?" William asked.

Jones leaned back in his chair. "Yes."

FOR THE NEXT HALF HOUR the house was all a-tumble with getting William ready to travel. Young Will and wee John woke with all the hubbub and even their sister slid down the steps as fast as she could to be part of the excitement. Catherine and Lucy held the youngest ones on their laps, out of the way of the men. Young Will ran back up to his room and reappeared as his father was opening the door, his hand behind his back.

"Daddy."

"No, Will. Your daddy has to hurry," said Catherine, holding the boy's hand.

They gathered together in the kitchen and he stopped to smile at each one in turn. "I'll be back soon."

BUT HE WASN'T. The hours passed, night came and with it the far-off sounds of cannon-fire. John sat on the porch with Lucy and Catherine, all of them fighting off the barrage of mosquitoes but reluctant to retreat inside. William was there in the midst of the fighting and in this small way they could each support him. Or so it seemed.

Soon the sky went darker and quiet and a few crickets braved the stillness with their annoying shriek. The adults moved inside to their beds although sleep did not come easily. John wondered what Catherine's thoughts were this night, the second without William. Lucy lay awake beside him; he heard the catch in her breath every few moments. In the morning he would ride towards the fighting. At Chippawa, he thought. For now, he must let his fears go and just sleep.

The morning came and with it a heavy quiet. The sun beat down on them as they went about their chores. John could hardly breathe for trying to listen for fighting but he heard nothing. The air was so still that just walking to the barn brought a tightness to his chest. The chores took little time with most of the animals in the pasture and William's horse gone. He dragged himself back to the house and sat on the porch again, even though the sun gradually baked its boards—and him—as he watched the road.

No one came.

Lucy and Catherine came out to bring him water and a slice of home-baked bread but he sat on. The children, kept inside by their mother, squealed and laughed and yelled and giggled, their high voices interrupted by shrieks or a shrill upbraiding from their mother or grandmother. He should be with William. Yet here he sat guarding his family.

"John," Lucy called. "Your dinner is on the table."

Wee footsteps and scraping chairs beckoned him.

"Papa," cried young Will. "Where were you?"

He smiled and sat, trying not to notice William's empty place at the table.

WILLIAM'S MILITIA UNIFORM STUCK TO HIS BODY. The heat came in waves like attacking soldiers. He mopped at his brow continuously, taking his hand off his weapon for precious seconds each time. The odor of boiled wool and terrified sweat came not only from himself but also from every soldier out there baking in the sun, waiting.

The regulars were drawn up beside them in an uneven line that left them all exposed to whatever the enemy might shower on them.

"Advance!" Alongside his fellow soldiers, he stumbled up and over the hilly terrain where trying to stay upright took his mind off the advancing line of Americans. He worked to shoot and reload, shoot and reload. Bodies dropped beside him in the long grass. His friends.

Artillery bursts took out whole groups around him but William kept running, tripping, loading, and waiting for the command to fire again. He landed on someone, slipped down into the bloody mire, righted himself and ran again, holding his weapon, its bayonet ready. With the Americans right in front of him, he stopped cold, waiting for the order to fire.

The line before him spread wide and advanced on the flanks of the British. Fire came from both sides. William's line fired back, over and over, the air so filled with it he could neither hear nor think, nor even worry. "Fall back!" The shout finally came. And the men did, their retreat covered by the heavy fire of another division. Back through the tall grass which slapped at his face and across the uneven ground slowing him and his fellows, William ran under the protective fire of British six-pounders and two-pounders from Chippawa.

Just when he thought the Americans had left off their charge, the terrifying yells and whoops of enemy Iroquois drove him and his fellow soldiers for cover at Chippawa. But the Americans did not pursue them, and welcome reinforcements soon took the place of those who had been killed or wounded or captured. Though skirmishes and phantom shots persisted, William and the others relaxed but he was not released from his duties for even a few hours to make the trip back to check on his family.

LUCY SLIPPED INTO THE BARN looking for John. His silent face at breakfast and supper the night before marked the measure of his fear and she needed to speak with him. John stood by the empty pen, one foot resting on its crosspiece, his arms still against the top rail.

"There are no pigs there that I can see," she said. "They're out in the pig run."

His foot fell to the dirt and he turned to face her. "No, my dear." His features relaxed into a smile. "I just thought I might be able to conjure some up if I stood here long enough."

She noted the lines in his face. His eyes, once tinged with more green, were now a washed out shade of gold. But they were still kind. He turned and studied the empty pen again, his scarred hands gripping the rails. She placed hers over his and leaned into him.

"It's not what we expected all those years ago, is it?"

He shifted but was silent a moment before he spoke. "No, it's not. But we've survived."

"And raised a wonderful family, don't forget." She thought of those they'd lost but didn't mention them.

"I never do, Lucy." His voice quavered. "I never will."

She held him in her arms, remembering. "Are you quite alright, John? Now, I mean?"

"Don't you worry about me. I'm strong. We'll get through this war just as we did the last one. And we'll survive, Lucy. We'll survive." His fists clenched the rail.

Sudden cries came from the yard. Lucy raced for the door but John overtook her and pushed her behind. "Stay inside!" He ran out and threw the barn door closed behind him. Lucy was left staring through a knothole.

Something crashed onto the roof and right through the open window not ten feet away. Flames bit into the dry straw and, like lightning, streaked across the pen in all directions. She hauled open the heavy door and ran outside.

Riders. In blue uniforms. What were they doing here? Flames… horses screaming…those pigs…squealing as though they'd been stuck. Young Will pushed wee John behind him as they tumbled down the steps from the house. Lucy ran into the smoke and pulled them to her. "Catherine! Run!" she called but Catherine just stood where she was, screaming and pointing at the flames coming out of the upstairs window.

The soldiers shouted and cheered at every new lick of fire, charging with their torches held high, only dipping to touch the wheat and the corn in the fields, the maple trees shading the fully flaming house until red was all she saw as she held fast to the two choking children.

From the mouth of the burning house came John, a blanket over his shoulders, stamping through the flames, clutching in his arms a small body tightly wrapped in a quilt. He stumbled on the steps and threw off the smouldering blanket. Catherine ran forward. She latched onto his arm and pulled him and his burden as far as she could before they both fell at Lucy's feet, away from the reach of the hungry flames.

Lucy still held fast to the two boys. "John, get up!" she screamed. Catherine grabbed for his bundle as he lurched to his feet and together they all staggered across to Catherine's clipped grass patch and fell into the chairs there. Gradually their breathing eased. John unwrapped Eva who screamed and screamed and no amount of Catherine's soothing could stop her. Lucy held the boys in her lap, the two of them shaking against her breast but not making a sound. John reached out to take young Will. His hands had all the hair burned off them but he took the boy in his arms and pressed him close.

....

The hooting and hollering had moved off. Lucy looked away from John's reassuring eyes a moment to see the horsemen galloping down Lundy's Lane toward their next target. Overhead the unscathed elm shaded them all from the searing sun but nothing and no one could protect them from their thoughts.

They watched the flames engulf the last of the house and barn. Clouds of grey smoke billowed up into the blue, the only signal to their friends and neighbours of what had happened. Lucy held wee John and Catherine rocked back and forth with the baby crushed to her breast. John and young William sat on the other chair, the boy for once absolutely quiet as his grandfather patted his back.

"Papa?" They all looked at young William. "Where will we sleep now?"

Chapter Thirty-One

July 25, 1814

THE DUST THICKENED with every soldier's footfall back along the Portage Road toward Queenstown. Regulars and militia kept pace on the sultry summer morning, which already was so hot William yearned to drop in the long grass beside the road. But he couldn't. Nor could any of the few hundred men enduring yet another forced march in this accursed war.

A couple of hours into the march, the order to halt came. The men sucked at their water bottles, and their superiors shouted to drink sparingly. He longed for home. No word had come nor had he sent any messages so dangerous were the roads with Americans and British moving back and forth. They weren't gaining or losing any ground but the tally steadily grew of dead soldiers hastily dug into shallow graves or burned on funeral pyres.

"Attention!"

They struggled once more to their feet and fell into line.

"About face!"

The whole assembly managed a one hundred and eighty degree turn. William exchanged looks with the man next to him, someone new since his friend had dropped from a freak shot.

"March!"

They were going right back where they came from. Apparently the Americans were now approaching. Why didn't we just stay at Lundy's Lane? The thought flickered through his mind but he let it go as so often he had done these last weeks. He thought instead of Catherine and the children, of his parents, and of the once-quiet nights of summer on his farm. He plodded on in the heat and tried to think no more.

The hill was just off the Portage Road at Lundy's Lane, a distinct advantage to whoever held it because it was the highest point in the area. The approach of the Americans could clearly be seen by all who assembled there. Under the scorching sun, William took his assigned position and the wait began. The cook wagon had moved nearer the hill and runners came with hastily heated plates of rashers and beans. He ate sparingly, knowing from experience that as soon as the fighting started the food would most likely find its own trajectory out of his stomach.

The Americans marched into view, their feet drumming in his ears. His stomach tightened and his fingers gripped the rifle. Their own artillery let loose; in front of him figures fell, others tramped over them, and the enemy line came on. More artillery, more fall-ing, more tramping until, in the intervals between volleys, the sounds of the tramping were all he heard.

"Fire!" He did. And he kept on, along with all of those regulars and militiamen beside, before, and behind him on the hill, over and over, without pausing to think until the dark came down and covered them all and almost hid the still-advancing enemy.

"Fall back!" William retreated with his fellows a short way along Lundy's Lane, towards his home, he realized. Those in the rear turned and fought, covering the gradual retreat in the dark of night. We're going to die, he thought. Close to home? If he had to die he'd rather it be here, now, and not where his family would have to watch. Or be killed themselves. Their running feet pounded on the dry ground.

The soldiers stopped their retreat. They pushed back at the enemy, once, twice, and a third time. Black as pitch the night was, as though God didn't want to watch their bloody battles. They straggled back along the road until a blessed halt came and the men fell to sleep where they lay. The Americans had turned tail, it seemed, although no one knew why.

In the night reinforcements arrived from Fort George and retook the hill, digging in their big guns. The sun came up the next morning on a much-reinforced British position and the Americans' attempt to retake it was futile. William helped to haul bodies to a large pile on the top of the hill where they were burned in a foul-smelling and gruesome funeral pyre.

Little food was eaten that day.

Having helped to hold the hill position on Lundy's Lane, the militia were released to their homes for much-needed rest. William walked the few miles as his horse had been shot dead several days earlier. For once he didn't mind the walk. He was alone and the sun not so hot with all the clouds scudding across the sky. He had orders to be back in two days' time.

As he cleared the first hill he looked with high hopes at the first farm where perhaps he might eat and drink. The thought of Mrs. Dunlop's ginger beer and a slice of home baked bread smeared with fresh-churned butter made him realize his stomach was long past just wanting food. He needed it and walked faster, ignoring the holes in his worn shoes. But the house was not there. He squinted in the distance but it was gone. Only black rubble was left. The barn, too, had disappeared as though an artist had smudged out the buildings from his painting and left dark holes.

He ran. When he reached the spot, puffing and sweating in the heat, the homestead lay silent and still before him. He shouted but only the crows cawed back at him from the trees. And what trees they were. Some green branches held on to the blackened trunks but most had fallen to the ground where they snapped and broke under his feet. A baby's clout lay soiled in the withered grass.

As the desolation before him sunk into his brain a stream of images and thoughts assailed him. He ran again, this time ignoring his hunger and his painful feet, driven only to prove his visions wrong. Two more miles he needed to go to reach home but his own travesty gradually took shape. First he smelled the acrid odor of fully burned wood. Then he saw what was gone from the landscape. His house, his barn, and even his crops in the fields, all were gone.

Like the Dunlop's place, his home was all blackened beams and stripped trees "Catherine!" He screamed her name over and over, as he looked and looked but could see no one. He fell to the ground, exhausted, his face in the dusty grass, and wept.

Two days later William reported back to his militia group, having found nothing or no one who knew of his family. He was not the only one. All who had returned home had found their farms devastated and most of them, like William, searched in vain for their families. For miles around the countryside was bare and burned, with nary a farm untouched, and no message to tell where any of the dispossessed had gone.

The militia men brought back an anger they hadn't had before. With the whole area laid to waste with no thought for the women and children who would suffer in the coming winter, William and his comrades now loathed the Americans. Where before settlers had been ambivalent in their feelings, now they lived and breathed a pure hatred, which gave them the stamina to dig in and fight as long as it might take. William felt it in his own gut and saw it in the eyes of his friends whenever the Americans were mentioned.

No sooner did August roll around on the calendar than he and his fellow militia were marching for Fort Erie, bent on reclaiming it from the Americans. Not a man among them was against this plan, so anxious were they to rid Canadian soil of their enemy as soon as possible. The march was slow in the heat, with many stops and a few small skirmishes along the way as they encountered pockets of enemy soldiers.

Where last year wheat had been ripening in the August breezes, now lay only fields burned black and stark remnants of once-strong timbers marking the graves of houses and barns. Only in the forests could the men breathe fresh air but, even there, the scent of wet smoke and freshly burned wood assaulted William's nose whenever they happened upon a section where the burning fields had consumed large sections of the once-green forest.

A cool breeze lifted his sagging spirits. Marching out of the trees toward a brilliant blue sky, William caught the scent he had known for most of his childhood. His legs seemed less tired. He lifted his gaze from the grey jacket of the man ahead of him and leaned out of line, trying to see what he knew was there: the lake.

He could barely see where the water ended and the sky began. He smiled for the first time in months. And even though he knew he would soon be embroiled in another battle, he felt his face crack and his heart swell.

The Americans had improved the fortifications of the fort during their time there. An additional earthen wall stretched to the south maybe half a mile and William could see the outline of a gun battery. To the north, a few hundred feet from where he stood, another earth wall ran to the lake and ended in a gun battery. The angry-looking spears of felled trees lined the outer side. Attacking there would be impossible.

They fell back some distance and constructed a secure camp. Besides the usual tents and cooking fires, small cabins were built from felled trees and officers soon moved into them. There was even a latrine for their use although the rest of the soldiers, militia and regular, were not so fortunate.

From the British vantage point the American ships in the harbor seemed harmless but as soon as the order came to move forward and construct siege lines and batteries, gunfire from those ships harassed the British mercilessly. Their own small squadron was unable to leave the Niagara River to come and help as the three larger American vessels blocked their way.

William finally got to sleep in the damp heat of the August night but artillery fire soon ripped him from his dreams. He grabbed his rifle and, with the other three in his tent, scrambled to muster. In the starless night trees loomed out of the dark. A light rain fell. He crashed into several other soldiers as they fell in to report. In a few moments the order came to go back to bed. The firing was directed at the ships in the harbor.

The next day the British commander opened fire on the fort although William could see the bombardment was having little effect. Undeterred, two nights later, the commander ordered attacks on the fort's three batteries. William's group stayed in the muddy siege lines to protect their position. The relentless pounding of their bombardment on the fort made talking impossible, even if there were anything to say.

And then it stopped. For some time the only sound was the rain splashing into the mud and filling up the soldiers' boot tracks until gradually they sloshed and slogged in inches of water every time they moved. Still William and his fellows stared through the blackness keeping silent watch in the wet night. He knew his part in the attack: guard the siege lines while the others attacked the batteries.

He had written a letter to Catherine that day, knowing what he faced, but he had not realized how difficult his role would be. Constant gunfire, searing screams, and long silences repeated over and over but he could only guess what was happening. Were the British breaking through at Snake Hill? At the Douglass Battery? That was the plan.

His trigger finger went numb. When he tried to move it, only a dripping lump of flesh pulled off the wet metal. Even if he could get the feeling back in his finger, would the rifle even fire in this deluge? To his left and his right, men all up and down the trench stood motionless waiting for an attack that never came.

That didn't stop the noises. Elsewhere cannons roared, rifles repeated, cries of battle and death filled the night and the rain just kept coming down on it all, mercifully muting the din just a little but not nearly enough. Behind him a lone scream pierced the night and before anyone could stop him, one of their own militia men threw himself out of the trench and ran yelling toward the solid wall of the fort, the flash of his one shot lighting up his fixed bayonet. Long before he reached the wall he went down, the target of dozens of fire flashes from slits along the solid wall.

AS DAYLIGHT CAME the rain still poured down but at least William could see what was happening. His sergeant had spent the rest of the night going back and forth talking to the men. No one else had resorted to a suicide run. The men, himself included, huddled in the wet but said nothing. Their eyes told the tale. And if that wasn't enough, their sluggish shifting back into line to face another day of battle mirrored their utter despair.

Word came that the British held the northeast bastion but the soldiers' weak-willed cheer was worse than none at all. Cannon fire from both sides filled the air and in the soupy sky, clouds of smoke hung like ethereal corpses over them all. With no food, no sleep and nothing about them dry, the militia struggled to stay alert. His thoughts drifted from Catherine to Robert to the cow and finally he lost interest in trying to make sense of them at all. His head slipped forward.

The sound came a split second before men and body parts fell from the sky, some off the walls of the fort and others from he knew not where. His ears exploded. He lay against the back wall of the trench under a barrage of stones and beams and arms and boots. His gun gone, he slapped his hands to his ears to protect them but the damage had been done. Where a second before the screaming blast had drowned out all else, now William heard nothing.

Time seemed to stop as he watched his fellows pull themselves from under the deluge. He sat up. Threw someone's arm off his bloody belly. Yelled at the bleeding man beside him but couldn't hear his own words. And neither could the man. He didn't even turn his dazed eyes. Scrambling he was. And running. And though he couldn't hear, the sound of the hounding fire in his head was a hundred times worse than the real thing.

Waves of flame leapt over the wall of the fort, turned to smoke, and reignited over and over, the fiery clouds expanding over them all. When he ran through the mud, the long grass, and up the small incline into the trees, though dozens ran with him, he screamed and screamed but heard not a sound.

Chapter Thirty-Two

Burlington Heights
August, 1814

THE ROWS OF LIGHT TENTS stretched all across the heights starting from just behind what had formerly been someone's home and reaching across to the edge of the cliff. They were symmetrical and laid out by companies, side by side, with the first tent opening from one direction and the next from the opposite. Catherine supposed it was to give a little privacy but in actual fact privacy didn't exist in the overcrowded camp on the Heights.

She and Lucy had done the best they could that morning to get everyone's clothes clean after the gruelling trip they had endured as they fled the fires all across the countryside. At least John still had his wagon and horses. Though most of their possessions were gone up in smoke none of their family had suffered the fate of many of those they had passed along the way.

Spindly legs stuck out of ragged short pants as bare feet trudged the trail. Filthy shirts, long outgrown, barely covered the wasted bodies of children straggling behind their beaten mothers. As if the fire had not marred them all for life, now the sun burned their bodies. She had stopped looking at their faces. John kept the horses trotting as though he could outrun the terror and despair etched in all of their minds.

When they finally reached safety, they were allotted one tent for all of them. John, Lucy, the three children and herself, and were lucky to get that. The influx of refugees was so great the military stores had run out of supplies and everyone watched the slip of land that fronted on Burlington Bay for ships to come across the water from York.

John had hurried off to confer with the soldiers as soon as they had their tent, leaving the women to their work and the children to their play. Young Will had been listless and quiet ever since their arrival. The other two believed their grandfather's tale—they were playing a very big game, leaving their home and travelling so far away.

Catherine glanced at her mother-in-law. Standing knee-deep in the bay, her skirts hiked up to keep dry, Lucy scrubbed John's shirt back and forth in the water. She must be tired. Bending almost double, though, she didn't stop, even when her bonnet slipped forward unleashing her almost completely grey hair. The curls hid her face so that Catherine couldn't see her features.

A shout went up behind them. John stood on the beach gesturing for them to come out of the water. The children gave off their splashing first and ran to him, little Eva struggling across the sand after wee John. Lucy gave the shirt a final swish, and straightened beside her. Together they made their way across the hot sand.

"I've come to give you all a ride." He pointed to the wagon.

Catherine nodded. "Thank you, father," she said. "Give your grandfather some air, boys. Eva, take my hand."

That night the three sat under the stars. John had put them off until the children were asleep but Catherine could see he had news. His hand had rested just a little longer on Lucy's arm as he helped her off the wagon and his face lit up with the first glimmering of hope she'd seen in his eyes since the fires. Lucy seemed content to wait but Catherine wanted to know just what her father-in-law had learned.

She peeked in the tent to check the children before sitting with her inlaws. "Father, what is it? What has got you so happy in the midst of all this misery?" Her arm swept across the camp.

"I wouldn't say I'm exactly happy," he began, "but I am hopeful." He sat on a stump, Lucy beside him, and reached for her hand. "William sent a message."

Catherine jumped up and ran to him. "Let me have it, father." She almost pushed her open hand right into his face. "Please!"

"No, not a letter, daughter." He leaned away from her hand and turned his head. "With Captain Crawford."

She couldn't see her mother-in-law clearly but she had heard a gasp. "What is it, mother?" Catherine resumed her seat.

"Just a name from the past, my dear." Lucy glanced from one to the other but said no more.

"What did he say about William, father?"

"He talked to him after the fighting at Lundy's Lane." He reached out and took first Lucy's hand and then Catherine's. "He is well, my dears."

Catherine's shoulders dropped and, with a strangled sob, she let the tension out of her whole body. In a flash it was back. "That's almost a month ago. And why did you have to wait until the little ones were sleeping to tell us?" She knew her tones were strident and regretted them but she had to know. "What else did the Captain tell you?"

"Yes, John. What else?"

He took his time, brushed his hand over his lengthening beard, and dropped his voice to a whisper. "Come closer."

They did, moving their stumps so their knees touched and their bodies formed a dark triumvirate bathed in the filtered moonlight of the warm night. John whispered softly that a major offensive was taking place, that the object was the retaking of Fort Erie in hopes of ending the war. He leaned away from them but reached for both their hands. "It will soon be over...we can go home."

In the ensuing silence Catherine thought of their home. A tear slipped down her cheek and then another.

John had taken Lucy's hand. "Aren't you happy, my dear?"

"Happy?" she shouted. "That another battle____"

"Shhh, Lucy." John dropped her hand and made a gesture of covering her mouth. Someone in the next tent hollered, "Silence! We're trying to sleep!"

Catherine leaned in and motioned them to do the same. "What about William?"

John said nothing.

"Yes, John. What about our son? Will he be fighting at Fort Erie?"

Catherine looked from one to the other. John's head drooped low. Lucy watched him squirm as he looked anywhere but at her.

"He will...won't he?" Catherine whispered the words under the constant hum of the crickets but John heard and gave one brief nod.

REPORTS CAME IN SPORADICALLY and so jumbled by the time the refugees heard them that uncertainty became their constant companion. August rolled into September, the crickets sang louder, and John slept little. Catherine and Lucy were right to worry. He had not told them all he knew about the explosion of the powder magazine during the siege at Fort Erie and he certainly didn't tell them how many had died.

Now no one had any news of William. Not Captain Crawford, nor any of the regulars John had come to know. And though Lucy and Catherine had started lessons for a small group of children including their own three, John knew they had done it more to keep busy than to impart learning. Finally, towards the end of the month word came back that the British had lifted the siege and the fort was still held by the Americans. Straggling back to Fort Chippawa, the British were at first pursued by the Americans. Soon, however, the enemy turned back to Fort Erie.

As cold days and colder nights set in, the camp faced the fact that winter would soon be upon them. The flimsy canvas tents that had housed them in the heat of summer were just not up to the job of protecting all and sundry from the approaching scourge of winter. And yet what could the refugees do? The conflict was not settled and even if it were, most of those at Burlington Heights, while they had land, no longer had any buildings on it.

The first snowfall covered the tents and the slivers of ground between so that the whole area resembled a white fairyland. No one ventured out. No one but the few guards who stood sentinel and John, whose body needed to answer the most ancient call of all. In his light shoes he shuffled away from the tents making a path for others to follow later. Maybe the children would see the joy in the snow although none of them had proper clothing for it.

As he stood looking back over the camp, tails of smoke spiralled out of the blockhouse, made over from some farmer's barn, and the smoky smell of wheat cakes in bacon grease wafted from the cookhouse. An odd silence settled over the Heights. He looked over to the bay but could see only swirling snow in the just-dawn light. Uneasy he finished his business, stood listening and looking, seeing nothing. A black crow squawked out of a fir tree a few feet away.

There. From the south came a muffled sigh as though a hundred men breathed in unison. Louder. Not a sigh. He ran for the tent. As he grabbed his rifle young Will sat up straight, his eyes wide and worried. "Lucy, Catherine. See to the children." He was back outside as fast as his stiff limbs would take him. He heard it again. By now others were up, looking and listening, their eyes, their movements harried.

Marching. Hundreds of feet marching. But no orders stinging in the wind. Only snow, now swirling, now driving, and still the marching feet came on. "Halt!" The sentries called their warnings and were answered with shouts. The marching stopped. The wide gates opened and John thought for a moment some fool had given the wrong command but as the cloud of snow-whipped walkers came on, he caught glimpses of red uniforms. His family beside him saw, too, and breathed easier.

"Are there militia men, too?" Catherine asked. The faces were impossible to see, so covered with beards and mufflers and snow were they. And the bodies, too, were all the same, their only motions their feet that shuffled more than marched and their arms swinging only enough to keep the bodies from falling. She wrapped her shawl tighter around her thin body, determined to see every single one of their returning soldiers. But no bright spark came to her eyes.

The long column marched right to the barracks buildings and the men were dismissed into the shelter. How they'd find room inside, John didn't know, but he intended to find out. Leaving the women and children to prepare for the day, he struck out across the snow, his feet already wet and his trousers, too. No matter. He needed to find William.

Others had the same idea and together they approached the barracks door where the soldiers had disappeared. Armed guards—six of them—stood shoulder to shoulder against the wooden doors. They obviously had no intention of letting anyone else inside. Taken aback John hesitated a moment with the others but soon stepped forward. Instantly the guards dropped their rifles, the bayonet points scant inches from his chest.

He forced a breath from his thumping chest. "My son," he began, but the guard closest to him pushed his bayonet against his chest, hard enough that John could not help stepping back a half pace. He studied the man's lined face. All around him mumbles and snarls erupted. The bodies pushed up behind him. The man's flint-coloured eyes shifted first one way and then the other but he did not lower his weapon. Neither did the other five.

The crowd pushed so hard that John was in danger of being skewered. "Sir!" He raised his arms above his head. "We only want to know. Have our loved ones returned?"

One of the doors pushed open wide enough for a uniformed soldier to come out. A captain, by his bars. From behind family members gave voice, pushing forward even more. The captain took one look at John's predicament and began to shout.

"Silence! You're going to kill this man. Move back and all your questions will be answered."

John stood close to the officer. The man's grey hair curled down over his collar and lines creased his leathery skin. He stared at John, looked away, and then back again.

"Do I know you?" he asked.

John pulled off his hat. "We meet again, Captain," he said.

"Garner...we do indeed." A ghost of a smile flickered across his face.

The whispering behind him began to rise again and the captain tore his attention away from John. He shouted the plan to let everyone meet the new arrivals but only after they had eaten and slept. No one would be denied. John nodded his head but stood his ground as one by one the others shuffled off to their tents, a low grumbling disappearing with them.

"I...is my son...?" His voice gave out and he saw the spark of sympathy in Crawford's eyes.

"Yes."

Just one word but John's relief overpowered him and he stood like a sentinel, motionless, as a line of tears trickled down his icy cheeks. The captain didn't move but stood with John. He opened his moustachioed mouth to speak but nothing came out. Instead he touched John's arm and retreated into the barracks once more.

SHAKES AND CHILLS TORMENTED William's fevered body. He lay on a hard bench covered by a threadbare blanket that he shared with the men on either side of him. All around him soldiers moved back and forth in a flurry of activity but he focused on the scenes playing in his own mind. Catherine came and went, whether real or not, he couldn't tell, his mother, too, and his father, but only one at a time.

Each time he woke, hands held him and fed him until he drifted away again, until he thought he heard a voice. And listened again for it. Familiar. Through wisps of eyelashes he tried to see. And smell. It wasn't her; his eyes closed.

"William."

"Wake up, dearest."

He pushed back the fevered weight of sleep and looked. In his head he ran and leaped and sang. "Catherine," he croaked.

Over the next weeks William and the others, too, who had marched that terrible journey of defeat, with no succour along the whole burnt-out way, gradually recovered under the ministrations of the women in the camp and the hours of rest. Because the enemy Americans had moved their armies out of Fort Erie, the British were able to stand down and go into winter quarters as well. No one had any intention of doing anything but try to survive.

ONE OF THE LAST SHIPS TO MAKE THE JOURNEY along the lakes before freeze-up brought blankets and, along with the furs traded from the Indians, these comforts made the survival of the dispossessed at least possible. Food was still scarce but hunting parties went out daily, returning with carcasses more often than not. The camp cooks became adept at feeding the refugees and soldiers from whatever was at hand.

John did not dare to think beyond the daily grind of keeping his family warm and the wolves of hunger at bay. When they talked at all, the conversation was not full of hope for the future but rather what they might do to entertain the three children who had no room to play in the tiny tent and little energy to venture outside in the frozen wasteland. When he recovered, William came to be with his family, one more to squeeze into the space, but not one of them complained.

The adults took turns walking to the fire built some distance from the rows of tents and bringing back heated bricks to nestle at their feet under the furs. John had traded for the furs by allowing the soldiers to use his horses and wagon, although as the snow deepened the wagon became useless. The horses, however, continued to pull dried tree trunks from the forest to be chopped for firewood in the camp.

Two ships were frozen in the harbour, cut off from their trade route down the lake. From time to time snow-covered messengers would stagger in along the trails, whether they be Indians from Brant's Ford, soldiers from Fort George, or more stragglers stripped of their possessions and almost their very lives by this war.

Winter had a tight hold on the Heights the day the news came that the war was over. The Americans and the British had agreed to end their fight in December. The treaty of Ghent, they called it, although what and where Ghent was few in the camp knew. Along with that welcome announcement came the news that the British had fought one more battle in New Orleans after the war was over. And they had lost. Had the commanders on both sides known of the treaty, they might have saved countless lives.

Still, the war had ended. John and William began to take walks while the children napped in the crowded tent and the women whispered as they watched over them. Miraculously their family was healthy when all around them others were not. Not much was said but John had seen the bodies of children wrapped in sacks and carried to a place beyond the barricades where, in a small shed built for the purpose, they were stacked, frozen, until spring.

On one such walk the men encountered a party of gaunt and haggard Indians making their way toward the Heights. Father and son helped the two men and three women pull their sleigh through the gates of the palisade to safety. They were on their way to a refuge on Burlington Bay, the home of Joseph Brant's widow. By the look of them, they wouldn't make it. They took the party to the cook's cabin and got them some food.

"You will be safe here," John said. He sat opposite one of the women. She said nothing. The other two were silent as well, but the older Indian, the one with streaks of grey and white in the parted hair along the top of his head, spoke in a rusty voice.

"We were there...with the others." He cleared his throat. "With Tecumseh." A shadow passed over his aged face and his eyes closed a moment as though he might keep the memories from coming back.

John and William looked at each other. "You've had a long walk," John said and William nodded but said nothing.

At first haltingly and then, as he regained his words, the man told the story of being at Amherstburg with Tecumseh and the British the previous summer. The women and children had been there, too, when the news came that the Americans had taken control of Lake Erie and the white father, Major General Proctor, immediately turned and fled. Soldiers, Indians, and militia followed, much to the despair of the Indians. "The great Tecumseh feared for his people without his British allies." The old man took a long drink from his cup. "He had to follow." He looked right into John's eyes. "Tecumseh said Proctor was like a fat animal that carries its tail upon its back until the first sign of danger; then it drops its tail between its legs and runs off."

Proctor led a speedy retreat instead of remaining with his troops to fight to ensure the survival of both Indians and white settlers. At Moraviantown, an isolated settlement along the Thames, he finally ordered a halt and prepared to meet the Americans in battle. Tecumseh drew up his five hundred Indians in a swamp alongside the British. When the attack began the British were immediately overrun as they had built no earthworks to stop the enemy. The American cavalry rode right into the British, whose one cannon failed to fire.

"The British soldiers turned and ran. Following the cowardly Proctor."

"And Tecumseh?" William spoke for the first time.

The Shawnee chief had fought on, his braves with him, until about twenty American cavalry charged into their position. Still the Indians did not give ground but shot most of the sallying force. The remainder bogged down in the muddy swamp.

"The great Tecumseh would not give up. He charged into the mass of horses and reeds and men firing, screaming his war cries right up until the moment he was shot."

"Did you see that?" John asked.

"No, but I felt the heart leave our warriors." His voice was but a whisper now. "We could not fight the mighty Americans whose guns just kept firing, no matter how many we killed."

Tears coursed down the cheeks of the woman across from John but no sound came. He didn't know what he could do but wouldn't leave them there alone. William was silent as well. He started to ask what had taken them so many months to get here with their sleigh but stopped. After a few moments he stood, gathered the empty plates and cups, and delivered them to the cook who had heard the whole exchange. Without a word the burly man took the dishes and turned to wash them himself.

The Shawnees accepted camp hospitality for a few days longer and through that time, John spoke often with the old man. He learned that the Indians were not related but had banded together after the debacle at Moraviantown. They had tried to stay in that area because of their log huts and their unwillingness to go somewhere new to start again but the Americans hounded them into leaving. Two children among them, they struck out for Brant's Ford along with a horse to pull the sleigh, a mangy dog and the one tent they had saved from the burning camp.

They might have stayed there but one of the women wished to go on to Burlington Bay where she hoped to find her family and the others agreed to accompany her. On the day before the group planned to set out again for the last leg of their journey, Lucy and Catherine learned the fate of the children.

In that universal way of women bonding with little ones, the Indians gave young William, wee John, and little Eva, each a piece of maple sugar to suck on. William's eyes had opened wide as he tasted the sweet. For the first time, the three women smiled. In a complicated mixture of signs and words, Catherine asked about their children. The smiles faded.

Taking Catherine by the hand the youngest of the three led her through the snow to the sleigh, which they had all been loading. Lucy followed. In one corner was a shaggy buffalo robe that the young woman grasped in her tiny hand. Catherine held her breath. Slowly the woman pulled back the covering. Two small bodies lay side by side—a boy and a girl—their eyes closed and their faces lifeless.

The young mother touched the children, about six or seven years old, and gently covered them again. Catherine thought of her own loved ones whom she had left buried on the farm. Immediately Lucy's arm linked with her own and pulled her close. Together they walked back to the tent where John and William had the old Indian deep in conversation.

When the Shawnees left the next morning, they took with them, untold, the story of how the children died. William had offered to accompany them but the old Indian's scornful look at the suggestion they might need help stopped him.

Chapter Thirty-Three

March, 1815

THEY TOOK THE QUEENSTOWN ROAD, passable already because of the early melt followed by solid cold again. The men thought if they waited any longer spring thaw would make the road mush for weeks. Besides, they were all more than ready to return to their homes now that the war was over. Lucy had watched the days lengthen and the sun strengthen and she longed to be in her own kitchen once more.

Thoughts of returning to normal after two years away helped keep her mind off the lurching, slipping wagon and the creaking and aching of her bones. She was getting too old for this. Fifty-six this year she was, as John had reminded her on her birthday a few weeks ago. She'd laughed but inside the piling up of the years caused her more than a little worry.

Her auburn hair was long gone and even in the dull mirror of the glassed windows at Burlington Heights she saw the lines in her face and the droop to her chin. The freckles on her worn hands had multiplied and her once-straight and smooth fingers now curved inward, the thumb joint on her right hand constantly swollen and sore.

"What are you doing?" John asked. "Keep your hands out of the wind or you'll freeze."

She slipped them back under the buffalo robe and snuggled closer to John whose own hands must be frozen on the lines even though he wore the mittens she had made for him back at the camp. "I wonder what we'll find," she said in a low voice. They would reach William's land first and planned to settle there a while before traveling on to their own land.

John shuffled on the seat and, for the first time in a long while, smiled at her. "Always curious, aren't you?"

"Yes. Isn't that why you married me?" she teased.

In the back William and Catherine rode with the children, all of them huddled together to keep warm, Catherine holding little Eva to cushion her against the rough ride. She had fallen asleep in her cocoon and the others were silent so as not to wake her. In exchange for John and William's months of work, Captain Crawford had managed to fill their wagon with goods.

All along the road few signs of settlers were to be seen. Rather, the thin layer of snow partially covered burned-out buildings and split-rail fences, the markers of what had been and was no more. Lucy tried not to look. Better to watch the woods and think of all the frozen trees preparing to live again in the spring.

The village of Queenstown was not much better although here and there stacks of logs and fresh cut lumber showed the inhabitants were beginning again. The family camped near the barracks and William told again the story of Robert huddled in the enclosure before being traded back across the river. No one mentioned the battle where Thomas had died but Lucy looked longingly to the heights and remembered.

There was so much sorrow, she thought, and hardship. Both in the past and for years to come. Catherine handed her a plate of hot stew. Her family spread around the fire as close as they could come to the flames. Lucy forced a smile to her face. Young Will sat beside her on the cold stump. She moved to give him room and he wriggled closer.

William remembered the stark black of the few timbers left from their neighbours' homes and their own. He had tried to prepare Catherine for what she would see as they came over the last hill before their farm. And, of course, she had reminded him of the day they were burned out, barely escaping with their lives. But neither was prepared for the sight that met them as the horses cleared the rise.

He had insisted on taking the lines for this last leg and nothing would do but Catherine would sit with him. His parents kept the children warm in the back and John's stories kept all three entertained. The soft drone of his father's voice, interrupted by occasional high-pitched laughs and excited questions, made a soft and steady counterpoint to his thoughts.

Though the war was over and he should be looking forward to peaceful times ahead, he wasn't sure he had the heart for what lay ahead. They had their land and they had each other. Would it be enough? At his side Catherine sat silent. What was she thinking? The horses steadily drew them up the hill and he held his breath, as did Catherine beside him.

Through the clouds of steam coming off the labouring horses he strained to see his land once more. They started down the other side. The roadway was cleared of snow all along Lundy's Lane past where their buildings had been and stretching into the distance. They were not the only returning family. But wait. Was that a thread of white winding up into the blue? In spite of the rough ride he flicked the lines and urged the horses faster.

"There's smoke, William." Catherine gave voice to his thoughts.

From behind, his father called out, "William. What do you see?" Not waiting for an answer he grabbed the back of the seat and pulled himself partway up behind his son. "Is that a cabin?" And, of course, it was. Situated right beside the ruins of their once lovely house a tiny structure sat square and solid, a steady plume of smoke streaking up into the blue sky above.

William didn't know whether to be happy or frightened. Catherine was absolutely silent as they rode past the burial place, both looking for a few seconds before turning back to the string of smoke curling into the air. He could smell it now, the scent of other homecomings filling his thoughts. He turned to Catherine and smiled. She was gently nodding.

As they drew nearer, the road curved around a lonely stand of white pines. He urged the horses on, by now feeling the anxiety of everyone in the wagon. At least he still had his large acreage of woods. They wouldn't freeze although how they would live until they could plant a garden and some crops he wasn't quite sure.

The horses needed no urging. They steadily clip-clopped along the rutted track. But his father reached under the seat for the musket. "Not too quickly, William," he said in a low voice.

The door in the front of the tiny cabin opened and a couple stepped into the snow, both wearing fearful frowns which soon collapsed into broad grins.

"Who...?" His father's voice spoke in his ear.

"I...I..." Catherine, too, was at a loss. She clutched his arm a little tighter.

From behind, his mother shrieked. "Helen!" Everyone began to shout and scream so loud that William had a job keeping control of the horses.

LUCY WOKE THE NEXT MORNING scrunched in between Helen and Catherine, the sound of water dripping near her head. In the small confines—the structure was twelve foot square, Timothy had assured them—the men and children had taken the floor and the women the bed.

Light streaked through the unchinked logs but did not dispel the heavy gloom inside. She pulled the blankets up over her cold nose and blocked out the smell of so many bodies in the room. John's heavy breathing with the occasional throat clearing and snuffling she recognized. Someone else snored softly. The children's solid sounds were clear and healthy, a blessing amidst all the sorrows they'd faced.

And there were other blessings. Her Helen lay so close in front of her she had to brush her daughter's hair away from tickling her nose. Catherine had insisted Lucy sleep in the middle, the better to stay warm. Just now, though, she wished to be on the outside so that answering nature's call might be easier. She'd just wait a while longer.

They had brought their buffalo robes and blankets and even the two rope-slung beds John and William had fashioned over the winter. Pots and spoons, dishes and tubs, all would find a place in the two households but for now, they were still on the wagon just outside the cabin. The men had built a temporary animal shelter using evergreens from the woods as a roof and a bit of a wind-break. She could hear the blanketed horses snuffling and periodically shifting on the other side of the wall. Even their scent carried through the gaps but Lucy didn't mind.

The sound of the dripping intensified though she wanted not to think about it. Melting snow. Spring was welcome but they would have to improve the makeshift roof before the rains came. Helen shifted beside her.

"Mama," Eva's small voice whimpered near the stove.

Catherine slipped out of the bed and picked her way toward the child, a comforting shadow crossing the room. Lucy, too, climbed out but fished under the bed for the chamber pot and, ignoring the lack of privacy, squatted.

ONCE THE BEDS WERE TIDIED AND EVERYONE FED, John felt all eyes upon him. He sat against the wall on a roll of blankets, young John beside him and wee Will between his legs. Eva was in her mother's arms holding her hands over the small stove which Timothy and Helen had brought. Lucy wasn't letting Helen get far away, although how she could in the crowded cabin was a good question, and Helen's eyes shone in the flickering candlelight. One of the first things they would do was cut a window. As soon as it was warm enough, and they could find some glass.

Timothy stood by the door. Ready to make his escape, John supposed, but he had no more hate or blame for his son-in-law. He cleared his throat. Everyone, even little Eva, turned his way.

"I'm not much of a praying man," he began, "but today my heart is full." He paused. No one spoke. "We've lost so many and so much." He looked at each of them in turn. "And we have so much building to do..." He couldn't go on.

Lucy dropped Helen's hand and stepped toward him. "But we have each other." She smiled at him and gestured around the crowded room.

"Timothy, we thank you for all you have done...for Helen and for all of us." John emphasized the last few words, his eyes fastened on his son-in-law.

William spoke up. "Father is right. We're a family again...and you're part of it."

Everyone spoke at once about the past and the future, about Robert and where his family might be, about Timothy and Helen's children left with his brother near Lewiston while they tracked down her folks, and about the mill where they had grown up. Timothy told them about finding a man in Queenstown who knew William and where his home was. Helen held his hand as he apologized for stealing her away from her family. The least he could do, he said, was help her find them all.

As the weather warmed up and spring stepped closer they worked and planned. Helen and Timothy helped wherever they could but, in the quiet candlelight moments when the chores were done and all the words were said, John saw their fleeting looks and knew they would soon be gone. He steeled himself for it by thinking of his other grandchildren and when he and Lucy might meet them. Much as he liked being here and helping William, in the back of his mind was his own place; he longed for it and for a return to life as it had been. And, truth be told, he ached for the feel of Lucy snuggled up against him in their own bedroom.

The advancing spring brought more changes. Helen and Timothy struck out on their horse, their belongings tied on behind them. For a long while the family waved and watched until they were specks going over the hill in the distance. They would cross the river again at Queenstown.

The next day John hitched up his wagon, loaded with what they had managed to procure, make, and haggle for with neighbours who had also returned, and together he and Lucy headed out to return to their mill.

Young Will and wee John ran after the wagon slipping and sliding in the mud while Lucy waved and called to them from her seat on the wagon, the tears streaking her cheeks so that John almost turned back. But no. They had their own life and must leave William and Catherine and their family to theirs.

Blotches of self-seeded grain poked through the chocolate earth. Thick-trunked trees, some scarred with fire and broken branches, budded above and beside them as the wagon lurched its way in the warming sunlight. Tufts of twitch grass poked up beside the road that was barely a track in some places. In others muddy detours around water holes threatened to suck them, their horses, and their loaded wagon right into the depths of the earth.

They drove on past the bloody battlegrounds at Lundy's Lane, along the Portage Road to Chippawa, all the while unable to escape the signs of the previous year's struggles. Crude markers in uneven rows or single solitary crosses marred the once-vibrant and vital route around the mighty falls. In Chippawa they searched in vain for a warm place to spend the night.

Beside the Chippawa river, John pulled up the horses, gave them their heads to nibble at the new shoots along the bank, and with Lucy's help fashioned a place to sleep in the wagon. In the morning they took the ferry across the narrow river and continued their journey along the treacherous road.

Again, they stopped along the roadside, Lucy cooking over an open fire the rabbit John managed to shoot in the sheltering woods. All talked out, that afternoon they rode in silence. Nothing along the trail seemed familiar to John. Where once had stood neat homes and snug barns surrounded by split-rail fences separating thriving crops, now lay devastation. They passed the McKie's farm. John stopped a moment to take a better look but no life stirred.

Beside him, Lucy sniffled and took a deep breath but said nothing. The path through the woods comforted them both as the buds promised new life but the open spaces breathed black despair. And they met no one. No other wagon bumped over the ruts nor slopped through the puddles. Nobody else breathed in that damp desolation of smoky loss. John held Lucy against him, trusting the horses to his one hand.

AS THE DAY DWINDLED she kept her eyes fixed on the road ahead watching for the gap in the trees ahead. "That's it," she called out. "Isn't it, John?"

"Yes." He breathed deeply beside her and flicked the lines over the steaming horses but said no more. The closer they came to the turn, the farther forward she leaned on the seat. And yet, part of her wanted to hold back, afraid of what they might find. Would anything be left? And if not, how could the two of them, tired and bone-weary, certainly not the young pair who had built a home twice before, how could they do it again?

John pulled the horses to the left into what had been their long laneway. The horses slowed as they picked their way along the unused path but Lucy watched ahead, missing the sniff of smoke always apparent by now. They came around the big oak.

"Whoa!" John shouted, and hauled back on the lines. Together they sat, his arm around her again, she leaning into him with tears streaming down her face as she drank in the scene. She couldn't speak.

Before their very eyes the setting sun threw streaks of pink and yellow and violet across the cloudy evening sky. The outline of the far side of the river misted into memory as sunlight streaming across the water lit the waves in bright spots of glass, floating a moment, and then disappearing. Almost immediately the sun slipped down taking with it the vibrant colors and leaving fading memories of what had been but a moment before.

Lucy straightened her back against the stiff wagon seat and closed her eyes. A second later she opened them again. Yes, her house was gone. And their small barn. But standing tall and dark against the azure sky the stone mill jutted into the sky. The wagon moved again as John drove the team closer. All was still. No birds winged above. But when the wagon stopped at the rail in front of the mill—amazingly still there—a whiff of water and wood and the musty smell of last year's grain filled her senses.

John was off the wagon like a shot, in his haste forgetting to help her down, but she didn't even notice. Up the steps and into the mill she followed him. A quick look around assured them it was safe and John hurried back outside to unload the wagon while the light held. She felt like a girl again lifting the barrels and bedposts with John and setting up their things. Eventually a new house and barn would come but for now she was thankful. The mill would be their home in the meantime. John tended the horses, she set out a meagre meal, and they reclaimed their home.

The one fireplace in the mill held a place of prominence in John's office and it was there they would stay for the moment. The bed fit in one corner and his desk became their table. John mended the broken chair with a newly shaped leg jammed up into the hole and made tight with wood shims. For their midday meal that next day, she insisted he take the chair and she sat on the edge of the bed.

They had barely finished when a shout sounded in the distance from the direction of the river. John grabbed the rifle and hurried as fast as his legs would take him down the wooden stairs. She dropped the plate in her hand back on the table and rushed to the only window in the room. Its glass broken, they had covered it with a piece of oilcloth last night to keep out the wind but she ripped one corner away and peered through the tiny opening.

She could see nothing but, at the wild shouting, hurried downstairs and out the door. The rifle lay on the loading dock. John ran for the water where a small skiff was nosed up on the shore. Someone was so close to John that she couldn't see who it was but she saw the outstretched arms of both men as they ran and clasped each other. Over John's shoulder, almost a head taller, with wild flying hair and a grin she would know anywhere, was Robert.

He dropped his arms from around his father and reached for her, folding her against his heaving chest as though he would never let go again. Robert. He was safe. He looked nothing like the young man she had lost before the war but his beard looked just like John's had those many years ago. She stood back; his eyes, once clear and calm, were red-streaked and framed with little lines.

"Come. Let's get your mother back inside, son." John took her one arm and Robert took the other; together the three of them hurried back to shelter.

When they had closed the door on the stiff breeze and hurried upstairs to the fire, Robert began to speak. "I've been across the water for over a week watching for a sign, any sign, you were here. I'd given up." He stopped a moment and looked into the flames.

"What do you mean?" Lucy asked, looking from John to Robert.

"The house and barn. I saw they were gone."

"And you thought we were, too," John said.

"Yes."

For a moment they were all silent.

"We have another cup, Robert. Would you like tea? I'm afraid it's bitter without sugar but it's warm." Lucy rummaged in a sack on the floor, brought out the cup and poured for Robert. "It's just like old times," she said and sat on the bed watching the same wry smile on their two faces.

That afternoon they worked at clearing out the mill and making it habitable. Though the water wheel outside had been torn off its support, the millstones inside were intact. They fashioned brooms from winterkilled branches and evergreen boughs and soon the whole building was alive with a smoky haze in the afternoon sunlight coming in the opened doors and window slots.

The men cleared the rubble and dust out of the mill room below while Lucy, having cleaned their living space in John's office, swept all the way over to the doorway of the room where Black Bear

Claw had lived. He was in her thoughts the whole time, another casualty of the cursed war. She tossed her head to shake away her dark thoughts and opened the door.

Almost black the room was, with just a slit of light from the window high above. She covered her nose against the dry odor, which made her cough, and backed out, letting the door swing shut again. At first she thought she'd leave that room until later but she wanted the whole place clean. The lantern lit, she pushed open the door again.

Chapter Thirty-Four

THE MEN IN THE MILLING ROOM had their own challenges what with the broken gear work and the partially burned stairway. The Americans had tried to destroy the place but, thankfully, had not done a very good job of it. John and Robert had just decided the stairs would hold for now when Lucy's scream rent the air. Robert took the stairs two at a time, John behind him, trying to keep up.

When he reached the top, Robert already held Lucy whose finger pointed into the Indian's dark room. Her skin was ashen and her eyes wide and white as she grabbed for John's outstretched hand.

"What is it, Lucy?"

Robert released his mother and holding the lantern high stepped into the tiny dark cell. With a soft pat on Lucy's arm John turned and followed. Immediately he covered his mouth against the odor. He couldn't believe the sight. Against the wall lay a body, or what had been a body before the rats and the worms had their way. The head was mostly mutilated down to the skull. Bits of grey hair lay where they had fallen still tied in a leather thong. And though a grey blanket covered the rest of the body, in the eerie glow of the lantern John could see the sharp jut of bare bones.

"Black Bear Claw," Lucy whispered behind him.

"Yes," he answered.

They backed out of the room and edged the door closed as though the spectre was just sleeping and they daren't wake him. In the office, Robert and Lucy sat while John passed a hot drink. One more shock for them to bear, John thought, his eyes on Lucy and Robert sitting side by side on the edge of the bed. No one spoke.

THEY LAID BLACK BEAR CLAW in the barely thawing ground at the edge of the trees. The last shovelful of earth thrown, John turned to go but Lucy stopped him.

"We need to say some words over his grave, John."

He hardly remembered much from the good book but did his best with the prayer taught by their Lord. He had no idea what god the Indian had followed, but his words pleased Lucy and he was content. Robert stayed strangely silent throughout the whole affair standing off to one side throughout the service. As soon as it was done he turned on his heel and headed back into the mill. They could hear his hammering and banging all the way out at the edge of the woods.

John took it upon himself to clear out the Indian's room while Lucy stayed in the office preparing their evening meal over the open fireplace. He uncovered the window and let in the fresh air while he scrubbed with lye soap even though his fingers were almost numb with the cold. When he finished, he closed the door but left the window open. The sun had moved to the other side of the mill.

ROBERT STRETCHED OUT NEAR THE FIRE that night on the buffalo robe that had seen so much use over the years. Lucy lay next to John watching her son twist and turn in his sleep and wondered what he was hiding. So far he had said not a word about his wife and children, not even how many he had, and he sidestepped any attempt on their part to draw him out. John shifted away from her, giving her room to turn from their son and she drifted into sleep.

She woke to an empty bed the next day. John, and Robert, too, had slipped out in the sunshine to chop the dead tree they'd felled.

The steady thunk, thunk of the axe carried easily in the clear air. Throwing off the quilts she hurried into her skirt and built up the fire. By the time the men came inside hot tea filled their cups and fresh-cooked bacon with Johnnycakes sizzled in the pan.

When they had downed the last morsel John spoke. "Robert." He leaned back in the only chair on the other side of the small desk. "Tell us about your family."

Beside her, Robert sat straight and stiff. His face seemed closed to the world, even to them, his parents. His eyes fixed on a point on the wall and his whole slight body seemed to channel his energy onto that one spot. Lucy followed his gaze but could not see what he was looking at. Still, he sat and stared. She lifted her hand toward him, held it a moment, and brought it to rest on his arm.

No word came from his mouth but he blinked a few times and turned to her. One lone tear slipped down his freckled cheek. She longed to wipe it away as she had so many times when he was young. Instead she stroked his arm but said nothing. John was silent, too. The tiny room itself waited.

At last he told of his wife, whom he had married soon after following Helen across the border, and his daughter, named Mary Anne for her mother. A ghost of a smile lit his face as he said the name but it disappeared as quickly as it had come. A log fell in the grate. Robert's glance flitted to his father.

"You know I was fighting, Father," he said softly.

"William told us about Queenstown, son."

"He couldn't tell you all of it."

"Of course not. There are things in war best not said."

"I shot…" Robert clenched his hands together.

"What is it, my son?" Lucy asked.

John immediately spoke. "Son, you don't have to tell us. Let it go."

"But I have to tell someone. About the soldier on the hill," he said. "The officer."

"We don't want to know, son." John stood up. "Tell us about your family."

At this Robert brightened a moment but immediately looked down at the floor. "I wasn't there, back in Buffalo." He straightened his shoulders. "When they burned it."

Lucy clasped his arm against the words she feared were coming.

"Where were you, son?" asked John.

"I wasn't there!" he cried in anguish. "What does it matter where I was? I wasn't with them."

John leaned forward and touched Robert's shoulder. "Tell us, son."

And he did. He told of being at Fort Niagara when the British retook it and of running away from the pursuing redcoats. And he told of waiting for orders in the snowy woods for days while the higher-ups made their plans and he decided to slip away since his service was up. And finally, in a voice low and flat, he told of walking with a friend the whole long way back to Buffalo. The cold froze their joints but they kept walking, seeking shelter wherever they could. He had not seen his family for almost a year. The child would be walking—he couldn't think what she might look like—and Mary Anne's eyes would shine with joy.

The closer they got, the less the two men talked as their feet followed the beaten path home. Robert's sole attention was on the road ahead but he was unprepared for the clouds of billowing smoke rising in the distance. Cannon fire followed and, soon after, the screams of women and children fleeing. The heat of the roaring conflagration stopped the two in their tracks. All they could do was watch and listen and feel their faces burn as their town disintegrated under the hands of the punishing British troops.

Robert dropped his gaze to the fire beside the three of them. Lucy still held his arm and it felt like a lifeless twig. She squeezed. With a look of longing and pure pain, her son stared into her eyes. "What happened? Did you find them?" She couldn't quite say the names even though now she knew them.

"We found them." Robert said no more.

"Tell us, son," said John.

"Mary Anne, my wife, I found wandering in the smoke the next day. She carried a bundle of rags in her arms." He stood up so quickly Lucy slipped off balance on the bed. Her son turned his back on them. "She didn't know me," he whispered.

"And the baby?" Lucy asked, her heart broken at what she might hear.

"Dead."

John and Lucy both went to him. The three stood together, struck silent.

That day and the next she tried her best to comfort her son even though her own heart was like to break. John hardly spoke. Robert managed to tell them he'd left Mary Anne with her parents but he needed to go back and care for her. Now that he knew his parents and William's family and Helen's were safe, he was desperate to go to his wife. God willing she would recover and they would go on.

A few days later, Lucy walked on one side of Robert and John on the other down the short path to the river. They loaded Robert's boat with his few possessions and watched as he pushed off into the swift current. Paddling hard he headed across the water away from them. He turned once and waved but the current immediately took the craft further down the river in the direction of the falls until he paddled hard again to make for the other side.

John's arms held her as the tears slipped down her cheeks but they watched until Robert was safely out of danger and hauled his boat up on the far shore. She thought he waved once more although the distance was too great to be sure. Presently the two of them walked back to the mill.

APRIL'S RAINS WASHED THE WINTER AWAY and green sprouted on the ground and in the trees. Even the evergreens gradually took on a brighter hue as spring took possession of the peaceful land. John's step quickened on the stairs and Lucy took to wandering the forested paths looking for edible shoots and plants. Day by day more neighbors and newcomers stopped at the sign of their chimney spewing smoke, each one more welcome than either John or Lucy could say.

All up and down the peninsula life began again. Everyone was hard pressed to rebuild and replant. Fort Erie had been destroyed but still the name survived and came to mean the grouping of stalwart settlers who developed a community once more. A blacksmith and a store sprang up and John got his mill wheel righted again, ready for the ripening of the newly sewn crops.

A lone rider pounded along the lane one day with a message from Robert. His Mary Anne had recovered and the rebuilding of their home was progressing as they had money and time. William and Catherine sent word that all was well although they had not decided whether to stay or to sell and move to their land in Nissouri. Lucy hoped they would stay but John persuaded her that their children must live their own lives.

They were thankful for the money John had earned back at Burlington Heights, as he was able to purchase what tools and food they needed to hold them over until the new crops would be harvested in the fall. Their own small field planted, John spent his days clearing away the debris from their burned house. Day by day the smoky smell disappeared as the wind from the west blew across the lake clearing away the horror of the last three years.

"We're lucky, you know," Lucy said to John one evening as they sat on the mill steps and watched the sun slide across the water, a dipping, slipping orange ball ending the day. He took her hand in his and slowly brought it to his smiling lips.

~~

Links to More Information About the Loyalist Trilogy

More about the Loyalist trilogy at
www.elainecougler.com

Find Elaine Cougler on Goodreads
www.goodreads.com/ElaineCougler

If you care to know more about The Loyalist Trilogy and its progress, join Elaine Cougler's email list to get updates and special extras.
http://eepurl.com/FCKL1

Notes Re The Loyalist's Luck

1. The land where John and Lucy landed was at the time known as Quebec and those settled there were under the French seigneurial system and code of laws. As more and more Loyalists settled the region they pushed for the English laws they were used to. Eventually this large region was divided into what is present-day Quebec and Ontario.

2. The Angel Inn name I've used for simplicity's sake and because today it is still in Niagara-on-the-Lake and called the Olde Angel Inn. At the time of the burning of Newark (NOTL), however, the inn was called The Harmonious Coach House, according to the Olde Angel Inn website. Burned along with the rest of the town, it was rebuilt in 1815 and opened as the Angel Inn.

3. Portage Road actually ran from Queenstown to Chippawa and was first built to bypass the great falls at Niagara. I have used the term for the whole road all the way to Fort Erie in order to simplify place names for my readers.

4. The name of present-day Niagara-on-the-Lake has worn many changes since Colonel Butler named it after himself. Again, for simplicity's sake I've used Butlersburg and then simply Newark, although the area's names included West Niagara as well as just plain Niagara. Finally the post office initiated the modern name to simplify mail delivery.

Sources Consulted By The Author

1. *Mrs. Simcoe's Diary*, Mary Quayle Innis, ed. 1965 MacMillan of Canada, Toronto, St. Martin's Press, New York.

2. *Niagara-on-the-Lake: Its Heritage and Its Festival*, James Lorimer & Company Ltd., Publishers, Toronto.

3. *History of Niagara*, Janet Carnochan, originally published by William Briggs, Toronto, 1914, this edition published by Global Heritage Press, Milton, 2006.

4. *Canada & the American Revolution 1774-1783*, Gustave Lanctot of the Royal Society, Clarke, Irwin & Company, Toronto, 1967.

5. *Eleven Exiles: Account of the American Revolution*, Phyllis R. Blakeley, John N. Grant, ed., Dundurn Press Limited, Toronto, 1982.

6. *The Loyalists: Revolution, Exile, Settlement*, Christopher Moore, Macmillan of Canada, a division of Gage Publishing Limited, Toronto, 1984.

7. *King's Men: The Soldier Founders of Ontario*, Mary Beacock Fryer, Dundurn Press Limited, Toronto, 1980.

8. *Joseph Brant and His World*, James W. Paxton, James Lorimer & Company Ltd., Publishers, Toronto, 2008.

9. *Loyal She Remains: A Pictorial History of Ontario*, published by The United Empire Loyalists' Association of Canada, Toronto, 1984.

10. *Pease Porridge: Beyond the King's Bread*, JoAnn Demler, Old Fort Niagara Association, Inc., Youngstown, New York, 2003.

11. *Much To Be Done: Private Life in Ontario from Victorian Diaries*, Hoffman, Frances, Taylor, Ryan, Natural Heritage/Natural History Inc., Toronto, 1996.

12. *The Administration of Lieut.-Governor Simcoe, Viewed in His Official Correspondence*, Ernest Alexander Cruikshank, originally published by Toronto: Canadian Institute, 1891, this edition produced by Project Gutenberg Canada ebook #445, December, 2009.

13. *Historical Atlas of Canada*, Derek Hayes, published in Canada by Douglas & McIntyre, 2002.

14. *The Niagara Portage Road: 200 Years 1790-1990*, George A. Seibel, published by the city of Niagara Falls, 1990.

Topics and Questions For Book Clubs

1. What kind of characters has Cougler created? Are they different in any way from characters in fiction that is not historical fiction?

2. Which character most speaks to you as a reader?

3. How do the death of Harper John and John's infidelity change Lucy's character?

4. How does the approximately two hundred years separating the events of this novel from our modern world add to the experience of reading *The Loyalist's Luck*?

5. John's trip to Detroit with Governor Simcoe might have been left out. What are the reasons for including it?

6. The settling of Upper Canada, specifically the Niagara area, forms a large part of the plot. Discuss how your own view of these early times has changed, having read this novel.

7. Which of John and Lucy's children did you most empathize with? Why?

8. William and Catherine marry at a most trying time and suffer many hardships because of the War of 1812. For each of them, identify how their characters grow as they suffer through these difficulties.

9. The two wars between Canadians (British) and Americans form bookends for this novel. With such a conflicted beginning, do you wonder just how Canada and the United States can today share the longest undefended border in the world? Does this make the history more or less interesting?

10. How has Cougler's treatment of Native peoples, specifically Black Bear Claw, added not only to the plot but also to our understanding of the past?

COMING SOON!

Book Three in the Loyalist series

The Loyalist Legacy

William and Catherine Garner find their two hundred acres in Nissouri Township by following the Thames River into the wild heart of Upper Canada. On their valuable land straddling the river, dense forests, wild beasts, disgruntled Natives, and pesky neighbors daily challenge them. The political atmosphere laced with greed and corruption threatens to undermine all of the new settlers' hopes and plans. William knows he cannot take his family back to Niagara but he longs to check on his parents from whom he has heard nothing for two years. Leaving Catherine and their boys, he hurries back along the Governor's Road toward the turn-off to Fort Erie, hoping to return to Catherine in time for spring planting.